STRANGE EMBRACE

Longing and tenderness rushed over me, and I ran across the room and into my husband's arms. His kiss threatened to burn the skin from my lips, and his arms pressed me close to his lean, hard body. Waves of feeling pounded over me, and I clung to him, inhaling his familiar scent.

But suddenly a chill came over me. Something was not right. Richard had never kissed me quite like this before, and the scent of him was not so familiar after all. I struggled and freed myself from his arms.

I blinked and rubbed my eyes. It was Richard's face—and yet it was not. Some indefinable thing told me this man was not my husband.

"Good morning," he said cheerfully. "Thank you for the welcome salutation."

My head rang; my blood pounded. The voice was Richard's, too, but not his. "Who—" I began.

"What are you doing here? I thought we were rid of you!" The angry male voice came from behind me. I whirled, not believing my eyes.

My husband stood there.

NINA COOMBS PYKARE

THE LOST DUCHESS OF GREYDEN CASTLE

ZEBRA BOOKS
KENSINGTON PUBLISHING CORP.

For Becki and Bill
with love

ZEBRA BOOKS

are published by

Kensington Publishing Corp.
475 Park Avenue South
New York, NY 10016

First printing: June, 1990

Printed in the United States of America

Chapter One

I had never thought to be a duchess. Most assuredly I had never thought to be Richard's duchess. And perhaps, had I known what was to come, I would have refused that honor.

It was all quite strange. And nothing was stranger than Caroline's mysterious death. But let me begin nearer the beginning.

I first saw Richard, duke of Greyden, when he was a dashing blade of five and twenty who had come to offer for Caroline's hand. I had escaped the notice of Vickers, my governess, and peeped between the bannisters to see what all the commotion was about. I was thirteen at the time, a gangling, gawky girl with carroty hair that was always escaping whatever constraints Vickers tried to put upon it.

But in spite of my tender years, I knew my own mind, and one look at Richard was sufficient. I knew immediately that this was a man above all men. Tall and dark, with a leanness that bespoke great strength and dark eyes that flashed wickedly, Richard was the prototype of the hero in the stories my maid Burdner whispered to me.

Vickers, of course, knew nothing of this or of my taste for tall, lean heroes, but she was a great authority on manners. And when she found me at the bannister, eyes wide at the sight of such a man, she promptly grabbed me by the ear.

"Ouch!" I cried, for once taken by surprise.

So my first meeting with Richard was humiliating, to say the least. He looked up, a smile of amusement on his handsome face. I thought I should die of embarrassment, but at least Vickers had sense enough to let go of my ear.

"Hello there," Richard said, and his voice thrilled my young bones. "You must be Miss Vanessa."

I managed to remember my manners. "Yes, Your Grace. And you must be the duke."

His eyes crinkled into the beginning of a smile, and he seemed even more handsome. "Please come down, Miss Vanessa, so that I may make your acquaintance properly."

I remember that I refrained from sticking my tongue out at Vickers. Being the hoyden I was, I felt very virtuous about it, too. And I moved slowly down the stairs until I was staring up at the most wonderful man in the world.

"I'm pleased to make your acquaintance, Miss Vanessa." And he kissed my hand! His touch was thunder and lightning, like nothing I'd ever known, but all too soon he withdrew his fingers.

I closed my gaping mouth and managed a small curtsey. "Thank you, Your Grace."

He smiled, and his whole face was lit from within. "Let's not be so formal. Soon I expect to be your brother.

Then perhaps you will call me Richard. And what shall I call my little sister?"

"N-Nessie," I replied, yearning with all my heart and soul to hear that diminutive fall from his lips.

"Nessie." Again that magic smile brightened his face. "A lovely name for a lovely young lady."

No doubt this sounds silly, the antics of a schoolroom miss, but I knew then that I would never marry any man but Richard, duke of Greyden. And, since he was quite intent on marrying Caroline, who had been the belle of that season and several past, it appeared that I was going to resign myself to a life of spinsterhood.

And that is, more or less, what I did. Mama passed away two years after Caroline became Richard's duchess. Without her darling, she had no more reason to live. We had not seen the married couple again. London was too far from Wiltshire for ailing Mama to travel, and Papa did not like cities.

I knew, too, though Papa did not say it, that Caroline would not welcome us with open arms. She had never had much use for Papa. In her eyes he had failed her by not coming of better stock. How she had supposed this to be poor Papa's fault, I could never understand. His "bloodlines," as he always called them, were impeccable, and the blame for his being a younger son could hardly be laid at his door; but Caroline was always wishing for a title and quite bitter about his lack of one.

At least, until she nabbed the duke and became a duchess. Then Papa and I knew that we were too far down Caroline's social scale to be invited to the great house in London. But we didn't really mind. City life was not where our hearts lay. Papa loved the country—his horses and his land—and I, who had always been a hoyden, fell

7

quite naturally into the habit of accompanying him on his rounds, especially after Mama's passing.

The matter of my marriage came up for discussion on occasion. Papa even tried to send me to London for a proper season, though not, of course, to Caroline, but I told him quite frankly that I didn't care to go, that I much preferred to stay in the country with him. Since this was what Papa wanted, too, it was not difficult to persuade him.

Several marriage proposals came my way, from fine decent men, but compared to my shining memory of Caroline's husband, they appeared in a very poor light. I could not love any of them; I was obliged to decline their kind offers.

The years passed, and Papa and I led contented lives. Five years after the marriage, Richard sent word of the birth of a daughter, Sarah. Papa considered a trip to London to see his only grandchild and to take in the celebration of our victory over Napoleon, but before he could arrange it, word came that the duke was removing his family to the castle in Cornwall. Papa decided we could equally well give thanks for Bonaparte's defeat at home. No mention was made of going to Cornwall, and I did not press the matter. I knew Caroline would not welcome us.

I could not imagine Caroline being happy in Cornwall, a place reported to consist of desolate moors and cold, gloomy castles, where the sea beat angrily against the great dark cliffs and life was often grim. Caroline hated the country, but even more she hated being removed from society. Its glitter and excitement were her life's blood. I wondered how Richard had managed to persuade his wife to leave the scene of her numerous triumphs.

But I wondered only briefly. Papa and I were much taken up with new land projects, and so one thing or another was always occupying our minds as another four years sped by, almost without our noticing it. Then another message came—this time a shocking one. Caroline was dead!

It was hard to think of the beautiful, vibrant Caroline as no longer existing. We had never been close, my sister and I. The years between us had contributed to this, but even more than that had been our other differences. Caroline was a petite beauty, a stunning belle of the ball who liked nothing better than being the center of attention, surrounded by admiring men. I, on the other hand, was tall and robust. Indeed, I had towered over more than one suitor, and I had never cared much for their compliments. Empty phrases I felt them. Those who compared me to a rose were most likely to feel my thorns.

I preferred the company of a few close friends to that of many competing admirers, and I had never particularly cared for the gossip that made up so much of society's calls. I was, as you can see, quite happy in my life with Papa, yet not so happy that Richard's new unmarried status did not occur to me, of course. But I had ever prided myself on my honesty, with self as well as others, and I knew that I was nothing at all like the wife Richard had loved and lost.

Papa and I put on the obligatory black, but we hardly knew how to mourn. Caroline had made no bones about her disdain for us, and I regret to say that I could dredge up no pleasant memories of my beautiful sister.

However, one memory did insist on insinuating itself into my mind. As a curious eight-year-old, I had ventured from the nursery into the apartments that were Caroline's. I wanted to know from which bottle my beautiful sister got one of the sweet scents that always surrounded her. To that end I was carefully lifting the stopper from each faceted crystal bottle and raising it to my freckled nose.

Caroline caught me with one halfway open. She grabbed it from me with one white hand and dealt me an open-handed blow with the other. "Don't ever touch my things again," she hissed, her face a harsh mask.

And I never did. With my cheek stinging, I ran from the room. I didn't want to smell like a garden, I decided then and there. For years after, I refused even to consider wearing a scent.

Papa's calm reaction to the news of my sister's death did not surprise me—she had been no better a daughter than she had a sister—but I do own to a little gasp of astonishment when I heard of the manner of her passing. "Stomped to death by that great stallion of his," Papa said, shaking his head sadly.

"But how?" We both knew Caroline for a wonderful horsewoman, renowned over the entire county for the slam-bang way she rode to hounds. There was no horse on the face of the earth that Caroline couldn't handle. I said as much to Papa that day as we gazed at the letter.

"I'm afraid she met her match," he replied sorrowfully. "A great stallion shouldn't be attacked with a riding whip. Not by man or woman." He frowned. "She was a wild one, that's for sure. Not like you, Nessie."

Papa's praise warmed me, as it always did.

"I do feel sorry for Richard, though," Papa continued. "He was besotted with the girl. And then there's the little one. Though the Lord knows I can't imagine Caroline as a mother."

Remembering that long-ago scene with the scent bottles, I had to nod. The Caroline I had known had always been concerned only for herself. To imagine her caring for someone else was virtually impossible.

We said no more about Caroline's passing. I knew Papa sent Richard a letter, commiserating with his loss, and then we went back to our land plans.

Another year passed. Green shoots were poking their heads above the ground. We had put off our mourning barely the week before, when Dickson came to me in the library where I was doing accounts. "A visitor, Miss Vanessa," he said.

I didn't look up. Papa and I had many visitors, all about our land reform plans. "Show him in," I said.

"Yes, miss."

I heard the sound of male footsteps entering the room, but I finished my sum before I looked up.

"Good morn—" I began. The words died in my mouth, and the pen fell from my lifeless fingers. Richard, duke of Greyden, stood before me. His riding breeches and expensive coat of superfine were crumpled and travel-stained, his Hessians covered with mud and dust. His lean, dark face was etched with lines of weariness, but in any condition he was to me a most beautiful sight.

"Your Grace." I struggled to my feet, inordinately pleased that that morning I had chosen my new apple-green gown with the velvet ribbons.

For a long moment his dark eyes stared deeply into mine. I felt rather like I was sinking, but it was a most enjoyable sensation.

"Nessie," he said finally, his voice even more thrilling than I remembered it. "The years have been good to you.

You have grown even more beautiful."

I blushed then. I, who had shrugged off other men's compliments with disdain, felt like the greenest schoolroom miss. "You are very kind, Your Grace."

My eyes hurried over his features. It was easy to see that the years had not treated Richard kindly. Gray dusted the dark hair at his temples, and there was a hardness to his eyes that I did not remember. There were more lines of strain on his face than could be accounted for by his trip or the decade that had passed. I longed to reach out and smooth away his cares. Instead, I dug my hands into my skirts, reminding myself that this rush of feeling was hardly seemly.

"We are pleased to see you," I said, summoning my best company manners. "Papa is away from home just now, but—"

"I'll be pleased to see your father," Richard said. His gaze was still on my face, giving me the strangest sensations. "But I'm glad he's away at the moment. I've a matter to discuss with you."

I stared. I knew it showed ill-breeding to do so, but I couldn't help myself. What possible matter could Richard, duke of Greyden, have to discuss with me?

"If you'll come out from behind that desk and sit beside me over here. . . ." He gestured with a lean dark hand.

"Of course," I mumbled, wondering if I could pinch myself without his noticing. I desperately needed reassurance that I wasn't dreaming the whole amazing scene.

I managed the pinch, but it was a useless effort. Richard was still standing there, watching me expectantly. I left the shelter of the desk and moved toward him. "You look weary," I said, perhaps sensing even then that something was not right in his life. "Would you care to wash, to rest? I'll have Franks fix a room for you."

My hand was halfway to the bellpull when Richard said, "Later. Come here."

I was not accustomed to obeying male commands— even Papa treated me more as a hunting crony than a daughter—but when Richard spoke to me like that, I went to him immediately. It was not because he was a man, of course; it was because he was Richard.

"Sit here, please," he said, indicating the sofa.

I sat, my heart dancing on my stomach. Or so it felt.

Richard seated himself beside me, so close my nostrils were filled with the good scent of him—leather and horses, and something else I could not quite define.

He reached over and took my hand in his. It was thunder and lightning again. The years had done nothing to eradicate that. The duke made me feel strangely unlike my usual no-nonsense self. Looking down into my lap, I reminded myself that I was no longer a gawking girl. "Yes, Your Grace?" I asked.

"Please look at me, Vanessa."

I looked. His eyes were dark pools of jet. I could read nothing in them.

"I am looking," I said, because his gaze was still making me out of breath.

"Yes," he replied, his voice low. "But now that you are, I'm not sure I can begin."

For a moment I forgot the dark hand holding mine. How could this man possibly have trouble speaking to me?

"Please," I said. "You may say anything to me, Richard." I almost gasped at my own audacity, calling

13

him by his given name, but the smile he gave me erased all my fears.

"Yes, Nessie," he said. "I believe I can." His dark eyes were solemn. "Please, though, hear me out before you make a decision. This is a matter of some importance."

"Yes, Richard." I wondered if he had forgotten that he held my hand. I had not. I could not. My heart continued its strange dance, and I found it even more difficult to breathe.

He inhaled deeply, and his fingers closed around mine. For all the world as though the man needed courage!

I stared down at the hand that held mine. Perhaps if I did not look at him, he would find whatever he had to say less troublesome.

"It's been a year since Caroline's death." His voice held no hint of emotion. Though I tried, I could tell nothing from it. "It was, of course, a great shock."

"To us, too," I replied, venturing a quick look at the face I had dreamed of so often.

"Yes, yes." He looked straight at me now, and I fought not to let the man see how his presence affected me.

"At any rate, the year of mourning is over." He sighed. "There's the child, Vanessa. A young child. She needs mothering." He looked at me earnestly.

"Yes, of course," I replied, not understanding any of this.

"Cornwall is a dismal place for many people."

I was bewildered. With Richard holding my hand, it was difficult to think properly, and I could make no connection between Cornwall and finding the child a mother. Because I could think of nothing to say, I said nothing.

"The moors are desolate. Society is meager. There are

few parties and fewer balls."

I simply could not stand it any longer. His meandering was raising such apprehensions in my breast that I thought I should have an attack of the vapors. I! Who was strong as a horse! "Richard, please! Come to the point. What is it you wish of me?"

His black eyes gazed deeply into mine. His lips formed into a thin line. He shook his dark head. "Matrimony," he said finally.

The breath went out of me in a great whoosh, and my eyes fell away from his. Richard had come to me to help him find a wife! If only he knew. . . . But he couldn't. He couldn't possibly. I licked my dry lips. "I am hardly a good maker of matches. I know few young women and very little about—"

The pressure of his hands on mine stopped me in midsentence. "No, Nessie," he said, and strangely enough he was smiling. "I do not want your help in matchmaking."

"But . . ." By this time I was completely bewildered. His presence so close to me, his hands on mine, his strange words—all combined to make me feel light-headed and more than a little stupid.

"Nessie, my dear." For a moment I heard only the dear, but then he went on. "Can't you see what I'm trying to say? I'm asking you to come to Cornwall with me. To be my duchess."

"I? A duchess?" I could not believe my ears. I clutched at his hand. It seemed the only solid thing in a world gone suddenly head over heels.

I pinched myself with my free hand again. I had dreamed of Richard often, especially in those first years after he had married Caroline. But never, ever, had I

15

dreamed anything approaching this.

Richard reached over and pulled my hand from my skirts. "What are you doing?" he asked, smoothing out my clenched fingers.

"I . . . I cannot believe this is happening." I could not tell him the childish thing I was doing. I could not think what to say to him; my mind was all awhirl.

His face darkened, and he withdrew his hand from mine. "I should have known I was asking too much. You've heard the rumors. You believe I had something to do with Caroline's death."

While I sat paralyzed at this astonishing piece of information, he leaped to his feet. "I don't blame you," he cried, bitterness lacing his voice. "I'll leave immediately. And Vanessa, there's no reason to bother your father with any of this. I should like to keep his good will, at least." Without looking toward me again, he started for the door.

It was the darkest moment of my twenty-three years. I willed the life back into my paralyzed limbs and commanded my tongue to obey me. "Richard! Stop!"

He swung on his heel, his face so hard and grim I could scarcely recognize the man I'd remembered with such longing.

"Please, Vanessa. There's no need for this. I fully understand."

I lurched to my feet and stood glaring at him. "No, Richard, you understand nothing."

His face grew grimmer. "I understand that my trip here was futile. You have refused me."

The moment seemed to call for dignity. I pulled myself to my tallest. "I have—" My hastily summoned dignity suddenly deserted me, and I became again a thirteen-year-old child. "Please, Richard." My voice quivered in spite of all my efforts to keep it from doing so. "I . . . I . . ."

My tongue simply refused to work, but fortunately instinct took over, blind feminine instinct. I literally ran across the library and threw myself against Richard's waistcoat. If his arms had not opened to catch me, I doubt that my legs would have held me; but his arms did open, and I was gathered tightly against a muscular chest where I finally managed to sob, "Yes, oh, yes. I *will* marry you."

Chapter Two

It was not settled quite that easily, of course. Papa had to be consulted. He seemed more than a little taken back when he came home and found the two of us ensconced on the sofa, deep in conversation about the moorlands and the varied uses to which they could be put.

"Papa," I cried, quite unaware that my hand lay possessively on Richard's sleeve or that my face shone with happiness. "Look who is here."

"Richard, my boy," Papa said, never being one to stand on ceremony, even with a duke. "It's good to see you again. How are things going for you now?"

Richard turned his smile to me. "Things are going admirably, sir. May I have a word with you before dinner?"

Papa cast me a quizzical look, but I could only beam in what I feared was a rather idiotic fashion. I knew that Richard meant to ask Papa for my hand in marriage, meant to do it even before the dinner Cook was so expertly preparing.

Later, looking back on those fateful moments, I wondered at my naiveté. I was no longer a gawking girl. As a mature woman of three and twenty, I ought to have had more sense than to go so giddy over a proposal from a man who had professed no stronger feeling for me than brotherly affection.

But I was as addlepated as any green girl, hardly even noticing that such a declaration was missing, intent only on being with the man I loved.

I did admit to myself that I was incurably romantic, and I blush to say that I even congratulated myself for not having settled for second best, never once giving thought to the fact that in me Richard was doing that very thing. Had I had my wits about me, I would have realized that a man who had been besotted by Caroline's charms could hardly find me an object of intense passion.

But I was too caught up in the fulfillment of my childhood dream to question any part of it. His astonishing words about Caroline's death meant so little to me that I didn't even bother Papa with them. It never even occurred to me to inquire about the other inhabitants of Greyden Castle or even to ask any questions about the place where I was planning to spend the rest of my life.

I didn't worry a bit when Papa and Richard sequestered themselves in the drawing room. I knew that Papa liked Richard. I knew, too, that my beloved Papa would put my happiness before his own.

And so he did. As quickly as the banns could be called, Richard and I were married. We left the same morning for Greyden Castle. Ours was a quiet wedding. There was none of the bustle and excitement that had marked Richard's first. He had wanted it that way, and for myself, I did not care. I would have married him any

19

place, any time.

I was sorry to part from Papa, for I loved him dearly; but I was all excitement about the new life that lay before me and the little daughter that I was soon to meet. Never once did I suppose that before many weeks had passed I would be wishing I had never left my sane, contented life with Papa.

But leave it I did. The journey was pleasant enough. Richard's carriage was one of the best, and his company made any minor discomforts hardly noticeable. We spent pleasurable hours discussing various methods of land use, but finally the subject seemed exhausted.

"Tell me about Sarah," I begged my new husband, placing a hand on the sleeve of his dark traveling coat. I was aware that I touched Richard perhaps a little too often for propriety's sake; but we were alone in the carriage, and we were man and wife, even if we had not yet had our wedding night.

At the mention of Sarah's name a curious thing happened. I felt the stiffening of the muscles that lay under my hand. His face did not change much. Only one who had studied it as closely as I had in the last weeks could have seen the faint withdrawal of warmth from his eyes. As he complied with my request and immediately spoke, I put what I had observed down to concern over the child.

"She is almost five," he said, in the rich deep voice I loved so well. "Her hair is long and fair. It falls in natural ringlets. Her eyes are wide and gray." He paused. "She looks very like her mother."

A shadow shivered over me, like a cold draft stealing under my warm furred cloak. There was something about the way he spoke, though his tone was even and his expression bland, that indicated great pain.

It came to me in a flash of understanding that turned my wildly beating heart icy cold. Richard still loved his wife—not the new one he was bringing home, but the first one whose daughter was a constant reminder of the joy he had lost.

For the first time I understood the concern I had seen in Papa's eyes. Well, I thought to myself, feeling the warmth of Richard's flesh through his coat sleeve, I am alive and I love Richard. I will make him forget her. I will make him love me.

I changed the subject then, discoursing on the countryside we were passing through, and Richard gladly joined me, his eyes regaining some of their warmth as we playfully argued over various methods of land use.

Why I did not think to ask him about his other dependents, I do not know. Why he did not freely tell me, I can now well understand.

We arrived at Greyden Castle just at nightfall. I must confess that I had fallen asleep, most comfortably, against my new husband's chest. Strange to say, I felt no embarrassment at waking there. However, this meant that I had no opportunity to view my new home from a distance.

I awoke just as the carriage halted by the great front door. Richard's face looked different in the shadows cast by the torch light—darker and with a sinister cast to it. For a moment I felt my heart pound with something very like fear.

Then I pushed such juvenile imaginings from my mind and smiled at my new husband. Desolate moors and cold gloomy castles meant little to me, I told myself. I intended to brighten his whole life with the warmth of my love.

Holding Richard's arm, I ventured into my new home. The entry hall was so huge I felt dwarfed by it. The roaring fire that graced the far hearth seemed too far away to give off any heat. Along the distant walls the flickering flames of many candles fought against the gloom and lost, and far back in the shadows stood the beginning of a great stone staircase, winding upward into encroaching darkness.

I shivered, and Richard glanced down at me, an amused smile on his dark face. "Don't say I didn't warn you. Castles are inevitably cold, my dear."

Had he known me better, Richard might have guessed that his casual "my dear" warmed me more than any fire ever could. I took it to my heart and kept it there, treasuring it as I was to treasure each smile, each little endearment, that came from my husband.

"I will get used to it," I said, smiling brightly and moving slightly closer to his side. "But where is Sarah? I am anxious to make her acquaintance."

Richard turned an inquiring eye to Gerson.

The butler's square face revealed no emotion, and his voice was equally bland. "Miss Sarah is in the nursery, milord. Asleep. The dowager thought the hour too late."

The dowager. I hadn't once thought of Richard's mother. But then I remembered her, and the memory was not an encouraging one.

I remembered most her steely gray eyes, eyes sharper and more penetrating than any I had ever seen. I remembered, too, her disdainful stare the one time I had chanced to become, very temporarily, an obstacle in her path. My new-found happiness was not to be entirely unchallenged, I thought. But if the dowager lived here, in

Greyden Castle, then why did Richard require a wife to care for the child? I turned an inquiring face to my husband.

His look made me draw a quick breath of surprise. Stark and grim, it seemed as cold and sinister as the castle entry hall. I had known Richard, really known him, only the few short weeks we waited for the banns to be called. Still, I had thought I knew all the moods and expressions of the man I loved so well. Never before had I seen such a look on my husband's face. There was anger there, and scorn. And pain, a great deal of pain. Something inside me curled into a tight ball, and I swallowed my question about the dowager. It was clear from Richard's face that his relations with his mother were difficult.

All of this happened in less time than it takes to tell of it. Then Richard's face assumed a dark, haughty look. "Send someone to Creighton. Tell her to bring Sarah. The child will meet her new mother tonight."

"Yes, Your Grace." Gerson's face was still expressionless, but something in his eyes indicated approval. "Immediately, Your Grace."

Soon a little noise came out of the darkness at the top of the stairs. "Good evening, Father. I'm happy to see you home safe."

A small white figure emerged from the gloom of the huge staircase. In the candlelight, her fair ringlets gleamed like spun gold. She paused some feet away, clearly awaiting Richard's reaction. I glanced from her to my husband and was surprised to find no welcoming smile on his lips. He might well have been facing some unpleasant and distasteful task. "You may come here, Sarah," he said formally, so formally.

The child advanced, slowly, carefully, putting one

small foot after the other. As she got closer, I could see her face. I swallowed quickly. Allowing for the childishness of her features. Sarah was a small replica of her mother. My heart lodged in my throat, and for the first time I considered that this was Caroline's child I had committed myself to love and care for.

Reminding myself that Sarah was in no way to blame for her mother, I stooped to her level. The child was less than a foot away. Her clear gray eyes stared calmly into mine, and for a moment her lips curved into a tiny smile.

"Is she my new mother?" she asked. As she looked at her father, the smile faded.

The expression on his face did not change. Why wasn't he warmer toward his child?

"Yes," I said quickly. "Will that please you?"

She tossed her small head, and my heart jumped. Just so had Caroline been given to tossing her blond curls.

"I don't know. Grandmother says—"

"Now that you have met, it really is time for bed." Richard's voice was not harsh, but it lacked affection. I could not help but wonder what the dowager had said about me and why he had felt it necessary to interrupt.

The child dutifully dipped her head. "Yes, Father. Good night, Father."

She hesitated.

"You may call me Nessie," I said, sensing that she was fumbling for what to say.

"Good night, Nessie." She paused as she reached the bottom step, a small white figure in the gloom. "It isn't true. You aren't like my mama at all."

She darted up the stairs before her father could reprimand her, and her last words floated out of the darkness above us. "And your hair doesn't look like carrots."

I turned to my husband with a light laugh. It was abundantly clear to me that his mother disliked the idea of our marriage. "Shall we be seeing the dowager tonight?" I asked, smiling to indicate that the child's words had not hurt me.

Any mother might well resent being displaced in her son's home, I reminded myself, and I could not imagine that Caroline's mother-in-law had many pleasant memories of her. Caroline had always been sure of her power, and she wielded it without mercy.

I supposed that the single exception to this must have been the duke. Still, I had read that men could be wrapped around a woman's finger if she knew the proper moves. As undoubtedly Caroline had.

My husband did not return my smile. "Has the dowager also retired?" he asked the butler.

"I believe so, Your Grace. The time of your arrival was not precisely known." This last seemed directed at me, almost as though Gerson were apologizing for his mistress's ill-breeding.

It was ill-breeding. Or, at least, premeditated discourtesy. The hour was not late, and Richard had sent word ahead of our coming. Still, I could not help feeling a little relief. I was weary, and the child's greeting had been rather disconcerting. I was just as pleased not to face the dowager at that moment, especially as this was my wedding night.

The duke tucked my arm through his. "I will show the duchess her rooms. Send her up a pot of hot tea."

"Yes, Your Grace."

I was glad to have Richard beside me as I approached the gloom of the staircase. He picked a candelabra from a side table and held it before us. "Tomorrow," he said, "I shall show you the whole place. It's most imposing in the daylight."

I nodded to this, but imposing was not the word I would have used to describe Greyden Castle. It was cold and gloomy; the very air seemed destructive, seeking to get under my fur cloak and into my bones. I tried to shake such thoughts from my mind. I was merely cold and weary. And I had been a little shaken—just a little—by the dowager's nonappearance and by the child's strange words.

I reminded myself that Sarah didn't know me. She must have time to become friendly, and the same applied to the dowager. She had only the memory of a carrot-topped hoyden—and the fact that I was Caroline's sister. Neither of which could do much to predispose her in my favor.

We ascended the great stairs, Richard and I. With him beside me the darkness was not so menacing. Surely in the next day's light, I would find this evening's feelings mere childish imaginings brought on by fatigue.

"The castle is very old," Richard said as we reached the top of the stairs. "Fourteenth century, in fact. Greyden's duke sailed with Raleigh against the Spanish."

I smiled, but momentarily I was thankful for the gloom of the corridor. We were approaching our wedding chamber, and though I knew a great deal about the mating of animals, I knew next to nothing of the first meeting of husband and wife. Even so, I did not suppose most wedding nights to include history lessons.

Richard pushed open a door and revealed a lovely room. Here the candles almost succeeded in relieving the gloom. A big state bed was hung with pale green curtains. I blushed as I saw they'd been pushed aside and the covers turned invitingly down.

26

The room's other appointments were equally attractive. Had Richard had this room redone especially for me? I could not imagine Caroline in a green room. Blue had always been her color. For the first time I considered that I would have not only Caroline's husband but her apartments.

"I hope you like it," Richard said softly.

My eyes looked to his face with longing, and my heart fluttered as I realized that my wedding night had finally arrived. "Did you . . ." I began, before common sense stopped me from asking the obvious question.

"I had it decorated with you in mind," he said. "I hope you won't think it vain. I . . ." Seldom did Richard falter, but at that moment he hesitated. "I think it was partly to keep my courage up. The way things had been here. . . ."

I recalled his hastily spoken words about people blaming him for Caroline's death. Of course they didn't know him as I did.

"It's lovely," I said, crossing the room to the series of crenellated windows that faced out toward the dark countryside. Through the space where my body blocked the reflection of the candles, I looked out. Moonlight bathed the dark woods below, touching the tips of branches and gleaming off trunks. Everything looked strange to me. The woods seemed different from any I'd ever seen, and the moonlight had a strange, eerie cast to it.

It must have been weariness that was making me so fanciful. I turned back to my husband. "Thank you."

He smiled. Now, I thought, now he would take me in his arms. At last I would be his in reality as well as in name.

But he didn't cross the distance between us. He didn't

come near enough to touch me. "The trip has been a tiring one," he said, "and your welcome was not what I would have wished for." His face darkened, and I was glad I was not the dowager. "Don't let my mother upset you. She's set strong in her ways, but I handle her."

He seemed about to say something else, and I waited with bated breath; but he merely indicated a door between two Chippendale side chairs. "My room is through there." He spoke as though this, too, were a piece of castle history. "Enjoy your tea and sleep well. I shall see you at breakfast."

While I stood staring in utter amazement, my husband went out, carefully closing the door behind him.

For a long moment I stood there, my heightened senses still feeling his presence. My first impulse was to throw something. Anything. I reached out toward a vase, then reminded myself that this was a habit Papa had deplored and which I had therefore suppressed. But, oh, how I wished to throw something then.

Frowning, I closed my gaping mouth and turned toward my boxes. At least the servants were efficient. While we had tarried with Sarah, my boxes and trunks had been carried up. I opened the one that held my nightdresses. A few tears spilled from my eyes as I laid aside the one I had stitched so carefully for my wedding night. Instead, I took out my warmest flannel.

The maid who brought the tea found me already in bed, my expression serene. I sipped while she scurried about hanging things. But as soon as I'd finished, she whisked the tray away, her expression one of anticipation.

I kept my face serene. At least the servants weren't aware that my husband was avoiding my bed. But where had he gone? Why hadn't he at least gone to his room for

28

the night?

No sounds came through the adjoining door, and I knew Richard was elsewhere in the castle. Probably with that mother of his.

I nursed my anger long into the night, another habit Papa had deplored and which I had tried to eradicate. But in this case it had one advantage. It kept me from remembering that in the morning I must face the dowager duchess of Greyden.

Chapter Three

Morning found me still tired and feeling rather put upon, but I pushed such thoughts aside. There must have been good reason for my husband's absence on our wedding night. I determined to make the best of things and subdue my temper, at least until I had heard his explanation.

I washed and donned my walking dress of gray merino, making a mental note to order some good warm stuffs for dresses. Though it was nearly summer, the castle was damp and chilly, and I did not intend to go about constantly shivering.

I pulled my cashmere tighter around my shoulders and surveyed myself once more in the cheval glass. Then I sighed. Where was the radiant face of a happy bride? The woman who looked back at me was sad and unhappy, her face white under the high-piled red hair. I pinched my cheeks, trying to put a little color in them, and turned toward the door.

I was not positive I could find my way back to the great staircase, but I determined to try. Certainly I did not want to be in this room when curious servants came to tend it. On impulse I leaned over and further disarranged the covers on the great bed. At least I could present the outward picture of a proper wedding night. With this in mind, I pulled my features into what I hoped was complacency and opened the door.

The corridor was still dark and gloomy; but at least it was possible to see, and the shadows seemed less threatening. I turned left, back toward the great staircase. Suddenly, without any sound or warning, he was there. A youth in black clothing blocked my path.

His huge dark eyes searched my face, and I felt a chill creep up my back. There was no welcome in those eyes, no good will. There was only animosity. "So you're that witch's sister," he said in a voice that rang like a death knell.

"I am Vanessa D—" I began, then belatedly remembered my new station in life. "I am the duchess of Greyden," I replied, returning his look without bothering to mask my distaste. "And who are you?"

He laughed, a most uncomfortable sound that held no merriment and, indeed, promised evil. "Some call me Penrose." His black eyes gleamed with unholy glee. "Some call me the youngest Greyden son." His full lips drew back in a smile straight from hell. "And some call me Satan's spawn."

A frisson of panic touched me. There was no denying he looked evil-born. Nothing relieved the dour blackness of his clothing, and even his skin seemed gray and ashen, as though he had risen from Hades' very depths.

I shook my head and called up my temper, a formidable weapon as Papa had often remarked. Looking straight into those gleaming black eyes, I laughed softly. It was

31

not my best cutting laugh, but he needn't know that. "As far as I'm concerned, you're simply a foolish young man. And, if you're indeed a Greyden son, you are most impolite to greet your brother's wife in this rude fashion."

Surprise flickered briefly in his eyes, but then he laughed again. How I was to hate the sound of that laughter in the weeks to come. "That witch's sister deserves no better welcome," he said. "Dear Caroline was not exactly beloved here."

I refused to let him frighten me. Was I not a duchess? "I am not Caroline," I replied, my tone flat. "And where I come from, people are judged on their own merits. Now, if you'll excuse me. . . ." I swept by him haughtily.

I made my way down the great stairs, my mind awhirl with questions. Where was Richard? Why hadn't he told me about this younger brother? Or that his mother disapproved of our union? I tried to remember what I'd heard about Richard's family, but I could recall nothing. Caroline's interest had been only in his title and his wealth. And, of course, ten years ago this Penrose had been still in the nursery.

I reached the bottom of the stairs and turned toward the smell of food. At least the people in this castle ate, I told myself, trying to dispel the sense of impending disaster that meeting with the youth had raised.

Fortunately, the smell of fried bacon issued from a small room down a corridor to the right. As I entered, I spied the figure of a man at the crenellated windows. His back was to me, and sunlight gleamed on his thick black hair.

Longing and tenderness rushed over me, but they had

to battle with irritation. I was not accustomed to such treatment as I had lately been receiving. "Richard!" I cried, hurrying to him. "I have met the most astonishing young man. And why—"

As I reached him, he turned, and in spite of my anger, I walked directly into his arms. This was my husband. And I loved him dearly.

His kiss threatened to burn the skin from my lips, and his arms pressed me close to his lean, hard body. Waves of feeling pounded over me, and I clung to him, inhaling his familiar scent.

But suddenly a chill came over me. Something was not right. There was a strange sweetness about him, a flowery scent that seemed almost womanly. And Richard had never kissed me like this before. I struggled and freed myself from his arms.

My knees quivered as I stood there, staring up into Richard's face. I blinked and rubbed my eyes. It was Richard's face—and yet it was not. Some indefinable thing told me this man was not my husband.

"Good morning," he said cheerfully. "Thank you for the welcome salutation."

My head rang; my blood pounded. The voice was Richard's, too, but not his. "Who—" I began.

"What are you doing here? I thought we were rid of you." The angry male voice came from behind me. I whirled, not believing my eyes. My husband stood there. His dark brows were furrowed, and his frown made me quiver, even though it wasn't directed at me.

"Mama wrote me the happy news," said the man who wasn't Richard and yet looked like him. "So I came home to see that my new sister-in-law receives a proper welcome."

He extended his hand to me and smiled. The warmth in his expression was as welcome as his words. "Congratulations, Vanessa. I hope you'll be happy here."

This was the first real gesture of welcome from anyone in this impossible family. Even though I felt Richard's displeasure, I felt constrained to return the man's greeting. "Thank you." His touch was warm, but I drew back quickly, mindful that this man's lips had been on mine in a salutation that could hardly be called brotherly.

"When are you leaving?" Richard's question was abrupt; his tone bordered on insulting. I turned to stare at him. How could he behave so rudely?

The stranger smiled at me. "Careful, Richard, you're shocking your little bride. Mama demanded my presence. And you know I can refuse her nothing."

He turned toward me. "No doubt she knows I've arrived. She'll be expecting me." He moved toward the doorway, and I saw now that he looked younger than Richard, his gaze more open, his features showing less wear. "Somehow I suspect you didn't tell your new wife much about us," he said. Then he was gone, and I was left staring at my husband.

For long moments he stood silent, apparently fighting some inner emotion. I tried to wait, but my temper was up. Why hadn't he told me what to expect?

"Richard . . ." I began.

He turned his dark eyes on me and smiled ruefully.

I felt again the pull of my longing for him. I shoved it down. I meant to have an explanation; I was certainly entitled to one.

"That was my brother Roland. My twin brother."

"Twins!" The word rushed out of me. "But why didn't you tell me?"

"He had left here. I had hoped he would never return." His features were grim.

My breath caught in my throat. "Your own twin?"

"My own twin," he repeated, his voice flat. "But, since he has returned, we will have to put up with him."

What a strange choice of words. I could not expect every family to be happy. But—twins! I had thought twins bore a special bond. And this Roland was warm and friendly, not like the dowager who hadn't deigned to greet me or the impossible young man who had blocked my way to breakfast.

"Richard." I was conscious of the rising inflection of my voice, a sure sign that my temper was also rising; but I had had enough of surprises, and I did not attempt to curb its sharpness. "Who else," I demanded, "lives in this castle?"

My husband smiled, but there was no light in his eyes. "I'm afraid you've the right to be upset, Vanessa, though I really didn't think Roland would return. And I had hoped that the dowager . . ." He paused, his look pained.

I felt a moment's tenderness, but I pressed on. "I met a most peculiar young man upstairs," I announced, letting my expression reflect my distaste.

"That was Penrose. Don't mind him." Richard's eyes avoided mine, as though he wanted to hide something from me.

But I didn't mean to be put off. "He said he was the youngest Greyden son. Are there still other members of your family that I know nothing of?"

Richard turned toward me and took my hands in his. "Only Rosamund, poor soul."

"Poor soul?" I echoed. What kind of marriage had I made?

35

Richard's hands were warm on mine, warm as his brother's lips. . . .

"Who is Rosamund?" I asked, trying to banish the feelings that had crept into my body. I had returned Roland's kisses only because I thought the man my husband. It was a natural mistake. And, actually, the fault should be laid at Richard's door. He had left me unprepared to deal with such a person.

"Rosamund is my sister," Richard said. "She suffered a loss when she was young. A terrible loss. It affected her mind."

A coldness seeped into my bones. What else didn't I know about this family? How foolishly I had agreed to share this man's life. "Her mind?"

Richard raised one of my hands to his lips and kissed it. "Don't look at me like that, Vanessa. Rosamund is harmless."

"Harmless?" My voice was still rising, my temper with it. I jerked my hand free from his and glared at him. "Exactly what is wrong with this sister of yours?"

He did not try to reclaim my hand—and foolishly, then, I wished that he would—nor did his expression change. My temper did not seem to engender any answering anger in him. "When she was seventeen," he said, coming to stand at my side, "she lost her heart to a young man. My father felt the man was unsuitable and made it worth his while to seek greener pastures."

I nodded. Many fathers had no doubt done the same. But if the young man had gone, he could not have loved Rosamund so much.

Richard's expression grew more troubled. "Rosamund refused to believe that he had taken the money. She insisted the duke had had him killed."

I could scarcely believe my ears. "She believed her father capable of murder?"

Richard nodded. "She was sure he had paid someone to do it. I tried to convince her otherwise. I saw the fellow later in London, but she would not believe me." He shook his head. "How she has suffered."

"But surely your mother—"

The anguish on my husband's face stopped my words.

"You may as well know now, Vanessa. The dowager is mother to only one of us. Rosamund and I mean nothing to her. To all intents, Roland is her only child."

"But Pen—"

"'Softly, love, softly. I'll come to thee soon. Darkness won't harm me.'"

The crooning song came from outside the door, the voice so slight and wavering one would have thought the singer elderly and frail. But when she entered, I saw a woman of indiscriminate age. Her rich sable hair, pulled back harshly, was the same color as her severe mourning garments.

"Good morning, Rosamund." Richard greeted his sister with warmth and affection, but her eyes held no welcome for him. Huge dark eyes, their depths haunted, stared out of a face as pale as winter's snow and just as cold.

"It's all right, beloved." The woman spoke to the vacant air beside her, putting her hand out to touch an arm that wasn't there. Revulsion shuddered over me as she gazed into nothingness. The huge dark eyes became earnest and tender. "I won't let anyone hurt you," she said softly. "We'll be together always."

"Rosamund." Richard reached out to touch her, and she looked up, her eyes widening with apprehension.

37

"You promised," she cried. "You promised."

"Rosie, really, it's all right."

The childhood name seemed to calm her, and she nodded. "Yes, Papa is gone. He can't hurt anyone now." She turned again to the empty space. It was terrifying to see the look of tenderness and love she lavished upon nothing. "He can't hurt anyone anymore. Ever again."

Her voice grew softer, and she raised her eyes, bringing them to bear directly on me. "He's in hell, you know. He was a wicked, wicked man." She smiled, and I shivered within the warm circle of Richard's arm. "He's going to burn forever. I'm glad."

The childish simplicity of her statement was almost more shocking than the words themselves. I was speechless. It was hard for me, who dearly loved my papa, to sympathize with a woman who thought hers capable of murder and who actually relished the thought of him burning in hell.

Fortunately, my lack of words made no difference to Rosamund. Her gaze fell and she turned away. "Come, beloved," she whispered softly, putting out a hand to clasp an imaginary one. "We'll go find Penrose. He's such a fine boy. So good at lessons. And he dearly loves his mama."

Rosamund left the room as quietly as she had entered it, all her attention focused on the vacant air she supposed contained her lover.

I shivered again, and Richard drew me closer. The heat of his body was comforting, and I found that my anger toward him had disappeared. Rosamund was indeed a poor soul. And what man, going courting, lays bare all his family's darkest secrets? Still . . . there were too many secrets here for my liking.

I turned toward my husband. "Richard, I—"

He bent his head toward me, his dark eyes warm with affection, and forgetting my questions, I lifted my lips to his. Our mouths touched. Sweetness like—

"So here you are." The voice was harsh, more like that of a fishwife than a duchess. It grated on the nerves like chalk drawn down a blackboard.

Richard stiffened, and I jumped, startled by this intrusion into our embrace. The voice was easily recognized, however, and I found myself transported back to the only other occasion I had seen the dowager. Her curt command still rang in my ears. "Get out of my way, you impossible child."

I straightened my shoulders, reminding myself that I was no longer a child. I was a full grown woman, the duchess of Greyden, and Richard's wife. The latter, especially, gave me courage.

"Good morning," I said, turning to face her.

She did not return my greeting. Eyes the color and texture of ice traveled over me, and it was only with difficulty that I kept myself from shrinking back against my husband.

The dowager duchess was a small woman, impeccably gowned in silver-gray, her graying hair skillfully dressed, but her majestic carriage and dignified mien were marred by the coldness of her eyes and her expression of complete contempt.

Finally, after long moments during which I drew solace from the nearness of Richard's body, the dowager spoke. "So this is her sister. This is the woman you've brought here to supplant me."

I gasped. I could not help it. Such rudeness was shocking in the extreme. If her eyes had really been the

39

icicles they resembled, I should have been instantly impaled. As it was, I merely moved a trifle closer to my husband.

I felt Richard pull himself to his full height. "You mistake me, Mother," he said with admirable coolness. "I had no intention of supplanting you. I brought Vanessa here for one reason. She is the woman I love."

His words started a warm glow deep within me. This was his first real mention of his feelings for me, and I gloried in this public statement.

The dowager shrugged her elegantly clad shoulders. "I thought you loved the other one."

The way she pronounced the words made them as insulting as any I'd ever heard.

Richard's arm tightened around me protectively, and I knew he wanted to comfort me. I smiled up at him as best I could. "Come, Richard," I said, determined to behave in a normal fashion. "Let us have some breakfast. The bacon smells especially good."

Actually, food was the farthest thing from my mind. How could I have an appetite when my new world was all so threatening? Not a person in this place had been glad to see me.

For a moment I recalled the touch of warm lips on mine. I tried to push the memory away. The kiss I had shared with Richard's twin had been a mistake. That was all.

The man beside me, the man whose strong arm was around me, he was the man whose kisses I should be remembering—except that I had not known many of them, I thought with a bitterness that would have alarmed Papa. And I still had no idea why my husband had left me to spend my wedding night in solitude.

The dowager's eyes were still upon me. Cold, speculative, angry. I could not help wondering at such obvious hatred. I had done nothing to this woman—except that one time as a child when I had inadvertently blocked her way. Yet now she gazed on me as though I were one of the world's lowest and most loathsome creatures.

I remained close to Richard. How could he live with such a hateful person in his household? It was obvious he had told me the truth. His mother did not care for him at all. Indeed, no one in this place seemed to care for him. No one but me.

I put my hand on his sleeve as we moved toward the well-set sideboard. Under my fingers I felt the faintest trembling, yet a glance at his face showed me that it revealed no emotion whatsoever.

Well it shouldn't, I thought, anger making me catch my breath. Richard was the master of this household, the eldest son; on his shoulders rested the responsibility for this entire family. Yet each of them seemed intent on making his life miserable. I could not, for the life of me, determine why this should be so.

The husband I knew was a good man. A little brooding, perhaps; occasionally a little sharp of tongue. Yet essentially a good man. It must be so, I thought, feeling a twinge of uncertainty. For surely Papa would know, and just as surely, he would never have let me marry the man had he felt otherwise.

Chapter Four

The sideboard was amply supplied. Food of all kinds lay there, ready to my palate. At least, I thought, with a resurgence of my ill temper, I should not starve to death in this desolate place. But, though I filled my plate with this and that and took my place beside my husband at the table, I found that my usual hearty appetite had deserted me.

Even the sturdiest soul may have difficulty swallowing steak and kidney pie when she finds she has married, in addition to the man she loves, a household of most peculiar relations—all of whom seem to hold her in the deepest aversion.

Richard filled my cup with more chocolate. "You must eat heartily," he told me. "The castle is always on the cold side, even in the spring."

I nodded, determined to be cheerful. "I shall order some warm stuff for some new gowns. No doubt there's a dressmaker in the village who'll be glad of the business."

The dowager snorted. It was a rude sound, most unladylike. Richard ignored it, and following his pattern, so did I.

But I would find that the duchess could not be ignored. She did not intend that we should escape her censure. Not then. Not ever. "Warm clothes won't help you," she said, fixing me with a baleful eye. "They didn't help *her*."

A chill crept up my backbone. What was this awful woman talking about? And what did she mean by speaking about Caroline in such a tone?

I glanced at my husband for support and was surprised to see on his face a look of such fierceness that it almost made me move away from his side. "Mother—" he began.

"She might as well know it," the duchess declared, returning his look with one equally fierce. "She's not welcome here."

The harsh words were uttered in the coldest tones. I could not help myself. I shivered again. My temper had never been such as to take insult lightly, as Papa had more than once regretfully informed me, so I faced my mother-in-law with all the severity I could muster—and it was considerable. "I do not know," I said, "why you dislike me. I have only just arrived here. You have had no opportunity to know me yet. I came here your son's wife. Why do you not welcome me as most mothers would?"

From the doorway came a harsh caustic laugh. I knew before I turned that the youngest Greyden male stood there. He was still dressed completely in black, as Rosamund had been.

"Being Richard's wife," Penrose said, "will not make the dowager care for you. Now or ever. On the other hand, if you were Richard's enemy—"

"Enough," said my husband. He fastened his eyes on the youth. "Treat Vanessa with some respect. She is not

43

her sister."

This last remark startled me. Was everyone treating me so rudely because they supposed me to be another Caroline? Well, if that was the case, I should have to disabuse them of such a foolish notion. Perhaps if I practiced patience. But, unfortunately, that was not one of my natural attributes.

Still, I put on my friendliest smile. "I really am very different from my sister," I said as cheerfully as I could. "And if you give me a chance, you will see that for yourselves."

The duchess did not bother to look up from her plate. It was obvious to all that she did not care what I did or said.

Well, I would have to give her time. I would exert myself to be pleasant. Surely after a while they would all realize that Caroline and I were as unlike as sisters could be.

I turned again to Penrose. I would start with him. "Does your sister like to arrange flowers? Perhaps we could go for walks together. She must be lonely here, so far from everyone."

Penrose laughed. I cannot, to this day, forget the harsh abrasive qualities of his laughter. "Rosamund is never lonely," he said. "She has her Jeffrey."

I so forgot myself as to say, "Surely you don't believe that—that—" Words failed me. I could not go on.

His eyes laughed at me, cruel, piercing eyes. They searched my face for weakness. "Believe that his spirit accompanies her? Why shouldn't I believe it? She does."

I mustered all my resources. I reminded myself that I was a grown woman. I was Richard's wife. "But she is— ill. She needs help."

Penrose's face changed. From being sarcastic, it became twisted and violent. "Rosamund is saner than most people," he proclaimed, "and she is not going anywhere." He turned angry eyes to Richard. "I warn you—"

"Penrose!" Richard's voice rose only slightly, but it was enough. The youth lapsed into sullen silence. "You know quite well," Richard continued, "that Rosamund will remain here. I have no intention of sending my sister away from her home. And that is not what Vanessa had in mind."

"Indeed, it is not." I hurried on, intent on making myself clear. "I would never advocate sending her away from her home. I only meant that perhaps some fresh air and sunshine, and the company of another woman might be beneficial to her."

Penrose smiled, a smile of pure evil. "The company of your sister was not."

At that my temper, which I had been struggling to subdue since Richard left me the night before, broke completely loose. "How dare you?" I cried, leaping to my feet with such vengeance that my chair hit the stone floor behind me with a sharp report. "How many times must I tell you? I am not my sister!"

There was silence in the room. My violent outburst seemed to have stunned them all.

Finally Richard got to his feet and set my chair upright. He put a steadying hand on my arm. "Sit down, Vanessa. Calm yourself."

"Calm?" My voice was going higher and higher, and so was my temper. I tried to curb it by counting all the way to one hundred, but while I counted, I could not prevent myself from thinking.

The people in this impossible household had been uniformly rude to me—a stranger in their midst. Where I should have expected welcome, I had received insult. Not one—for a moment my mental tirade paused, and I remembered a kiss that had stirred my senses. But that, too, I reminded myself, was an insult. A kiss from my husband's twin—about whose existence he had conveniently neglected to inform me.

Then there were the circumstances of my wedding night. To leave me to spend my wedding night all alone— and without so much as an explanation. Now, when his nephew offered me insult, my husband wanted me to stay calm!

I was about to burst forth with some words unsuitable for a lady's tongue, when from behind me came Roland's smooth voice. "So, I see she has a temper like Caro's."

The shock of this hit me like a bucket of cold water. How could I ever expect to win these people over, to persuade them that I was not like my sister, if I let my temper so easily erupt? I swallowed hastily and reconsidered what I would say.

"I am not like Caroline," I repeated in as moderate a tone as I could manage. "And, given half a chance, I shall prove it to you."

The dowager looked about to make another disparaging remark, but from the hallway came a childish voice. "I want to see her!" It was evident from the tone that Caroline and I did not have all the temper in our family. "I *will* see her," the child cried. "She's my new mother."

This last warmed my heart, and I half turned in the chair, expecting the onslaught of a small body. Some childish hugs and kisses such as the village children had often given me would be tonic for my aching heart.

But the child Sarah did not run into my arms. She went straight for her Uncle Roland and climbed up on his knee. To my surprise I saw that she, too, was wearing black. I swallowed my disappointment and smiled at her. "Good morning, Sarah."

"Good morning." She cocked her head to one side and stared at me. "I was right. Your hair is not like carrots. But it is a funny color."

Beside me I felt Richard stirring. He must not reprimand the child over me. "Yes," I said quickly. "It's red."

"My hair is like my mama's." She twisted and looked up at Roland as she said this. Perhaps he was the one who had told her so. He smiled at her warmly. Well, at least there was one member of this incredible household who knew how to respond to a child.

"You're right," I told her. "Your mama and I were sisters."

Sarah nodded. Evidently someone had already told her this. "I wish I had a sister. I'd like someone to play with. Creighton isn't any fun."

Thinking of my escapades with poor, long-suffering Vickers, I swallowed a smile. "Perhaps you and I can do some things together."

The child's eyes—eyes so like Caroline's—widened, and she tossed her curls in that way her mother had had. "Why?"

The simple question left me momentarily speechless, but one thing was eminently clear. Richard had been right about it. This child was sadly in need of a mother.

I took a deep breath. "We shall do things together because I am your new mother. And I care for you." I tried to remember the pursuits of five-year-old girls.

47

"Have you a doll baby?"

Something flickered in Sarah's eyes. I thought it was eagerness, but I could not be sure. "No," she said, her tone so like Caroline's that it was uncanny. "Babies are an awful bother."

How could Caroline have told her own child such a terribly hurtful thing? "That is not true," I said firmly. "Babies are quite the most wonderful thing ever. A gift from God. We shall have babies here, I expect. And I will need you to help me with them."

"You will?" The child's eyes lit with excitement, and she clapped her little hands.

"Of course. You will be the big sister." And, I vowed silently, she would not be the kind of big sister her mother had been. "In the meantime," I continued, "your father will get you a doll baby, and I will show you how babies are cared for."

Through this whole exchange the dowager had continued to eat. Now she took the last of her chocolate and left the table, as silently as if the rest of us did not exist. No one else appeared to find this at all unusual, but I had no time to speculate on the dowager's nonexistent manners.

Though what I had said to Sarah had been spontaneous, occasioned by her strange remarks, I fully expected to give Richard children, many children. In my innocence then, I saw them running and laughing through the castle's gloomy halls, bringing joy and cheerfulness into Richard's life.

I turned to my husband. His expression was inscrutable, and I recollected that it was perhaps premature to speak of children when our marriage had not yet been consummated. "You will get Sarah a doll baby, will you

48

not, my love?"

"If you wish it, Vanessa." His eyes did not change. They did not warm when he looked at me. In some strange fashion they seemed to shut me out. Another shiver threatened to overtake me. Richard was my rock. In this strange household he was the only one I could trust. So why did he look at me as though—I could not finish the thought.

I was being foolish. My husband cared for me. He just seemed distant because of all the animosity in this household. I bristled to think of the way his own mother treated him. Would it not be natural for him to learn to withdraw into himself, surrounded as he was by those who gave him no honor, no love?

That was going to change. Richard now had me for a wife, and his life would be better for it. I would see to that.

As I glanced up at them, Roland smiled at the child on his knee. My mind went again to Richard's strange behavior. Why was he so cold to his only daughter? Could he be the sort of man who only valued sons? But that did not seem like the Richard I knew.

I wished I had Papa there to give me the benefit of his wisdom, and in a way I did: I knew exactly what Papa would say. "When you want the answer to a question," he had often told me, "the simplest thing to do is ask straight out. Nine times out of ten the person'll be glad to tell you."

I was not sure Richard would be glad to tell me, but at least I meant to try.

Well, I thought, turning my attention to my breakfast, I had been in Cornwall less than twenty-four hours, and already I had several questions that needed answering.

49

First and foremost, of course, was the matter of my lonely wedding night.

I felt my cheeks growing warm as I thought of it. Perhaps Richard had been concerned for me. The trip had been long. I had been tired. Probably tonight—

I had the uncomfortable feeling that someone was staring at me. When I looked up, I caught Roland's smile.

For a moment in my confusion, I imagined that he knew my thoughts, and my blush deepened at the memory of his kiss. Then I recollected myself. I returned his smile with a friendly sisterly one of my own, but I drew my eyes away from his. It was most disconcerting to have the only friendly person in the household so resemble my husband. Roland's kiss had been sweet, but I had no desire to kiss any man but my husband.

Sarah finished the roll she'd been eating and scrambled down from Roland's lap. She ran toward me with that little skipping gait children have. "Will you come to the nursery later?" she asked. "Nurse Creighton will want to meet you." She wrinkled her small nose. "She knows lots of stories."

"Yes," I said, longing to hug the child, but afraid to move too soon. "I shall be along to see your nursery later."

She skipped out, and Penrose looked up from his plate. "You will love Creighton's stories," he said with malicious delight. "Be sure to ask her about the haunting babe."

I looked at my husband, but he did not seem upset. "You know how servants are," he said with a shrug. "They're given to seeing spirits everywhere."

Now, if we'd been at home in Wiltshire, I'm quite sure I would have nodded in agreement and dropped the

50

matter. But in this castle, whose coldness even then gnawed at my bones, the idea of haunting babes did not seem so farfetched. Still, I did not intend to let Penrose frighten me. He was nothing but a nasty boy. I looked straight at him as I said, "I do not fear ghosts."

He laughed and bit into a roll as though it were a living creature. "Perhaps not," he said. "But I should stay out of the North Tower if I were you."

My patience, never particularly strong, had been stretched to the breaking point. I no longer cared whether I made a scene or not. I intended to get to the bottom of this frightening thing.

Again I turned to my husband. "Richard, I believe this has gone far enough. However silly the stories may be, I wish to hear them."

Richard frowned, his dark brows meeting in a fierce line. "Very well, Vanessa. If you insist."

I did not like seeing him angry, and for a moment I considered withdrawing my request. I did not really wish to hear any more unsettling stories, but since Greyden Castle was to be my home, I had to be prepared to deal with it. So I said, "Tell me."

"Creighton, Sarah's nurse, claims that a babe haunts the castle. The woman is growing old. She's probably just hearing the usual unexplained noises."

"And the North Tower?" I might as well have all the bad news.

His expression grew darker. "Caroline claimed that it was haunted."

He sighed as though the memory pained him. My heart ached for the man who had loved my sister so.

"At first she liked it there. But then one day she said she saw a ghostly figure, and she refused to use that part

51

of the castle again."

This did not sound at all like my sister. No ghost living—or perhaps I should say dead—would keep Caroline from anything she wanted. I was about to say so when I remembered something else.

Once Caroline had wanted to keep me from a certain place in the woods where she was in the habit of seeing a neighbor boy. So she had told me a frightening story of the witches who made that very clearing the scene of their gatherings—and who were fond of the flesh of young girl children. The ruse had worked, of course. I was too young to understand her machinations.

But I was older now, and wiser, and I was quite sure that Caroline had wanted everyone to stay away from the North Tower. Therefore, she had circulated a story certain to frighten the servants.

I decided to keep my peace about my conjectures. Little would be served by my voicing these suspicions. Whatever Caroline had been doing in the North Tower, it could have been beneficial only to her.

It pained me to think of my sister in such harsh terms, but I had always been a realistic person. It seemed that Caroline had not changed. The woman who told her little girl that babies were an awful bother was the same woman who had struck her little sister for smelling her scent bottles.

There was no use my denying the fact. The evidence was everywhere around me. Caroline had deserved every bit of the dislike these people felt for her. And to change their minds about me was going to be quite a strenuous undertaking.

Chapter Five

Several times I was like to choke at the thought of what I had heard that morning, but I forced myself to continue chewing and swallowing. I would show Penrose, and the rest of these horrid people, that they could not frighten me.

When we had finished eating, I said to my husband, "Will you show me my new home now?"

He put down his cup immediately. "Yes, my dear. But since the weather is nice, perhaps you would like to see the outside first."

The prospect of fresh air and sunshine was most encouraging, and I nodded in agreement.

Moments later we stood together outside the great front door. Made of solid oak, it looked strong enough to withstand any battering ram. We walked a way down the tree-lined road, so that I could view the castle as a whole from the distance.

The road slanted downward, so when we paused and turned we were looking up. The castle rose against the blue morning sky. It was built like a great box, with a tower at each corner and a series of parapets running between. There must be walkways up there, I thought, where the old defenders had stood to withstand the onslaught of the enemy.

The stone had darkened over the long years, until the building looked weary and aged. Though the spring sky was beautiful, bright and clear, and the sun was casting dapples on the road at my feet, the castle was grim and foreboding. A frisson of fear skittered over my skin. The place looked a fit home for its strange inhabitants.

"It is so—huge," I whispered, clutching my husband's arm. It was not like me to be weak-hearted, but there was just something about the place. Even the cheerfulest heart would have paused at such a sight.

"This was not the whole of the original castle," Richard told me. "This was only the keep. Originally the battlements ran out in both directions and made a huge walled rectangle which surrounded the bailey. You may find pieces of the wall even yet. It was let go to disrepair when the constant fighting stopped."

"Was there much fighting here?" I asked.

Richard frowned. "I suppose so. It's on the coast. And there were many petty little wars."

I shivered again, thinking of all the blood spilled, all the lives lost. All the women who mourned and wept. I sighed deeply.

He looked down into my eyes. "Are you all right, Nessie? The family can be a little overwhelming at times."

Overwhelming was hardly the word for this horrid family. Still, I only said, "Yes. But if you had warned me, I should have been better prepared."

"I meant to, but the time never seemed right. You

were so happy. And away from here, so was I." His frown deepened. "I had hoped to make you happy here, too. Caroline hated it, you know. She hated me."

"Oh, Richard, no!" The pain in his voice was like a stake in my own heart. How could I make Richard love me when he was still mourning her?

He frowned. "It's true. She told me so many times."

"She—she must have been angry. That's all. She didn't mean it."

He laughed, a bitter sound that carried no amusement. "She was angry, yes. But she meant what she said. She hated me."

"But why?"

He slipped an arm around my waist, and I felt warmth stealing through me.

"She was not like other women, Nessie. Not like you. She needed the admiration, the adulation of men."

His expression grew so wretched that I longed to tell him to stop. I did not want to hear this terrible story, but something bade me hold my tongue and listen. I had to know what had happened.

"I brought her here, away from that," he continued. "And so she hated me."

"But if you knew she hated it . . ."

He sighed. "I had no choice. She was becoming the talk of the town. She had taken—taken—"

It seemed he could not go on. Emboldened by his arm around me, I whispered, "Lovers?"

He turned, his eyes dark and full of pain. "How did you know?"

I decided to be truthful. "She always had them—at home. Papa didn't know, but she sneaked out nights sometimes, and she met boys in the woods. From the time

55

she was first grown."

"I had to put a stop to it," he said, "and so I brought her here. Away from the city. Away from everyone."

He looked so distressed that my heart ached for him. It was not good for him. This discussion of Caroline was too painful. It was painful for me, too—the second wife seeing how much he had loved the first. Besides, I had heard all I needed to hear. I decided to change the subject.

"Can we walk around the castle?" I asked. "I should like to see all of it."

He favored me with a warm smile. "Of course, my dear. We cannot go all around, but come this way. I'll show you why."

With his arm around me I would have gone anywhere.

"The castle is built on the cliffs," he said as we walked. "It dates from the time of Raleigh. But I told you that."

He squeezed my waist. "We can go around this way. To the North Tower. The back wall faces the sea. The North Tower looks out over the cliffs."

I suppressed a shiver and managed a little giggle instead. "Is that the haunted tower?"

He nodded. "I'm glad you don't believe in such foolishness." He swung me around to face him. "Oh, Nessie, I'm so glad you're here. My life has been empty for so long."

"I'm glad, too," I whispered, raising my face for his kiss. It was a sweet kiss, heartfelt, and I returned it happily, wishing that nightfall would come rapidly.

But there was a whole long day to be gotten through first, before my husband could come to me and really become my husband.

Richard released me and took my hand. "You must not

go this way alone," he warned.

I would not have thought of doing so. Stunted trees and wild grasses pressed in upon the castle, leaving only a narrow stone walkway. It was not a place anyone would wish to go alone, even in broad daylight.

"It is too dangerous," Richard continued.

My thoughts flew immediately to Sarah. I was already thinking as a mother. "The child—"

"Sarah does not come out alone. Creighton always accompanies her." He squeezed my fingers again. "Sarah seems to have taken to you. But be careful. My mother and Roland—they have too much influence over her."

Now was the time, I thought, to ask him why he treated his daughter so coldly. But then we rounded the corner, and I gasped.

A narrow wooden railing bridged a gap in the ruined wall. That railing was all that kept a person from stepping right over the edge of the walkway and falling to a horrible, smashing death on the sea-washed rocks below.

In spite of the sparkle of the sea foam, the scene was sinister. I could almost see bruised and broken bodies draped over those rocks.

I clutched my husband's arm. "Oh, Richard, this *is* dangerous. Can you not close it off?"

Richard patted my hand. "Nessie, my dear. I didn't know you were afraid of heights."

I shook my head. "It is not the height. I had quite a reputation as a tree climber in my childhood. It is just—it looks so—and the rocks—" I felt ridiculous, unable to even voice my fear.

"Come," he said. "We'll find the path and go down to the beach."

I could not stop the shiver. "Down there?"

"No, dear. That beach is too rocky. But farther on there's a path, and the beach there is sandy. Shall we go?"

"Of course." I had followed Richard into this impossible household. Why should I not follow him to the beach?

The path lay through a wood. I had my shawl, but though it was spring, I wished for my heaviest cloak. The wood was dark and chill, shutting out the sun's light and warmth. And the trees were strange—their branches and exposed roots twisted like creatures in mortal agony. I shuddered, and Richard drew me closer.

"There's no need to be afraid, Nessie. It's the elements that make the oaks grow so strangely twisted. The soil and the sea wind."

I nodded, and I did not voice my thoughts that perhaps it was not the elements at all, but the pervasive evil of the castle reaching out to twist all within its purview.

In a little while we came out of the wood into the sunlight. Then I was glad I had kept my foolish dark thoughts to myself. Just because my husband had a few peculiar relations was no reason for me to start conjecturing evil at every turn.

The sun was warm on my face. The sand shone like spun gold. The wind and the sea had conspired to pile the sand in graceful sloping dunes. Some were barren and others were dotted with tall, graceful grass. And down by the ocean's edge, the foaming water kissed the golden sand.

I felt like a child again, released from the prison of the schoolroom. The dark gloom of the castle and its distressing occupants fell away like the shawl I let drop into the sand. I began to run—down toward the golden shore, the sparkling water.

The sand pulled at my flying feet. The wind blew my hair down into my eyes. My husband called after me, "Nessie, stop!"

Still I ran. I ran and I ran until the ocean itself stopped me.

I stood there, panting, drinking in the glory of the sea, the sharp salt tang in the air, the sunlight dancing on the waves.

Then Richard came panting up beside me. He clasped me to him in an embrace that eliminated what little breath I had left. I struggled to free myself, to breathe properly.

He looked down into my eyes, and his face was white with terror. "Don't—ever—do that—again," he gasped.

I did not understand. I frowned. "Do what, Richard?"

Slowly he regained his breath. "The sand. Don't run."

I did not like having my simple pleasure criticized. "Why not? Who's to see?"

"Not see. The sand—quicksand."

The words struck terror in my heart. Even at home in Wiltshire we had heard stories of the sucking sands that could swallow whole cows and horses.

"You mean—right here on the beach I could get—" The words would not come.

Richard had regained his breath. "Yes," he said. "You could get swallowed up."

"But can't you tell where it is?"

He shook his head. "Not always. Sometimes it looks just like the other sand."

"So inviting," I murmured.

"And so dangerous."

Though the sun was still warm on my skin, I felt a

coldness deep inside. In this awful place even beauty was suspect.

"So you see," Richard continued, "you must be careful."

I nodded. "Yes, I shall be." With determination I pushed away my feelings of foreboding. I had loved Richard long and truly—much longer than he had any reason to believe—and I did not mean for anything whatsoever to come between us.

Putting a smile on my face, I turned to him. It was then I saw it, looming like a prison house over the golden beauty of the beach—the castle, high on the cliffs.

Home. I tried to form the word in my mind. In my heart. Greyden Castle was my home. But the idea refused to take root, until Richard looked at me and smiled. I knew then, that for better or worse, wherever Richard was, *that* was my home.

His smile grew. It was amazing how much younger he looked when he smiled, like the dashing blade I had first seen and loved.

"Nessie," he said. "Let's do something childish."

I was game for that. It was good to see his eyes light up, to see happiness on his face. He looked more like the Richard I had come to know in Wiltshire while we waited on the banns. "All right," I agreed. "What shall we do?"

His eyes danced like the sunlight on the waves. For a moment I imagined the two of us naked on the golden sand. I could almost feel his kisses.

Then he said, "Let's walk in the ocean." He frowned, his happiness suddenly fading. "But I forget. You might get your gown wet."

It was almost as though Caroline had snapped at him. I hated to see the light go out of his eyes. "I have plenty of gowns," I cried gaily. "Surely a little sea water and sand will not harm this one. I have never walked in the ocean, Richard, and I should very much like to do so with you."

His smile came back then, and I thought I should walk anywhere, do anything, if only I could make him happy.

He led me to a comfortable rock, and right there in the sand he knelt and removed my shoes. He looked up at me, his face as sheepish as a boy's. "Perhaps you should do the rest." While he took off his Hessians, I removed my stockings.

The sand squished delightfully between my bare toes, warm and comforting. With my husband beside me, I could push the thought of sucking sands from my mind.

Richard stood up. His bare feet looked strong and masculine. Looking down at my own toes, I felt suddenly undressed, but I pushed the thought away. This man was my husband. Soon he would see much more than my bare toes.

I stood up, too. "Show me how I must fix my skirt."

"The fishermen's women do it this way," he said. He took the back of my skirt and pulled it through my legs and up the front, where he tucked it under my belt. The result was a trifle bulky, but I did not care. I would have run naked on this beach had Richard asked me to.

"Ready?"

"Oh, yes!"

Like two children we ran squealing into the waves.

It was a wonderful golden hour, the first truly happy time I had spent since I reached the castle. Greyden was still there, of course, looming over us, but I refused to consider it or its baleful influence. I wanted only to be happy with the husband I loved.

The sun was high in the sky when Richard drew me

into his arms and kissed my nose. "Your freckles are coming out," he said with a laugh. "And I love them."

If Richard loved them, that was enough for me. "I shall come out into the sun every day, then," I said pertly. "And soon I shall be nothing but freckles."

He kissed me again, this time on the lips, and I thought to ask him about the previous night. But the moment was so golden that I hesitated. Why should I ruin this precious time with recrimination? Richard loved me. I could feel it.

He looked at the sun. "We must be getting back," he said, his voice heavy with regret.

I felt as though a dark cloud had passed overhead, but I resolved not to let my fancies take control of my mind. "Yes," I said. "I promised Sarah I would come to the nursery."

His expression changed; his eyes went cloudy. "And I shall attend to some things in the village."

I was not imagining this. I had felt the slight stiffening of his body at the mention of Sarah. But I was too happy to pursue the matter then.

So we dried our feet as best we could, and I put on my stockings. Richard insisted on kneeling to replace my shoes. As I gazed down at his dark head, my heart overflowed with love for him.

My happiness carried me through the dark wood, but in the front hall, when Richard dropped a kiss on my forehead, I wanted to throw myself into his arms and beg him to stay with me. I did not do such a childish thing, of course. How he would have stared at me if I had. Instead I smiled pleasantly and wished him godspeed.

The castle's interior was still grim; the candles still did not give enough light to banish the feeling of gloom that hung over everything, but I would not let that bother me. I was Richard's beloved wife.

With that thought to armor me, I set out for the nursery. I could have asked the butler for directions, but I did not want to look foolish in front of the servants. As I went up the great stairs, my unfortunate temper took hold again. A good husband would not have run off to the village. He would have stayed to show me around the castle, not left me here to feel like an utter stranger.

When I realized what I was doing, I tried to laugh at myself. Only moments ago I had been all choked up for love of Richard, and now I was growing angry with him again.

I hoped Sarah would not become a bone of contention between us, but this matter had to be resolved. Thinking of my papa and the love between us, I was brought almost to tears. It was not decent for a man to treat his child in this strange fashion.

He had loved his wife, loved her very much. Why did he not love their child?

I found the nursery without too much trouble. Since the castle was constructed in a great square, I just kept walking. The nursery was below the South Tower, far away from the rooms that Richard and I shared.

This tower, too, faced the sea. What a strange choice, I thought, putting the child in such a place—and so far from her mother.

I peeked around the door and announced, "Sarah, I have come to see you as I promised."

For a moment there was silence. Then an old woman appeared from an inner room. She was slightly bent and wearing black. In the gloom, her eyes seemed to gleam. "Good day, Your Grace."

"Good day."

"'Tis sorry I am about the child," she began.

"The child?"

Creighton nodded. "This morning at breakfast. She had to come down to see you."

I smiled. "That's all right. I wanted to see her, too."

The nurse's face reflected bewilderment. "He didn't tell you," she said finally.

Obviously she was talking about Richard. I disliked gossiping with the servants, but how could I function here if I didn't know what was going on? "Tell me what?" I asked, keeping my voice calm.

"The child's not to go down there. She's to stay out of his sight. In the nursery."

This was terrible. I thought of Richard's passion for Caroline, of the way Sarah so resembled her mother. Could the sight of their child be too much for him to bear?

"But surely, now that the year of mourning is over," I began.

"It ain't got to do with mourning," the nurse said. "'Twas *her* orders. Since the babe was born."

"My sister's orders?"

"Aye."

Even Caroline could not have been so heartless. "Then she must have come often to see the child."

The nurse shook her head. "She weren't no more eager to see her than he was. The only one as cares about her is Mr. Roland. Now, there's a good man."

I was inclined to agree with her, but Richard was my husband. "There must be some reason . . ." I murmured.

The nurse shook her head. "All I know is, I got my orders. And I bide by them."

"Yes, of course. Where is Sarah now?"

"She's sleeping, Your Grace. She takes a little rest after lunch." She covered her mouth with her hand. "I usually lays down myself for a while. The haunting babe was noisy last night. Kept me awake."

I knew I should walk away, but my curiosity overcame me. "Tell me about the haunting babe."

She nodded. "Whyn't you sit down here by the fire? And I'll tell you all I know."

I followed her to a chair. The fire gave off little heat, but its glow was cheering.

Creighton settled into a battered rocker. "'Tis a babe dead afore its time. In the first days, when this castle was new built, the lord sailed off with Raleigh to fight the Spaniards. He left his lady with two young ones and another on the way. When he didn't come back, she lost the child. And after that, the babe could be heard crying."

She clasped her gnarled hands together. "'Tis said that if a member of the family hears the babe crying three nights running—" her voice fell—"then Death will come calling."

"Death?" The tale shocked the word out of me.

"Aye." She looked around fearfully. "They say *she* heard it before—before—"

For a moment I thought *I* could hear the babe crying. Then I straightened. This nonsense had gone far enough. "I hope you have not told Sarah such fearful stories," I said, getting to my feet.

"'Course not," Creighton replied, struggling erect. "I wouldn't be frightening the little one."

I found myself smiling at her. In spite of her superstitious stories, I liked Sarah's nurse. "Listen,

Creighton, has Sarah no other dresses? That black—the year is over."

Creighton's lined face creased into a smile. "I was waiting, Your Grace, but no one told me to change them. Her old ones—they're too small now."

I nodded. "We'll get some material and make her some new ones. Something bright and cheerful. And Creighton—"

"Yes, Your Grace."

"I do not want Sarah confined to the nursery any longer. She is growing up now and will need to learn manners."

"Yes, Your Grace. But the dowager—"

"I am the duchess now," I said. "The duke expects me to care for his child."

The old nurse nodded. "And about time it is, too. The little one's been sad neglected."

I did not want to criticize my husband. "Well, we shall remedy that. And now, I shall leave you to your rest. Tell Sarah I was here. I shall see her later."

"Yes, Your Grace."

I left the nurse to her tea and stepped out into the corridor. I paused for a moment to get my bearings. Richard would be gone for some time. I turned left, away from the great stairs. I had a sudden urge to see the North Tower.

Chapter Six

I followed the outer wall around. The North Tower was come to by a spiral staircase. It was not hard to find. The arch at the bottom of the stairs had no door to bar it.

No wonder Caroline had been successful with her ghost stories, I thought as I carefully mounted the twisting stair. The castle stones were so thick that only a little light came through the slits in the walls. Nowhere in this place had I seen a cheerful, sun-filled room. It seemed I would have to get used to living in gloom.

The door at the top of the stairs opened to my touch, and I smiled. No wonder Caroline had liked the place. It was small and therefore more easily lighted. I wished I had thought to bring some candles along.

I went to one of the apertures that served as windows. Glass had been set into it, but I could see that the castle walls must be six or eight feet thick. The windows here had not been enlarged as they had in my room. Sunlight would only reach the room if the sun was in a direct line with an opening.

I looked around. A fireplace built into the ocean wall

had a pleasing herringbone design. A small rosewood writing desk and matching chair sat near one of the window openings. An armoire stood against one wall, awkwardly because the wall was rounded and the cupboard was not. And against another wall, out of view of the door, was a cot covered by a royal blue coverlet.

I was sure of it then. Caroline had used this room as a rendezvous. Bringing her to the country had not stopped her. Removed from the London dandies, lacking the adulation that had always been her food and drink, she had simply turned to some servant.

I frowned. Perhaps more than one servant. After all, Caroline had never been particularly nice about such matters.

I sank down on the cot to think. There was still no point in telling my husband what I was certain was true. The living Caroline had given him enough pain. Let the dead one rest in peace.

Papa had always said that my imagination was far too healthy. Now I could see Caroline, beautifully gowned as always, opening the door to her lover. I knew she would be there first. It was always her nature to play the queen bee.

She would offer him her lips to be kissed and on this cot— My overheated cheeks turned scarlet.

I knew Caroline had been with many men. Why had she wanted so many? Had she suffered from some sickness that drove her to such strange behavior?

My own body was filled with a fierce longing, but it was all for Richard. It was Richard's embraces I wanted. Richard's kisses—

I jumped up, my lips burning at the memory of that fiery kiss from Richard's twin. But, I assured myself, it had only affected me so because I thought the man was my husband. . . .

I moved restlessly around the room, Caroline's room. For a moment I could almost smell the scent she habitually wore—the cloying sweet scent that she had struck me for seeking among her bottles.

Less light was coming through the apertures, but I was not ready to leave. It was almost as though Caroline wanted to tell me something. I could feel her presence so strongly! It was as though she were standing there in the room with me.

I laughed at such farfetched childish musings. Caroline had never told me anything, except to stay out of her things. I sat down and opened the desk. Since the cot still held the coverlet, perhaps the desk had some candles in it.

The drawer held writing paper, quills, and ink, but no candles. I told myself that when I came here again—as I knew somehow I would—I would bring a candelabra.

The desk's drawers offered nothing else, and I rose and went to the armoire. It was very old, and I paused to admire its intricate carving, running my fingers over the figures done with such infinite care. Without its distressing inhabitants, Greyden Castle might be made quite livable.

But I knew that Richard would never shirk his responsibility to his dependents. He was the head of the family, and caring for them—however difficult he might find it—was his task in life.

Certainly they could not fend for themselves. The dowager might be given a small annuity and be set up elsewhere, but Richard was not the kind to turn his mother out. Rosamund could not function properly even here; in the real world she would never be able to survive. And Penrose—I could not be sure if the boy was genuinely evil or just tainted by this strange household.

Of one thing I was quite certain, though. However peculiar Richard's family might be, I meant for Sarah, and for my own babies, to grow up as normally as possible.

Normal. The word rang in my ears. The only normal person in this entire household was Richard's brother Roland. And Richard hated him.

Certainly I could understand filial dislike. Had I not suffered much with Caroline? But I would have thought twins shared something better, something very special. If that were ever true here, something had gone very wrong. For all Roland's friendliness, Richard treated him most rudely.

My fingers went to the latch of the armoire—and hesitated there. I could swear I smelled it again—Caroline's sweetest scent. The room was growing darker. I almost withdrew my fingers, almost left the room without opening that cupboard door. But Papa had always said I had more courage than was sensible for a woman, and so, even then, with the premonition of evil heavy upon me, I did not back away.

I jerked open the door as though I expected some demon to leap forth at me, and immediately I fell to laughing. So much for my premonitions of evil; Caroline's dressing gown hung in the armoire. I recognized it from the old days, and from it came the sweetness of her scent.

The armoire held no other clothes, but down in one corner rested a small chest. I knelt to lift it out. Inside nestled a bottle of her scent, almost full, a mirror, and a hairbrush. Now my suspicions were absolutely confirmed.

Suddenly the hair on the back of my neck began to rise. Someone was watching me. Was Caroline angry that I had invaded her private domain? Still on my knees, I turned swiftly, almost expecting to see the wraith of my sister glaring at me.

But it was Roland who stood in the doorway. Relief washed over me at his friendly smile.

"I have been exploring," I said.

"Are you truly not afraid of ghosts?"

I felt his question showed genuine concern for me. How nice it was to feel comfortable, to converse with a normal human being. To have someone smile instead of glower at me.

"Truly I am not," I said, with perhaps not total honesty. "My papa is a very practical man, and he raised me to be practical, too."

"Yet Caroline—"

"Papa did not have the raising of her. She was Mama's favorite." I hoped the old childhood pain had not made itself known in my voice. I had outgrown that long ago, and I had been blessed with Papa's love.

"So, what have you discovered?" he asked, coming farther into the room.

"Nothing much." I returned the chest to its corner and got to my feet. "I think Caroline used this as a writing room."

"Until she saw the ghosts."

I shut the armoire door. "Of course. Till then." I was not going to discuss my sister's frailties with this man who was to all intents a stranger. Still, I was curious to know his opinion of her. "Did you live here when

Caroline did?" I asked, making my voice casual.

He shrugged. "Yes. But she was not an easy person to know. To admire, perhaps, but not to know." He sighed. "She caused poor Richard a great deal of heartache. Her escapades—"

"Oh, no! Were you in London, too?" The words escaped me before I thought.

"Yes. But I was speaking of her behavior here. It was common knowledge—over the whole countryside, I'm afraid—but the talk has died down now."

I could not help myself. I had to ask. "The talk?"

"Yes. You know, because he refused to destroy Mercury, the stallion that killed her. Some said—" He paused and frowned. "It was all foolishness, of course. Richard loved her madly. He would never have done anything to hurt her."

My heart rose up in my throat. If what Roland said was true—and why should he tell me an untruth?—the neighbors had suspected Richard, my Richard, of murdering his wife!

I strove to control my expression. Richard could not have done such a horrible thing. "That can't possibly be true," I said. "Richard would never—"

"Of course not," Roland said sincerely. "But then, we know him better than most. We know what trials he's had to bear."

It was on the tip of my tongue to ask him what was the cause of his brother's dislike of him; but it seemed too personal a question, and so I did not.

"Yes," I said instead. "We know he loved Caroline. And besides, Richard would not—could not—"

"Of course not." Roland's smile was so friendly, so comforting. What a good brother he was! His behavior made Richard's churlishness seem doubly unmerited.

Suddenly I decided to take the risk. "Roland?"

"Yes, Vanessa?"

"I—have you any idea why Richard is so—so rude to you?" Having asked, I colored at my temerity. "I—I'm sorry, I had no right to ask such a question. Forget that I mentioned it."

"No, my dear. You have every right to ask. Coming here must have been quite a shock to you." He indicated the doorway. "But let us go back to the main part of the castle. No doubt by now there's a nice cheery fire in the library."

"Yes, of course." The tower room was growing darker, and I suddenly wanted to get away from the memory of my sister. I loved my husband and I did not intend to let her memory ruin my marriage; but even as I thought this the smell of her scent seemed to grow stronger. "Yes," I repeated. "Let us go."

Like the gentleman he was, Roland preceded me down the twisted stairs. They were even darker than when I had ascended them. "You must be careful here," Roland said. "A fall could be very dangerous."

I nodded. Still another danger. This place was fraught with possibilities for disaster.

Soon we were in the library. Roland was right—it was more comfortable. A cheery fire blazed in the hearth, and Gerson came bearing a silver tea tray.

The tea was most welcome. I sipped at its comforting warmth. "Now," I said to Roland, "you were going to tell me. . . ."

He nodded. "Yes. I'm afraid it's not a happy story. But then, you expected that. It happened when we were boys."

73

I leaned forward, my heart in my throat. At last I would get some answers to the questions that plagued me.

"Vanessa!" Richard's voice, echoing through the great hall, so startled me that tea shot out of my cup and onto the carpet. With shaking hands I set down my half-empty cup.

"I'm coming," I called. With an apologetic smile to Roland, I hurried out.

Richard was just removing his gloves. "There you are," he said.

I went to him and raised my face for his kiss. It was ridiculous of me to feel guilty. After all, Roland lived here, too. Certainly there was nothing wrong with having a cup of tea with my husband's brother. Nevertheless, I was quite aware that Richard would not like it, and for that reason I did not want him to know about it.

"How have you spent your afternoon?" Richard asked.

"I visited the nursery, but Sarah was napping."

His face took on that closed look, and I knew he wished to avoid the subject. Still I chattered on. Sarah was his child. I meant for him to acknowledge her. "I talked to Creighton. The child needs clothes. The mourning year is over."

He nodded. "Do as you please," he said. "I will not object."

"But Richard—" A father must have some interest in his child's welfare. How could I say this? "Richard—" I began again.

Then I saw his expression. Just so might I have looked had Caroline's ghost really appeared to me in the North Tower. But it was only Sarah. She ran to my side and slipped her little hand into mine. "Nessie?"

74

I thrilled to think she had come to me of her own accord. "Yes, dear?"

"I want to go see the horses. Will you take me?"

I looked down into the eager little face. "I cannot take you myself, dear. But I'll ask your father."

Her face fell, as if she already expected his refusal. But I would not accept that. "Richard, please. I should very much like to see the stable. I shall enjoy a good ride now and then."

I tucked my free hand through his arm, all the while talking.

He looked most unhappy and about to refuse, but I smiled again. "Please?"

He sighed. "Very well, Vanessa. If you wish. But you must not go riding without me."

I nodded happily. "I would not dream of doing so, my dear."

We did not speak more as we made our way out the front door and down the path to the stable. It sat on the far side of the castle, the opposite side from where the break in the wall looked down on the cold wet rocks.

The stable seemed new, strong and snug, as it would have to be to withstand the fierce winds from the sea. I smiled as the comforting smell of horses surrounded me. As a child, whenever Mama scolded me for not living up to her expectations, I had escaped to the stable and my friends, the horses. They did not yell or scream. They always understood.

I looked down at the child. "You must hold tight to my hand," I cautioned.

"Yes, Nessie," she said. "Oh, look. Such a pretty horse!"

I felt Richard's arm stiffen, and I knew. The horse was

beautiful—a smoky blue-gray with a lovely head and deep intelligent eyes. I simply could not see this horse as a killer. "This is your stallion?" I asked.

"Yes. Mercury. I wrote your father about what happened. It was strange."

"Yes, we thought so at the time. Caroline was such a good horsewoman."

"Yes." Richard looked around. "Toby!"

A stableboy popped his tousled head over a stall. "Yes, Yer Grace?"

"Take the child to the other end. Show her the new filly."

The boy came round the stall and extended a grimy hand. "Here you go, young miss."

I watched the boy lead Sarah away. Then I turned to my husband. "Is the horse vicious?"

He frowned. "No. He had never harmed anyone before. I raised him from a colt, and he had always been gentle."

We moved toward the stall, and the horse whuffled a greeting. Richard rubbed the soft nose. "Hello, boy. Be patient. We'll ride tomorrow."

"Oh, good," I cried. "I should much enjoy a ride."

"I didn't mean—"

"Oh, please, Richard. You must take me along."

The stallion whuffled again and stretched his nose toward me. Without thinking I reached out to stroke his neck.

Unexpectedly, Richard smiled. "I should have known you'd understand."

"You mean because you didn't have the horse destroyed?"

He nodded, his face becoming grim again. "Yes. You'll

76

hear all about it sooner or later. The whole countryside was up in arms. But, Vanessa—I could not do it."

I pressed his arm. "Of course you could not. He's a beautiful animal, Richard. And—" I hesitated. I knew this was a painful subject for him, but it was something we needed to talk about. "Papa told me she was found— found—with a riding crop in her hand."

"Yes," he said. "And the horse had welts. On his flank and on his withers." He shook his head. "I cannot believe she would beat a horse like that. It made no sense."

A chill crept over me. "I know. Even Caroline—" I stopped. I did not wish to malign the dead. "Caroline loved horses. Why should she abuse him?"

"I don't know." His frown deepened. "Unless she wanted to get back at me." He sighed. "She was capable of that."

The horse shoved his nose into my hand. "You were right not to have him put down," I said. "Why, look! He wouldn't hurt anyone."

Richard pulled me into his arms. "Oh, Nessie, Nessie, I'm so glad you said yes."

He pressed his lips to mine, and I responded happily. It was good to hear my husband speak kind words to me.

But my happiness faded just a little. He had yet to say the words I longed most to hear. Except for that morning, when he had announced to the dowager that he had married me because he loved me, he had yet to say, "I love you." But he would, I assured myself. Tonight he would come to me.

Chapter Seven

The evening did not begin auspiciously. I dressed for dinner in my gown of apple green with the darker ribbons. It was the dress I had been wearing the day Richard proposed to me, and I was very fond of it. Besides, I had decided to behave in as normal a fashion as possible.

So I chose my brightest cashmere—it was impossible to go about the chill castle without a shawl—and put a smile on my face.

Acting on my decision to be pleasant to everyone, I greeted each member of the family cheerfully. In return I received only sullen looks. Whatever was wrong with these people? None of them knew how to behave with even a modicum of decency.

Poor Caroline. I found myself startled by the thought. My sister must have found this place utterly unbearable. She was a creature of light and glitter, noise and gaiety, and there was none of that here. Nothing but unrelieved darkness and gloom.

The dowager was wearing deep charcoal gray, unrelieved by even a touch of white. Penrose and Rosamund were dressed all in black. I would not have been surprised had they owned no clothes of any other hue.

Roland was absent from the table, and though I missed his cheerful face, I was glad not to have the tension between him and Richard so in evidence. If Richard had not come home when he did, I should already have heard what Roland had begun to tell me; I should have known the reason for my husband's unusual animosity toward his twin. Now I would have to wait.

But I did not intend to wait for long. I was determined to ferret out the truth. I meant to mend Richard's relationship with his twin as well as with his daughter. There was much work to be done at Greyden Castle, and since I was an eager and loving wife, I was the one to do it.

Richard came down as I was striving to make conversation with Rosamund. I felt sorry for Richard's sister. Living in this oppressive atmosphere could not be any help in overcoming her illness.

I had been talking to her for some while with no response when Richard entered. "Hello, Rosie," he said. "How are you this evening?"

She smiled. When I spoke to her, it was as if she didn't hear me, but for Richard she smiled.

"You're looking very pretty tonight," he said.

I stared at my husband. This pale wraith of a woman with her great sunken eyes was a far cry from pretty.

But her smile broadened, and she said, "Thank you, Richard. Jeffrey thinks so, too." She bestowed another bright smile on the empty air beside her.

"Have you been talking with Vanessa?" he asked.

Her expression grew bewildered. "I don't remember Vanessa."

Richard put an arm around her. "This is Vanessa," he said. He pulled me closer. "She's my wife."

Rosamund's eyes widened. "Wife? Your wife is wicked. Oh, no. The bad wife is dead. She's burning with Papa."

Our Rosamund seemed rather eager to populate hell with her own special choices, but I did not say so. No doubt Caroline had plagued her a good deal.

"Vanessa is good," Richard said patiently. "She wants to be your friend."

"Yes, yes, I do," I added. "We can talk together. Maybe take a walk now and then. I imagine the woods are lovely in the fall."

"Penrose takes me for walks. He's a good boy."

"Yes, I'm sure he is." It was a white lie, said to placate her, but it was a lie nevertheless. To my mind Penrose was *not* a good boy. He was evil, and what was worse, he delighted in being so.

Richard gave his sister another squeeze. She smiled up at him as a child might. "You are so good to me, Richard. Much better than Papa was. You let me have Jeffrey here."

"Yes, dear." He patted her hand. "Jeffrey may stay as long as he likes."

"He will never leave me," she said, and strolled off, talking with great animation to the emptiness beside her.

I faced my husband. "Richard, are you sure you should encourage her in her illusions? Will that cause her condition to worsen?"

He shook his head. "I tried telling her that he wasn't there, that she had imagined it all, but she grew so hysterical that we had to send for Dr. Sanderson. As long as we do not contradict her, she remains docile. So that is the course we have had to follow." He sighed. "I know that it seems strange, but so little is known of illnesses of this kind. We must do whatever seems to work best."

I nodded. "I understand, my dear." I looked around the room. "Perhaps I should converse with your mother."

My husband's expression grew grim. "I'm afraid it's no use, Vanessa."

I was not ready to concede defeat. "But perhaps I can make her see that I am not like Caroline."

He sighed again. "It is not because of Caroline that she treats you so poorly."

"It is not?"

"No, it is because of me."

"I do not understand."

He took my hand. "Of course you don't. But I shall try to explain. My mother was married against her will. She loved another man, but her parents insisted she marry the duke, my father. Her parents thought she would grow to care for him, but she hated him with a passion some women reserve for love."

He ran a hand through his hair. "When I was born first, the heir, my father was overjoyed. But my having my father's love was enough to set my mother against me. Then Roland was born, ten minutes later, and she lavished all her love on him."

Tears came to my eyes as I listened. Though my own mother had not been that harsh, she had been quite obvious in her favoring of Caroline over me, and the wound still festered.

"Oh, Richard, how dreadful. But it was not his fault. Roland couldn't help it." I thought at last that I had discovered the cause of my husband's dislike for his twin.

"Of course he could not," he said. "But Mother's love

81

twisted him. It made him believe he could do no wrong."

Richard's censure of his brother seemed too strong to me. Many a nobleman was utterly convinced of his infallibility, but Richard must be mistaken about his brother. I had experienced Roland as a friendly, helpful person. He had not appeared to be unyielding or proud. Indeed, he had been most affable.

"Why—" I began, but Gerson announced the meal, and having no wish to discuss it in front of the others, I let the matter drop.

After the meal Penrose and Rosamund went off, walking arm in arm. The dowager returned to her apartments without even deigning to tell us good night.

"Is she always like that?" I asked, as Richard and I moved into the library.

"With me she is." The bitterness in his voice pained me. "With Roland she is all sweetness. He is her cherished son. As I said before, to all intents he is her only child."

"But it's not fair," I cried. "You have all the burdens of the dukedom. You have protected and cared for them all, and they treat you so poorly."

He shrugged. "It has always been this way," he said. "I'm sorry, Nessie. I shouldn't have brought you here. Into this household."

I looked up into his beloved face. I only wanted for him to be happy. "Perhaps we could go somewhere else to live."

"I would like nothing better." He looked so wretched I was sorry I had mentioned the subject. "But I must look after Rosamund," he continued. "She would not fare well at all in the city. Here I can protect her. I promised my father I would do that. He was not a bad man. He tried to love us all. And what he did to Rosie—it really was for her own good. The man was a fortune hunter. A bad choice for a husband." He looked into the fire. "I'm sorry, my dear, but I cannot leave Greyden Castle. It is our home."

This was the very thing that I had already told myself. Still, I yearned to run into his arms and plead with him to leave this awful place and these terrible people. I did not, of course. I could not adjure him to desert his solemn duty. Nor would I have loved him as much if he had.

The evening passed slowly. I made a trip to the nursery to see Sarah tucked in for the night. I asked Richard to accompany me, but as I expected, he declined, pleading some estate work he had to do.

The child raised her little face to my kiss. "Nurse says you will come every night to tuck me in. Is that really true?"

"Yes, Sarah. That is what moth—" I paused. Whatever good memories the child had of her mother, they should be left inviolate. I did not intend to disturb them. "That is what I mean to do."

She smiled. "I am glad. Nessie?"

"Yes, dear?"

"Why do you like me?"

The odd question startled me. "Because—because you're my little girl."

"My father does not like me," she said. "Do you know why?"

I patted the small hand. "I think you must be mistaken, Sarah. Your father is a very busy man, but I'm sure he cares about you."

She sighed. "I wish I knew why he doesn't like me. Maybe then I could change. So he would."

The child's simple desire wrung my heart. She had had a mother like Caroline, and now she was denied her father's love. It just was not fair.

I hugged her tightly to me. "Don't worry about it, my dear. I'm here now. We'll work it out."

"Yes, Nessie." She settled back among the covers with a satisfied smile. "I'm very glad you came here. You're better than my real mother."

I heard the sharp intake of Creighton's breath behind me. "Your mother loved you, Sarah." I told the lie with all the sincerity I could muster. "It was just that she was very busy."

"I'm glad you're here," Sarah repeated. It was obvious she did not believe me.

I blew her a kiss and retreated from the nursery, Creighton on my heels. "Ain't no use, Your Grace. The child knows her mother weren't no good."

"Creighton! You must never say such a thing within the child's hearing."

Creighton frowned, but she was not to be denied her say. "Ain't me as says it. I know a child needs her mother's love."

"Then who?" I demanded.

"The dowager for one. And that Penrose. He's a mean one."

My temper started to rise. My boiling point had always been low, and my first day at Greyden Castle had not improved it. "Penrose has been saying hateful things to Sarah?"

Creighton nodded. "Ain't no one in this household as hasn't said hateful things about the child's mother." She hesitated. "And begging your pardon, Your Grace, you being her sister and all, but she deserved every bad word as has been said about her."

"Perhaps. But it's not necessary for the child to know that. She should have good memories of her mother."

Creighton shook her gray head. "'Tis hardly any memories she'll have. Truth is, like I told you afore, her mother rarely came near her."

"And her father?"

Creighton's creased face reflected distress. "Him I don't understand. I had the raising of that boy. The dowager—she would have let him die, she would."

"Oh, no!" I couldn't help myself. The thought of Richard so abandoned by his own mother made me want to cry.

I turned to the servant. "So you raised him?"

"Aye. Me and his father. That man surely did love the boy. But it weren't like the dowager said. The duke, he loved all his children." She sighed. "He did all that he could for them. That's why he paid off that man who was after his daughter. Weren't no way to know she'd take it like she did."

"Yes. It's a sad case."

Creighton frowned. "And so is the way the present duke treats his child."

"Has it always been this way?"

Creighton shook her head. "No, Your Grace. When the child was newborn, he doted on her. Came every day to hold her and play with her. And then—one day he just stopped coming. She could just talk then. She was saying Dada."

She wiped at a tear. "Pitiful, it was. Her calling after him all the while like that. She did it for months, but finally she stopped."

I swallowed over the lump in my throat. How could

Richard do this to his own child? Didn't he remember what it had been like to be virtually motherless?

I patted the old nurse's hand. "Thank you, Creighton. You have been a good friend to Sarah. And to my husband."

She sighed and wiped at her eyes again. "'Tis sorry I am about the duke. I thought I'd raised him better than that."

I put an arm around her shoulders and squeezed. "Don't worry, Creighton. I am here now, and whatever is wrong, I will fix it."

She sniffled. "I hope so, Your Grace. He was a dear lad, he was. So bright and loving in spite of that mother of his. And now, to do the same thing to his own babe—I can't make it out, I can't."

"It will be all right," I repeated. "You just keep on loving Sarah."

I left hurriedly, before I should break into tears and fall to weeping on the old servant's shoulder.

Perhaps I should have let myself weep then, for tears were surely to be my lot that second evening in my new home.

I returned to the library, but Richard was not there. So I went looking for Gerson.

"His Grace has gone out," the butler told me. "A message came from the vicar, and the duke ordered his horse."

My heart skipped a beat. "He rode the stallion?"

"Of course, Your Grace."

"Did he say how late he'd be?"

"No, Your Grace." It was plain from the butler's tone that he thought this a poor question from a lady of quality; but I had not been a lady long, and I was every

86

inch a woman in love with her husband.

Nevertheless, I asked Gerson no more questions, but went back to the library to await my husband's return. I let my gaze travel over the expensively bound books.

I sighed. The late duke's taste had run to volumes on the proper conduct of military campaigns. It was not a subject I could find to my liking.

Finally I selected a volume by Dr. Johnson about a mythical kingdom where everyone was supposed to be happy. But somehow I could not concentrate. My ears were ever alert for the sound of my husband's footsteps, and my eyes often left the printed page and turned anxiously toward the door; but Richard did not appear.

My eyes grew heavier. The previous night I had not had much sleep. Twice my eyelids fluttered shut, and the book falling from my hand startled me awake. The second time the fire had died down, and the library was no longer cozy and cheerful. Shadows lurked in every corner, and I found myself feeling distinctly uncomfortable.

Before I could decide what to do, there were sounds in the front hall. My heart leaped in anticipation, then fell again in disappointment. It was not Richard who had come home, but Roland.

He came into the library, smiling pleasantly. "Vanessa. Are you still awake?"

"Almost," I returned with an attempt at humor. "I'm afraid Dr. Johnson has been putting me to sleep."

Roland chuckled. "I find he has that effect on me too."

By then I was more fully awake. I leaned forward in my chair. "This afternoon you were about to tell me—"

"Yes," he said. "But it will have to wait. Richard was only a little behind me on the road. He'll be in shortly."

I sighed. My every effort to untangle my husband's life

seemed thwarted.

"I will tell you," Roland said. "I promise."

Richard came in five minutes later. "Vanessa," he said as I went to greet him. "There was no need to wait up for me. You must be tired."

"I am fine," I said, vainly trying to smother a yawn.

"Of course. But we shall go up anyway. Good night, Gerson."

"Good night, Your Grace."

I could hardly believe it. There I was, my arm through my husband's, climbing the stairs to our wedding chamber. At last. I leaned closer to him. "I missed you," I whispered.

He looked almost startled. "I'm often called away, Nessie. The local magistrate calls on me for help. And the vicar."

"Yes, I know."

We had reached my door. Richard opened it for me. My heart almost stopped in my chest. "Oh, Richard," I breathed.

He dropped a kiss on my forehead. "Go to bed, Nessie."

There was something about his voice that warned me. "But Richard—"

"I have to speak to my mother."

"Now?" I could not help it. I could hear the outrage in my voice.

He did not respond to it. "Yes, Nessie. Now."

"But—"

Richard did not wait to hear my comments. He left quickly, shutting the door behind him.

My temper erupted. I threw my pillows on the floor. I uttered every masculine curse I had picked up from

Papa's cronies. I stomped and raged around the room.

Finally, after I had paced for some time, I summoned the maid to help me out of my gown. While she was there, I controlled my tongue, but as soon as the door closed behind her, I gave vent to a string of curses that would have done credit to the lowest cutthroat.

Then I climbed into bed and prepared to wait. Richard had to sleep. Sometime tonight he would return to his room, and when he did, I meant to thrash this matter out.

Sitting there, propped up among my pillows, I fretted and fumed. Richard had made no mention of a marriage of convenience. Indeed, he had led me to believe that he cared for me. Not, of course, with the passion he had felt for Caroline. I understood that, or I tried to; but I also understood that Richard had made me his wife. And I meant to be just that—or know the reason why!

The hours passed. I was weary, but I could not sleep. I did not intend to let another night pass in which my marriage remained unconsummated.

Finally, after midnight, when I had just about despaired of ever achieving my purpose, I heard sounds coming through the connecting door.

The moon was full, and it silvered the coverlet and reflected off the intricately chased back of the mirror that sat on my dressing table. A beautiful romantic sight—except that I was viewing it alone.

My unstable temper slipped the rein again, and I felt ready to explode. I threw back the covers and leaped to the floor. The cold stone chilled my bare feet, but did not cool my temper. I marched across the room and yanked open the connecting door.

"Richard, I—"

He had removed his coat, his cravat, waistcoat, and

shirt. My startled eyes came to rest on his naked chest, and I forgot what I intended to say.

"Nessie, what are you doing here?"

I struggled to find my tongue. "I have come for some answers."

He sighed. "It is late. You should be sleeping."

My anger came back to me then, full-fledged. "Sleeping? How shall I sleep?"

He did not seem to comprehend my meaning. "Is something wrong with your bed?"

"Yes!" I lost all sense of decorum then and blurted it out. "Yes! My bed is empty! You are not in it!"

He stared at me. "Vanessa, such—" he faltered.

I was beyond caring about politeness. I meant to have some answers. I crossed the cold floor till I stood directly in front of him. "Have you changed your mind?" I demanded. "Do you no longer wish me to be your wife?"

"Vanessa, stop now. This is unseemly."

"Unseemly?" My voice was rising higher and higher, but I was powerless to stop it. "Isn't it unseemly to leave your wife alone on her wedding night?"

To my chagrin, tears came into my eyes, but I ignored them and ranted on. "No one in this miserable household treats me decently." Even in my anger I knew better than to mention Roland. "I can cope with them if I have your love. But without—"

The tears would no longer be denied, and great sobs tore through me. To make matters worse, the cold had traveled up my legs to chill my whole body, and my teeth began a wild chattering.

Suddenly Richard swung me up in his arms. "Don't be foolish," he said, carrying me back through the connecting door. "Of course I care for you. I should not

90

have married you otherwise."

"Then why—"

"It's Rosamund." He put me in the great bed and covered me carefully before he sat down beside me.

"Rosamund?"

"Yes. The moon is full, and when that happens, it affects her mind. She wanders about the castle. Once she even went outside."

I shuddered, thinking of that break in the wall that looked down on the rocks. "But you have servants."

He shook his head. "They make her nervous, and she gets even wilder." He kissed my forehead. "I beg your pardon, Vanessa. I should have told you before, but I didn't realize. . . ."

The things I had said returned to my mind, and I blushed almost scarlet. "Oh, dear," I mumbled. "Now you will think I am like Caroline." I sighed. "And you will be disappointed, for I know nothing."

Richard chuckled. "Nessie, you darling. I should never have imagined otherwise. Go to sleep now. I promise you, we shall soon be man and wife in every way."

With that I had to be content.

Chapter Eight

I'm not sure what awoke me, but I had been deep in a lovely dream where Richard shared my love and all was golden and beautiful.

From this joy I struggled slowly upward toward consciousness. As my wits returned, I grew aware that something was amiss. My room reeked of cloying sweetness. My heart threatened to stop in my breast. It was Caroline's scent! Caroline's scent was hanging heavy in my room.

While I was yet trying to come to terms with this, distantly, but clear and distinct, came the mewling cry of an infant. A cold sweat bathed my body. Three nights running, Creighton had said, and the hearer could expect a visit from Death. I lay there, not knowing whether to open my eyes or to keep them tightly closed.

I decided to keep them closed, to pretend sleep. I was being silly, I told myself. That was something else I had heard, not the haunting babe.

Under the covers my body shivered and shook. My heart raced in panic. Even if I had mistaken the sound I had not mistaken the scent that hung in my room. The air was thick with it. So thick I wanted to cough.

But if I made a sound—if I moved—whoever had left the scent might still be there, waiting for my reaction.

I told myself that it could not be Caroline who had brought her scent into my room while I slept. Caroline was dead and buried, and I did not believe in ghosts.

Papa had always laughed at tales of the supernatural. How I wished I had him there with me. He would soon have had me laughing at such silliness. And Papa would not lie there, his eyes squeezed shut, while someone tried to scare him out of his wits.

Taking courage, I opened my eyes. Moonlight was coming in through the windows. I half expected to see some lurking figure in the shadows, but the moonlight was bright; there were no shadows. And the room was, except for me, quite empty.

I lay there, shivering under the covers Richard had heaped on me. I did not—would not—believe in ghosts. So the next question was, which of Richard's distressing relations had done this thing? And why?

Of course, given their dispositions, asking why was perhaps unnecessary. I ran over the possibilities in my mind. The dowager could have done it, though I thought her inclination would be to more direct methods. She did not strike me as the kind who would resort to skullduggery.

Rosamund might have done it. In her deranged condition, she might have any number of strange reasons for wishing to frighten me. But earlier in the evening she had not even known who I was. And besides, Richard was with her.

Or Penrose might have been the one. Doubtless that

nasty boy would find the thought of terrifying a woman great fun.

It did not occur to me that Richard or his twin would wish to drive me from this place. Richard had said he loved me, and Roland had been very kind.

Of the three I suspected, I decided that Penrose was the most likely candidate.

My heart had slowed its pounding. Now that I had eliminated the supernatural, I felt more at ease, though I did not know how I could prove that Penrose was the culprit. He was such a thoroughly disagreeable young man that it seemed entirely possible he would resort to such nastiness.

I decided to try to sleep again. I would need all my strength in the morning. It took a great deal of energy to keep my temper under control when dealing with these people.

I closed my eyes. Where was my husband now? Sitting at his sister's bedside, calming her disordered mind? I tried to imagine Richard's beloved face. In my mind I reconstructed it, feature by feature. For long minutes I debated the exact shade of his dark eyes, the proper color to designate his darker hair.

Finally, I relaxed and drifted once more into sleep. Then it came again. There was no mistaking it—that was the cry of a baby! My heart pounded so that I found it difficult to think clearly. My limbs quivered with terror, and all my new-found confidence disappeared in one swift instant.

The haunting babe was the harbinger of Death. Creighton had said so, and she had said that Caroline heard it before—

Panic seized me, and I leaped from the bed and raced to

the connecting door. I did not stop to think whether Richard might have returned. I moved without thinking at all.

The moment I jerked open the door, I knew his room was empty. Still, there was a feel of his presence there, a comfort. I closed the connecting door behind me. I would stay in Richard's room until his return.

On my previous visit, I had not noticed anything but Richard; everything else in the room had been unimportant. Now, trying to distract my mind, I wandered curiously around.

This room, too, had large windows. The moon illuminated a big curtained bed, a writing desk and chair, and a carved wardrobe. The room was furnished sparingly. I saw nothing of Caroline in it at all, and this gave me a surge of pleasure.

Perhaps Richard had kept this room for his exclusive use. Caroline would have preferred that he sleep somewhere else. She had always liked her privacy.

I went to gaze out the window. The moonlight made strange shadows in the darkness outside. Figures seemed to lurk where no figures were. My imagination had become so inflamed that it was creating impossible things of the most frightening kind.

I moved away from the window, toward Richard's wardrobe, where I stopped and sniffed. I thought I could detect Caroline's scent. Had that person brought some in here? I moved on and no longer smelled it. Imagination again.

I scolded myself. I was held to be the sanest and most sensible young woman in all of Wiltshire—Papa had said so repeatedly—but I certainly was not behaving very sensibly now. There I was, reduced to looking for ghosts and sniffing for their perfume like a dog after the fox.

I sniffed again, but I smelled nothing. To the best of my knowledge, a wraith did not wear scent. I was feeling so much better that I actually smiled at the thought.

My mind was in a better condition, but my feet were nearly frozen, my teeth beginning to chatter again. I thought about returning to my room, but I felt better in Richard's room, stronger. He, too, had a bed—a big, heavily curtained affair. The covers had already been turned down.

I stood there looking at it. This was Richard's bed, and I was Richard's wife. I had every right to be in it, so I told myself as I climbed in and began rubbing my poor chilled feet. If only Richard would return and take me in his arms. Then I would feel safe.

I had been badly frightened, but if the person behind this deed thought to scare me away from Greyden Castle, he would be much disappointed. I was not a person given to quitting. When I put my hand to the plow, I stayed till the furrow was done.

I had married Richard to be wife to him and mother to Sarah, and I intended to let no one and no thing interfere with the performance of those duties.

I settled myself among my husband's pillows and prepared to wait. I wished, momentarily, that I had put on my prettier nightdress, the one I had made for my wedding night, but I was grateful for the warmth of the heavy flannel. Though a fire burned on the hearth, it was small, and its heat did not carry far.

This infernal castle, I thought with some petulance, was like to freeze my very bones. Why couldn't something be done to make the place warmer?

I snuggled down, prepared to let sleep overtake me. I

had always been a light sleeper, and I felt I would awaken on Richard's return. I shoved the pillows about, preparing a warm nest for myself.

My feet were still cold, and I turned sideways so I could pull them up under my gown. I took a deep breath to relax myself—and stiffened instead. There it was again—Caroline's scent. Not so strong, this time, but definitely Caroline's scent.

I lay there, my body aquiver, while the most impossible thoughts chased themselves through my mind.

Perhaps Caroline's ghost had come back to claim the husband who had once been hers. On the face of it, this was not even sensible. Even if ghosts did exist, Caroline had not loved Richard. Though it pained me to admit it, I was well aware that Caroline had loved no one but herself.

Then, there was also the memory, vivid as though it had happened yesterday, of Caroline striking me across the face and commanding me never to touch her things.

Of course I did not believe in ghosts. Could the tension I had been under have affected my mind? Could I be imagining that I smelled Caroline's scent?

This did not seem like a reasonable conclusion either. I was not a vaporish miss given to purple imaginings, but a grown woman of stable character, as anyone in Wiltshire would have been willing to attest.

But, if neither of these suppositions was true, then the scent must have a physical origin. Determined to think this thing through, I curled up again. In doing so, I slipped my hand under the pillow to cradle my head as I always did.

My fingers touched something different—something

soft and lacy under Richard's pillow.

I sat up, my skin gone suddenly cold. The moonlight was still strong in the room. I pulled the pillows aside and uttered a cry of pain.

There lay a lace-edged handkerchief. The familiar scent rose to my nostrils, and I *knew* before I picked it up. It bore a monogrammed C. *My husband slept with his dead wife's handkerchief beneath his pillow.*

Tears rose to my eyes, but I held them back. Carefully I replaced everything just as I had found it and returned to my own bed.

Once there, I twisted and turned, my mind an agony of thought. I knew Richard had loved Caroline—with a passion he had never felt for me—but to find such evidence that his love lived on, when she had been long dead, was like a dagger in my wounded heart.

I was not amazed that Richard still loved her, even after all she had done, for I already knew that love was a most mysterious occurrence and one over which we mortals have very little control.

What was I to do? Should I tell Richard I knew his secret, that our marriage was a farce and I meant to return to Papa and see it ended? In my pain I considered this for some minutes, soon realizing there were several reasons why it was unfeasible.

First, however Richard felt about it, our marriage was very real to me. I knew that Richard was the only man I could ever truly love. Second, if I left, that would mean Caroline had won. Even in death she would cheat me of the one man I could love.

There in the great bed I lay frowning. Caroline had always gotten everything she wanted. From the newest fashion to becoming a duchess, Mama had seen that she succeeded. But Mama was gone, too, and unless the two of them were conspiring to haunt me, she could no longer help Caroline.

Caroline was dead and I was alive. This, of course, could be considered an unfair advantage; but I had not caused Caroline's death, nor had I been the one to propose that Richard and I marry.

With these thoughts in mind, I calmed myself and dried my tears. I would not run away like a faint-hearted coward. I would stay and *make* Richard love me. Even then I was aware that love cannot be so conveniently forced, but I meant to be the best wife in all of Cornwall.

Perhaps—someday—he would find to his surprise that the image of Caroline that he carried in his heart had been replaced by one of me. Admittedly, it was a foolish dream, and much more fitting for a green girl than the mature woman I liked to think I was. But I did love my husband, very deeply and far too much for my own good.

Therefore I determined, drying my eyes on my pillow, that I would not let Richard know that I had been in his room. I would certainly not let on that I had found the love token he kept under his pillow. Not a word about any of this would pass my lips. Perhaps someday, Richard would see fit to tell me, but until then, the secret would be mine. Finally, I slept.

I woke late the next morning. Sunlight was streaming in through the windows—a beautiful sight.

I leaped from the bed and hurried to the connecting door. Richard's bed was empty, but it showed signs of having been occupied. He had come in sometime during the night without my hearing him.

99

I turned back into my room and began to wash and dress. The water in the pitcher was cold, but I did not wish to take the time to order hot. I wanted to get dressed and find Richard.

I hurried into my clothes, choosing a gown of azure that I hoped gave me a bright look, and a paisley shawl to go round my shoulders.

I opened the door to the hall—and screamed. In my haste, I had almost stepped on the bloody—and quite dead—bird that lay there. Its mouth was grotesquely open, and projecting from it was a piece of paper that read, "Go home."

No ghost had left such a gory calling card. This looked a great deal like the work of Penrose. It was just the sort of thing that would appeal to his sense of the grisly.

I considered what to do next. I definitely did not intend to remove the bird myself. With a shudder, I stepped over it and continued on my way to the dining room. Someone was going to pay for this outrage.

Seeing the dining room was empty, I almost stamped my foot; but I recollected my new status, and instead I filled my plate and sat down to eat. My stomach felt definitely queasy, but I forced myself to chew and swallow. I was determined to behave as normally as possible.

As I ate, I mused on the night's events. I should have taken up the bird, kept it to show Richard. After all, I had no proof of Caroline's scent or the cries of the haunting babe, but the bird was tangible evidence. Foolishly I had let it lie there where the perpetrator could go back and remove it. Well, I would return after I had eaten and take up the evidence to show my husband.

Just as I finished emptying my plate, the dowager

entered. "Good morning," I said, putting on a cheerful smile.

"There is nothing good about it," she said grimly. "My son made a mistake in marrying you, and you will rue the day you set your cap for him."

This outrageous accusation brought out the worst in me. "I did not set my cap for him! Our marriage was Richard's idea."

She snorted. "Indeed!" Then she fixed me with a glaring eye. "You're cut from the same cloth as that sister of yours."

"I'm—"

"There's no point in denying it." She pointed a bony finger at me. "But you'd better not behave as she did, or you may come to a similar end."

"I—" I stared at her. How could she say such terrible things to me? "You are very wrong!" I cried. "I would never behave as Caroline did."

"She's right, Mama." Roland came in, gave us each a smile, and stepped to the sideboard to fill a plate. "Vanessa is a very different sort."

It was the most amazing thing. Right before my eyes the dowager changed. The harsh-featured harridan was transformed into a doting mama. "Now, Roland," she said, with more sweetness than I had ever heard in her voice, "you know you are far too tenderhearted."

He gave her a sheepish smile. "Perhaps so, Mama. But, nevertheless, you have misjudged Vanessa. You really ought to be kinder to her."

"But she is *his* wife."

"Mama, you know Richard cannot help being the duke. It was not his fault that he was born first." He put an arm around her shoulders. "Just be happy, Mama.

101

Richard works hard taking care of us, and I am free to do other things."

For a moment I was curious. What "other things" was Roland speaking of?

Then the dowager turned to me. "Perhaps I have misjudged you," she said slowly, the skin around her eyes crinkling into a frown. "But you married the wrong son. Roland would make a far better husband."

The memory of a fiery kiss pushed its way into my mind, and with it came the momentary consideration that perhaps the dowager was right! I could not imagine that Roland would let his bride languish for two nights. My lips seemed to feel again the intensity of that brief kiss. Roland's nature must be more combustible than Richard's. What would it be like to wait for Roland to come through the connecting door?

The thought heated my cheeks. Dear God, I could not begin acting like Caroline! I loved my husband, and he said he loved me. Any speculations on the activities of other men must remain purely that—speculation.

I knew that it was useless to argue with the dowager. She had long ago settled that Roland was to be the darling of her heart. Nothing I could say or do would change that. And indeed, Roland seemed to deserve every accolade his mother gave him. He was kind and considerate, tender and generous. A woman could not ask for a better son. Or husband. The disloyal thought was difficult to silence, but I worked very hard at doing so. My heart belonged to Richard, I reminded myself. It had been his since I was a girl.

I turned my thoughts in another direction. What could I do to make things more cheerful in the castle? I looked to Roland. "Does Rosamund always wear black?"

Roland nodded. "The poor dear is perpetually in mourning."

"But why—"

"She lost her love, her Jeffrey."

"Yes, I know that. But why does she wear mourning now when she believes her Jeffrey to be always there, with her?"

Roland looked startled. "Why, I don't know." His forehead wrinkled in concentration. "I believe she first put on black when Papa paid Jeffrey to go away. She did it then to spite my father. And she did believe he had had Jeffrey killed." He shook his head. "Such a course was hardly called for. Jeffrey was quite happy to take the money and run."

"I see." I hesitated. I did not want my only friend in this place to think me interfering. "I was thinking—perhaps we could get Rosamund some more colorful gowns. They might improve her condition."

Roland smiled. "That's an excellent idea. She always loved bright colors as a girl. How kind of you to think of poor Rosie."

I basked in his admiration. "Thank you."

"But you'd better check it out with Richard," he continued. "He takes complete charge of Rosie, you know."

"Yes, I will. Thank you, Roland, ah . . ."

He smiled at me. "Come, Vanessa, speak out. You can say anything to me."

I truly felt I could. "Well, it's your brother—"

"You must already have observed, Richard is not—"

"No, I mean Penrose."

A strange look crossed his face. "Penrose?"

"Yes. He needs a better example. Should he not be

away in school?"

"He refuses to leave his mother."

I couldn't help it. I looked at the dowager. "But she—"

The dowager drew herself up. "I am not Penrose's mother," she said.

I was truly confused. "But—"

"Penrose is Rosamund's son," Roland said softly.

Of course, now all seemed clear. Rosamund and Jeffrey's child. That was what had finally unhinged Rosamund's mind.

"I thought Richard would have told you." Roland sounded offended for me.

"Perhaps it slipped his mind." The words came out of my mouth in a far more caustic tone than I had intended; but my husband had been remiss in a great many areas, and my feelings on the subject were quite tender.

"Don't be too hard on Richard," Roland said, leaning across the table to pat my hand. "He has a great many responsibilities."

I knew this for the truth, but somehow it did not ease my sore feelings. Indeed, in some strange way it made me even angrier. After all, I was one of Richard's responsibilities. So was Sarah. And he was neglecting us both dreadfully. Besides, the news that Penrose was Rosamund's son, though it now made perfect sense, was a shock to me. Why hadn't my husband seen fit to tell me these things?

I could not think about that at the moment. It was too painful. "Do you think Penrose will be agreeable to our buying Rosamund some new gowns?" I asked, getting back to the subject at hand.

Roland shook his head. "With Penrose it's hard to say. I'd just ask him."

"Ask me what?"

I jumped. Must these people always be creeping up on me? "I was telling your uncle that your mother might like some new gowns."

To my surprise, Penrose smiled—and it was a genuine smile, not the evil leer he usually affected. "Yes," he said. "She might at that. I will talk to her about getting some." He gave me a strange look. "But you must let her pick the colors. She gets agitated if she's crossed."

"Of course." I was so gratified by this, my first relatively normal transaction with these people, that I decided to forget about the gory missive lying outside my bedroom door. Perhaps when Penrose saw that I was not like Caroline, when he realized that I genuinely wanted to help his mother, he would come over to my side. For the first time since I'd come to Greyden Castle, I felt optimistic about the future.

Chapter Nine

When I returned to my chamber after breakfast, the bird had been removed from before my door. I decided to dismiss the whole incident from my mind. After all, I did not want to disturb the newly found amity between Penrose and myself. We were on our way to accomplishing something good. If I could help his mother. . . .

Sadly my optimism did not last long. Till midafternoon, to be precise.

I was in the library, before the cheery fire. Creighton had brought Sarah to me, and the child was curled up in my lap while I told her stories.

She was listening quite contentedly, and I was feeling the glowing warmth of motherhood. At last things were going in a better direction. It looked as though I might be able to deal reasonably well with Richard's relations, and Sarah was clearly beginning to like me.

Then Gerson came to the door. "You have visitors, Your Grace. The vicar and his sister."

There was something about Gerson's expression that indicated to me that the visit would not be a pleasant one.

I straightened my shoulders. "Of course, Gerson. Better have a maid take Sarah back to the nursery."

"Yes, Your Grace."

I kissed the child. "I'll send for you again, when the visitors are gone."

She wrapped her little arms tightly around my neck. "I don't want to go, Nessie. I want to stay here with you."

"That's not possible," I said, prying at her fingers. "The visitors will not be interesting to you."

"I want to see my father," she insisted, far too loudly for my comfort.

"Your father is away from home now, Sarah. You know that."

"I want to see him!" Her voice was still rising, and I realized quite abruptly that I knew much less about bringing up children than I had supposed. I tried to recollect how Papa had raised me. Firmness, I thought. Firmness was the key.

"Sarah," I said. "Listen to me. If you want to see your father, you must learn good manners. You return to the nursery now as a proper young lady should, and you may come down again later, when your father has returned home."

"Do you promise?" the child demanded.

"I always do what I say I shall," I returned, and my air of injured dignity was only half assumed. I was not accustomed to having my word doubted by anyone, least of all a five-year-old.

For a moment the child stared at me, and it was plain that promises to her had not always been kept. "I'll go," she said finally. "I'll be waiting for you to send for me."

"And I shall." I gave her another kiss and watched her walk out, her small hand in the butler's. Then I took a deep breath and prepared to meet the vicar and his sister.

The vicar was a short man, round as a ripe apple, but his face was not as cheery as his shape might lead one to suppose. Above his plump and ample body, his wrinkled and lugubrious face looked like some kind of caricature by Hogarth.

Accompanying him was a woman wearing the most outlandish bonnet I had ever seen. It looked big enough to hold a picnic lunch for a dozen people and was decorated with artificial flowers in every shade of the rainbow. The woman beneath it was nondescript except for her eyes. They were very black and darted incessantly around the room. I recognized the type—a gossipmonger whose stock in trade was little bits and pieces of others' private lives.

I immediately determined that I should give her no new stock. I put on my sweetest smile. "Vicar, do come in. How kind of you to call."

His smile was warm and friendly and quite took me by surprise. Two days and nights in Greyden Castle and already I was surprised by kindness, but I pushed that from my mind as the vicar spoke.

"It seemed only fitting, Your Grace, you newly arrived and all. It's my duty, you know, to call on new parishioners."

"Yes, of course. Do sit down. Gerson will be bringing tea."

The vicar selected a comfortable chair close to the fire. His sister took a lyre-backed chair and sat down, erect as an army officer on review. She coughed and favored her brother with an accusing glance. "Oh, ah, Your Grace," he said. "This is my sister, Cressadine Varish."

I nodded. "I'm pleased to meet you, Miss Varish."

108

"Yes," she said, giving me a slight nod. "You poor child. It must be just dreadful for you here."

I knew her type well—this was the direct frontal attack—but I also knew how to withstand her assault. I put on my most innocent look. "Well, I do miss my papa." I glanced at the fire. "And I must admit that I didn't expect the castle to be quite so cold and dark."

Miss Varish's lip curled. "There's no need to pretend," she continued in a low raspy voice that grated on my already overworked nerves.

I feigned amazement. "Pretend, Miss Varish? I'm afraid I don't understand."

"Certainly the man must have told you." One pencil-thin eyebrow arched superciliously.

I was fast losing patience, and my temper, fiery in the best of times, was rapidly reaching the boiling point. "It is difficult for me to tell," I said in my haughtiest tones, "which *man* you refer to. And as for telling me, there are any number of things I might be told."

Miss Varish raised the other eyebrow. Her temper, it seemed, was no stabler than mine. "Really, Your Grace—"

I almost expected her to say "my girl" and grab me by the ear as Vickers had so often done; but just then Gerson came in with the tea tray, and I busied myself with pouring and serving. When that was accomplished, I leaned back, sipped my tea, and smiled. "You were saying." I nodded to Miss Varish.

She gave an aggrieved sniff and rattled her cup against her saucer. "I have come offering help," she said in plaintive tones. "And you pretend that you need none."

"Oh, no," I said, with an innocent look. "I do need help."

Her eyes gleamed like a hawk's before it pounces on the prey. "Tell me, my dear. Let me help you."

"Oh, that would be most kind," I gushed. It was not good of me, I know; but I have always abhorred gossips, such mean people, always trading in the world's misery, and I badly wanted to give this one a good set down.

She leaned forward eagerly, almost forgetting her tea. I knew she was ready to snatch up each tidbit and even readier to enlarge and elaborate on it before making her next stop.

"Who," I inquired in my most dulcet tones, "is the best dressmaker in the village?"

For a moment my words did not seem to register. Then her expression hardened. "Dressmaker?"

"Yes, I find I need some new gowns, something on the warmer side. Castles are such chilly places, don't you think?"

Evidently she could not believe her ears, for she repeated the word once more. "Dressmaker?"

"That's right. Sarah needs some new clothes. And so do Rosamund and the dowager."

"How is poor dear Rosamund?"

I sipped my tea and pretended ignorance. "Poor dear? Rosie is fine."

Miss Varish shook her head. "There's no need to pretend with us, my dear. Everyone knows about poor Rosamund. Such a tragic tale. Tell me, how do you deal with such a person?"

"I deal with her as I should any human being." My temper was still rising. What an obnoxious woman the vicar's sister was! But I must remember that I had a position to uphold.

Miss Varish sipped her tea and nodded sagely.

"Sometimes these people must be sent away. For the good of the family."

Rosamund had not exactly endeared herself to me, but the thought of sending Richard's sister to a bedlam was appalling. "No good is served by such an action," I said firmly. "Rosamund is quite happy here, and we are happy to have her."

While his sister stared open-mouthed, I turned my attention to the vicar. "I wish to do my share of work in the parish. You must notify me when there are things to be done."

The vicar nodded approval over his cup. "Of course, Your Grace. There is one thing that comes immediately to mind."

I hadn't expected him to ask favors so soon, but I had offered. "Yes? What is it?"

"You could perhaps persuade His Grace to return to Sunday services."

"Richard has—" I caught myself as Miss Varish leaned forward again—"Richard has just been telling me how much he enjoys your sermons."

The vicar shifted uncomfortably in his chair. His sister cackled. "I wonder he can remember. He has not been to services since *she* was found."

The vicar frowned. "That is not entirely accurate, Cressadine. As I recall, the duke came for several Sundays after—after—"

"After she was killed," finished his sister. "But he hasn't been there since."

The vicar nodded. "Perhaps, Your Grace, you can discover why."

Miss Varish snorted. "Discover? Why it's plain as day. He didn't like the things folks were saying." She drew

111

herself even more erect. "It ain't Christian, him not putting down that ferocious animal."

"Mercury is gentle," I said. "He would not hurt anyone."

Miss Varish's eyes gleamed with delight. "If that is true, then someone else, some *person* killed her."

I shivered and was glad I had been safely in Wiltshire at the time. I had no doubt she would gladly have pinned the crime on me. I had never once supposed that Caroline's death was other than an accident; but Cressadine Varish had other ideas—and she had no doubt spread them far and wide.

The vicar frowned. "Really, Cressadine, that is enough. Her Grace is new here. You must give her time to settle in."

"Time will not change this," Miss Varish said, waving her tea cup for emphasis.

And indeed it would not. Not as long as she was going about adding fuel to the flames.

"People will continue to talk as long as he keeps the horse," she went on.

Perhaps they would, but I did not intend to urge Richard to put down a beautiful gentle animal to satisfy this dried-up stick who battened on other people's misery. I contemplated telling her so in no uncertain terms, but I remembered my position in the community and replied more moderately. "I am sorry, but I cannot suggest that the animal be destroyed."

"Good for you," said the vicar, ignoring his sister's dark glance. He smiled at me good-naturedly. "You must be patient, my dear. People do talk, but it blows over eventually." His eyes grew cloudy with sympathy. "The duke is a good man. There's hardly a soul in the county who hasn't known his help. They should all be grateful to him."

Miss Varish sniffed. "That hardly excuses murder."

"Cressadine!" The vicar seemed to swell, and his gentle voice turned to thunder. "Let her who is without sin cast the first stone. It is not up to us to judge. Only the Lord knows what drives a man to do the things he does."

My heart stood still in my breast. For a moment I thought it might never beat again. It sounded—could I be imagining it? It sounded as if the vicar suspected Richard of killing his wife!

Finally I found my tongue. "You do not mean—you cannot really believe that Richard had anything to do with Caroline's death?"

The vicar looked uncomfortable. As a man of God, he could not lie. "My dear, no one knows. But if in a moment of anger the duke—" He paused and swallowed. "We all know how great the provocation could be."

He put down his cup, pulled out a huge white handkerchief, and mopped his brow. "She was a wicked woman. A Jezebel. I'm sorry to say this, Your Grace. I know she was your sister, but she was very bad. The parish had never seen her like."

I could not contain myself any longer. "The fact that my sister was the talk of the parish is no reason to suppose that Richard killed her. If she was as bad as you say, there must have been many who wished her harm."

"Quite so, Your Grace." The vicar got to his feet and wiped his brow again. "This is an unseemly subject." He glared at his sister, who remained strangely quiet. "We should not be discussing such things. I meant this to be a friendly, welcoming call. And now"—he wiped his brow yet again—"we must be going, Your Grace."

I could not leave it like this. I blocked the vicar's way to the door. "Surely you cannot believe—you know Richard very well. He's a kind, generous man. You yourself told me how much he's done for the people of the parish."

The vicar nodded. "Indeed, he has. But many people have short memories." His sister paled, and I wondered what Richard had done to help her. "But others have more gratitude." He looked around and lowered his voice. "The truth is several people have been to the magistrate to ask him to bring charges, but he refused to listen to them."

I could not believe it. Richard's friends and neighbors, people who had known him for years, actually thought him capable of committing murder.

The vicar edged toward the door. "We really must be going," he said.

I decided to put a good face on things. "Of course. Please come again." What inanities politeness compels us to utter! "I shall talk to the duke about coming to Sunday services. And do let me know what I can do to help."

"Yes, yes." The pair made their exit in nervous haste, and I sank back in my chair. Things were getting more and more tangled. A little gossip was one thing, but people pressing the magistrate to bring charges—that was serious business indeed.

I sat there for some time, sipping lukewarm tea and trying to think of something I could do. But I was no closer to a solution when Roland appeared in the doorway. "There you are," he said. "I hoped I might find you here." He scrutinized my face. "Vanessa, you are looking pale. Whatever is wrong?"

I put down my cup. "I have had a visit—from the vicar and his sister."

His smile was comforting. "No wonder you look ill. What did they have to say?"

I sighed. I was glad to have Roland to talk to, but it was hard repeating such terrible things. "Miss Varish believes the stallion should be put down. And when I said he was gentle, she suggested that some *person* had killed Caroline."

Roland shrugged. Evidently this was not news to him. "Cressadine Varish is the scourge of the parish. She will accuse anyone of anything."

I was beginning to feel better. Roland was so sensible. "I thought as much and did not pay much attention to her," I went on. "But then the vicar began to talk as though Richard had done this thing. He said people had been to the magistrate, urging him to bring charges."

Roland looked surprised. "I've heard nothing of that."

"That's because the magistrate refused to do it. Or so the vicar claims."

Roland nodded. "Of course. Pemberton knows Richard well."

I discovered that my hands were shaking, and I hid them in the folds of my skirt. "The vicar sounded—he sounded as if he believed it himself. He talked about provocation. He called Caroline a Jezebel."

Something flickered in Roland's eyes—distaste, no doubt. "I know she was bad," he said. "That she caused Richard no end of pain. But to suppose that he would kill her—that is outrageous."

Roland rose and put a warm hand on my shoulder. "Calm yourself, my dear. Varish knows which side his bread is buttered on. He will defend Richard, never fear."

115

I stared up at my husband's twin. "You mean he will defend him even if he thinks him guilty?"

"Of course. The vicar's living comes through Richard."

I felt as though right and wrong no longer had any meaning. "But he is a man of God, surely—"

"Vanessa, my dear." Roland patted my shoulder. "You are elaborating too much on this. Richard is quite safe." He pulled a chair up close to me. "You wanted me to tell you the cause of the animosity Richard feels for me."

I had almost forgotten that in my mental chaos over the vicar's remarks. But I did want to know. "Oh, yes, please do tell me."

"It happened when we were boys—eight or nine. I don't remember exactly. But we were up in the stable loft. Not the present stable. Richard had it built new several years ago. He had the other one torn down."

He paused and poured himself some tea. "Well, as I said, we were up in the loft, playing highwayman, and Richard fell."

I found this story bewildering. "If he fell, why should he be angry with you?"

Roland looked embarrassed. "He says that I pushed him. Deliberately."

"Oh, no!"

Roland nodded. "Actually—no, never mind."

"Tell me. Please tell me."

He sighed. "We were struggling. And he said—" He paused and looked slightly ill. "He was only a boy, you understand. And he was wild with jealousy because Mama favored me."

He looked pained. How difficult that must have been for him. "When I got old enough to understand, I could

116

see what it was doing to Richard, but I could not get her to change."

He sighed again. "At any rate, as we were struggling, Richard whispered that he meant to kill me. Then he would be Mama's only son. I laughed, thinking he was joking. And—and he tried to push me out of the loft."

Cold terror clutched at my heart. If Richard had done such a thing then. . . .

"It was when he tried to push me that he slipped and fell. He hurt his leg and was in bed for several weeks. He told Papa that I had pushed him, and our father punished me; but I didn't care, I was just glad Richard had not been more badly hurt." He sipped his tea and frowned. "I don't know what went on in his mind. Perhaps he truly believes that I pushed him. As Rosie believes she is talking to her Jeffrey."

This story was not at all what I had expected to hear. For some moments I sat in stunned silence. It was difficult to believe that Richard could have done such a thing. That my Richard, whom I had loved for so long, had tried to kill his twin.

Roland patted my arm. "Please, my dear, don't let the story distress you so. Remember, we were just boys. No harm was done, and we get along reasonably well now."

I did not reply to this. I could not. For the first time I was entertaining serious doubts about my husband's character. It was not a pleasant feeling, and while I was still trying to deal with my emotions, the dowager entered.

"I heard the vicar was here."

"Yes," I replied. "He and his sister."

"You mean the viper." It was one of the few times I found myself in agreement with the dowager.

"The vicar spoke as though Richard might have been responsible for Caroline's death," Roland told his mother.

"I would like to think so," the dowager replied with a hard glance at me. "It would greatly redeem him in my eyes."

"Your Grace!" For a mother to wish her child to become a murderer. . . .

She shook her head. "If ever a woman deserved to die, it was Caroline, duchess of Greyden. She had carnal knowledge of nearly every man in the parish. Richard *should* have killed her."

Suddenly I could stand no more. I leaped to my feet, and without even offering an excuse I rushed out. As I used to when I was upset as a girl, I headed for the comfort of horses. They were much more decent than people. And far far kinder.

Chapter Ten

The stable was warm. Sunshine streamed in the open tops of the stall doors. Richard's horses, I thought angrily, lived better than his wife and daughter.

But I could not stay angry long, not when Mercury whuffled a greeting and the other horses joined in. Not when the comforting smell of horses, and leather, and hay was all about me.

"Toby?" I called.

"Here, Yer Grace." His face was still grimy, but his smile was friendly. I liked the boy.

"The duke did not take the stallion today?"

"No, Yer Grace. He took the carriage, you see. Something about an old woman wanting to visit her husband's eternal resting place. And her too old and sick for walking that far. 'Tis a good man, the duke is. Always going about helping folks as needs help."

"Yes." I was no longer sure about Richard's motives, but I did not intend to discuss them with the stableboy.

The great blue-gray stallion shifted and pranced in his stall, throwing his head about and tossing his mane. I knew he wanted some exercise. "The stallion is restless today."

Toby grinned. "Aye. He needs his run every day, or he fidgets about somewhat dreadful."

I smiled. "Then perhaps I should take him out for a ride."

Toby's face turned so pale his freckles stood out through the grime. "Ah, I can't be letting you do that, Yer Grace. He'd have my skin, the duke would."

I tried for dignity. I drew myself erect. "I'm a very good horsewoman."

"Aye, Yer Grace. I've no doubt of that. But I got me orders. No one rides the stallion but the duke himself. Not Mr. Roland. Nor yet Mr. Penrose. And *she* weren't allowed neither."

My heart skipped a beat. "Toby, are you talking about my sister?"

Toby nodded. "Aye. That's what made it so strange. Her being in his stall and all. She never rode him—not never. So why was she in there with him?" Toby shook his head. "It don't make no sense, it don't. She had a sharp tongue, the lady." He grimaced. "Sharper'n any whip. And she beat a horse now and then. But I never seen her go into a stall to do it. It don't make no sense."

It made no sense to me either. Caroline had been strong-willed, selfish, even cruel, but not stupid. Never stupid.

I stroked the stallion's smooth gray neck. Toby's eyes widened. He was obviously impressed by my nerve. "Since I can't ride the stallion," I said, "I'll take out the black mare—Fancy."

"But Yer Grace—"

I was sorry to be rough on Toby, but being there in the

stable was not enough for me. I badly needed to feel a horse under me. "Didn't His Grace say the black mare was to be mine?"

"Yes, Yer Grace." Toby didn't look at all happy. But he was a stableboy, not a barrister. He knew how to follow direct orders, and it was clear he'd had no orders on this.

"Yer Grace, I ain't so sure—"

"Saddle the mare," I commanded. "Or I will do it myself."

His mouth gaped and he stared at me.

"I mean it," I said firmly. "I have saddled many an animal in my day. I mean to have a ride today, and no one is going to stop me."

It was unfair of me to put the boy in such a position. I knew very well that Richard did not want me to ride alone, but the pressures of the day's events, added to those of the previous night, made me ready to explode. I had to get away from the castle and its inhabitants. I needed some time to myself—to think about the shocking revelations of the day. To be on horseback had always helped me to think more clearly.

Toby looked doubtful, but he capitulated. Fancy was saddled and led out.

"You ain't dressed for riding," Toby said.

I realized he was right, but the need to ride was strong within me. "I don't mean to go far," I said.

Toby knew when he was beaten. He offered me his cupped hands. I put my foot in them and was tossed up.

"Don't worry about me," I repeated as I hooked my leg in the proper position and settled my skirt. "I'll be back soon."

He went to hold open the stable door and stood watching me as I rode off. The sun was bright, the breeze from the ocean tangy with salt. I thought of going to the sea, to the golden beach where Richard and I had spent such a happy hour, but the thought of the quicksand put me off.

The mare was feeling her oats, lifting her heels in sheer joy at living and moving. There on the road I could control her, but the beach was a different matter. If the waves were high, she might shy at them. And with quicksand lurking. . . .

That decided me. I turned the mare's head away from the sea and took the road down from the castle. Without my boots the stirrup was uncomfortably hard against my ankle, and the sidesaddle suddenly seemed an instrument of torture. As we got farther into the shade, the breeze grew more chill, and I had to stop and tie my shawl in a knot about my shoulders.

Of course, any sensible woman would have admitted defeat and turned back; but when I was upset, I was far from sensible, and I desperately needed this brief escape. So in spite of everything I rode on.

Sunlight coming through the leafing trees dappled the road, and gradually my distraught thoughts slowed their racing. I wished I could simply enjoy the day—the sun, the breeze, the buds of spring—but the things I had heard kept reverberating in my mind.

Cressadine Varish could be discounted. She would accuse her own brother if it earned her an *entree* into enough homes. Her bitterness and sharp tongue might be the result of her spinsterhood, but somehow I felt they were more the cause than the effect. No sane man would marry a woman with Miss Varish's tongue. The vicar had no doubt already earned his sainthood simply by living with her for so long.

No, if Miss Varish had been the only one to accuse Richard, I should have paid her little notice, perhaps even have laughed at her. But she had not been the only one. It was clear that the vicar supposed my husband, if not guilty, at least capable of killing his wife.

I still could not understand the vicar's behavior. If he believed Richard had done this terrible thing, why did he not add his voice to those who wished the magistrate to bring charges?

Of course I knew that there were venal men in all walks of life. But Papa valued honesty. And for Roland to tell me that a man of God would protect the guilty in order not to lose his living—this was a piece of intelligence that did great damage to my ordered perceptions of right and wrong.

Then there was the story of Richard's fall. How could I believe that my beloved husband had tried to kill his twin? That was a horrid thing.

Perhaps Roland was mistaken. Perhaps Richard really had been joking. Boys that age were often rough in their play. It could be a misunderstanding on both their parts. I wanted desperately to believe so.

The road from the castle led into a larger thoroughfare. I turned left, away from the sea, and urged the mare on.

I don't know how long I rode. Without my boots, I was most uncomfortable; but my body was no more uncomfortable than my mind, and it was good to be away from the castle.

Up ahead the trees lining the road grew smaller and fewer, and suddenly there was the moorland. I drew in my breath. Such beautiful country. The gently rolling land stretched into the distance. It looked so peaceful, so free of evil and pain. Without thinking, I turned the mare off the road.

The land was not as gentle as it had first looked. Here and there outcroppings of stone reared above the furze and sedge, and in the distance shadowy peaks hinted at mysterious and ancient inhabitants; but I had no thought to spare for people of ancient times.

I wanted most fervently not to think at all, to retreat to those happier hours when none of these terrible stories had yet been known to me.

No matter how I tried, I could not forget what I had heard. I could not go back to those days of innocence when I had looked with joy to my coming life with Richard.

While I was lost in my musings, I let the mare follow her own inclination. Finally, the fact that her walk had slowed reached my troubled mind. Looking up, I saw that she was picking her way among huge tumbled rocks. I roused myself to look behind me for the road, but it had disappeared.

I did not let this frighten me. Papa had early taught me how to use the sun for direction. It was now throwing my shadow to the right. I had only to turn the mare around, keep my shadow on my left, and retrace the route to the road. A simple matter.

Except at that moment the sun went behind a cloud, and I had no shadow. I turned the mare anyway and headed her in what I hoped was the right direction. The sun would soon come out again.

But the clouds above me continued to darken. Gray and sullen, they gathered in ever greater masses, and in the distance thunder rumbled.

I looked around, but there was no place to take shelter. The scattered stones offered little or no protection from the elements. I pulled my shawl tighter and rode on. Soon now, we must come upon the road, and I would be safely on the way home.

As the sky darkened and the wind rose, even the castle began to take on pleasing aspects. Our squabbles seemed petty and trivial in the face of nature's rising fury. But the castle was far away, and I was not at all sure in which direction it lay.

Still, I kept the mare moving. I thought, too, of giving the animal her head. Perhaps she would turn homeward. But I did not know how long Richard had had her. Would she return to his stable, or would she perhaps take me back onto the barren and now frightening moors?

The wind grew rougher, loosening the pins in my hair and blowing wild strands down to sting my eyes. It tugged at my shawl and my skirt, flapping them furiously.

Then the heavens opened. The rain fell in great soaking drops. Soon my hair hung in sodden strands, my gown was plastered to my shivering body, and my teeth began a mad chattering.

The rainswept moor was barren and empty, my clothes were soaking wet, and I had no idea of how to get back to Greyden Castle.

In spite of my fiery temper, I had always been a believer. And so I thought to pray. But to be truthful, I did not see why the good Lord should be bothered to help me extricate myself from a position into which my own stupidity had taken me.

Only a fool—or a very distraught woman—went riding alone into unknown territory. Richard had warned me against that very thing, and I had promised I would not do it.

But I had let a mean-mouthed, hateful woman's words

and the tale of a boyish misunderstanding make me doubt my husband, and now I was paying for it.

I raised my hand to push the dripping hair from my eyes. A terrible clap of thunder seemed to shake the whole earth, and a bolt of lightning sizzled into the soil not twenty feet away.

The mare decided she had had all she could manage. She took the bit between her teeth and ran for dear life, almost unseating me in the first leap.

I am indeed an excellent horsewoman; and I had often ridden to hounds; but then I had been properly dressed. Not only did I lack boots, but the rainsoaked gown dragged at my limbs, giving me difficulty in keeping my seat.

The heavy rain made it impossible to see where we were going, and I grew fearful that in her wild flight the mare would crash into some stones or trip over something and throw me.

Suddenly she gave a great bound and we were on the road. I had no time to be grateful for that discovery, though, for through the pelting rain I could see a carriage bearing down on us.

The mare reared and neighed in terror. I knew instantly that I would not be able to keep my seat.

The driver swore—a nice round oath Papa would have approved of—and hauled back on the reins.

I suppose I guessed this last because by that time I was flying through the air. I hit the road with a dull thud and lay there, eyes closed, struggling to regain my breath.

The rain was cold on my face. I knew I was lying in a puddle of cold, wet mud, but all I could think of was getting air into my tortured lungs. Like an animal in pain I whimpered and moaned.

Suddenly the rain stopped falling on me. I opened my

eyes to find someone bending over me.

"My God! Vanessa! What are you doing out here?"

I could not answer, of course, and he seemed to realize this. "Harry, go catch the mare."

One by one, Richard tested each of my limbs. I indicated that I felt no pain. Then he was lifting me in his arms. I felt the heat of his body, so strong, so comforting. How could I ever have doubted him? He lifted me onto the seat and wrapped me carefully in the carriage robe.

His dear features twisted into a frown. "I know you've had the wind knocked out of you," he said severely. "But you are fortunate to have gotten off so easy. Why were you out on the moor in a storm like this? Whatever were you thinking?"

By this time I had regained a measure of breath. I had never liked being scolded, and I did not like it then. "I did not go out during the storm," I protested. "When I left the castle, the w-w-weather was sunny and b-b-bright."

Though my breathing was more normal, my teeth went on chattering.

Richard continued to frown. "The weather changes rapidly here. And you might well have lost your way or fallen into a bog."

"A b-b-bog?"

"Yes. The moor is notorious for such places."

Sucking sands on the beach. Quaking bogs on the moors. And in the castle. . . . Everywhere I turned dangers awaited me.

But I did not say so to Richard. He was angry enough already. And, since I had already regretted my headlong flight from the castle, and been giving myself a severe scolding, I had no wish to receive another from my husband.

My teeth continued to chatter, and I was too cold and

weary to control them, even if I had been able.

Richard's frown turned to a look of worry. "Vanessa, you're soaked." He put an arm around me and pulled me closer to him.

"You'll get wet," I protested.

Richard shook his head. "That matters little. I want to keep you warm till we reach home."

And keep me warm he did.

He did not scold me any more either, and I was grateful for that.

When we got back to the castle, Richard insisted on carrying me up the great stairs to my room. He dismissed the maid who brought the pitcher of warm water and with his own hands began to unknot my shawl.

For some reason I felt embarrassment. "Richard, I can undress myself."

"Of course you can," he said. "But you are shivering. And to do so will take much longer. You're already chilled through. I want to get you warm as soon as possible."

He dropped the shawl to the floor and began on the hooks to my dress. "I am sorry to have been gone so long," he said. "But it was the anniversary of Mrs. Carmody's marriage, the first since she lost her husband, and she had no way to the churchyard."

I nodded. "Toby told me."

Richard had taken off my blue gown, now sadly soaked with mud and rain, and knelt to remove my shoes and stockings. Though the room was chill as ever and my chemise was sopping wet, a warmth began to steal through my body.

"Richard, please do not be hard on Toby. He tried to stop me."

Richard smiled. "I'm sure Toby did what he could. At least he didn't give you the stallion."

"No. I tried, but he said he had his orders."

Richard looked up. "You wanted to ride the stallion?"

"Of course. He's a beautiful animal, and he was restless today."

Richard nodded absently. "He fidgets when he hasn't been out." He took the cloth and warm water and began to wipe my face. "I'm sorry, Vanessa. This whole thing is my fault."

Astonishment made my mouth fall open. "Your fault?"

"Of course. I should not have left you to your own devices. You're used to an active life. Being shut up must be galling to you."

I hesitated. Should I tell him what had upset me so, what had driven me to act in such an unusual way? "I—I was not bored," I said. "I was a little upset. The vicar was here. And his sister."

Richard's expression changed. His eyes, which had been warm and loving, grew cold and cloudy. He got to his feet and stood looking down on me. "What happened? What did they say?"

I kept my tone calm. "Miss Varish believes that you should have the stallion put down, and when I told her that I disagreed, she did not like it."

"Was that all?"

"Yes," I said. In that split second I decided not to tell him about the complaints to the magistrate, or to let on that I knew anything about the incident in the hay loft.

His expression grew less guarded. "I'm afraid Miss Varish is going to be disappointed. I've no intention of destroying a beautiful animal to please the likes of her."

129

"I should hope not." I moved closer to him. "Richard?"

His eyes grew warm again. "Yes, my dear?"

My heart was pounding, but I made myself ask the question. "Do you really love me?"

His eyes looked deep into mine. "Yes, Nessie, I do. And I mean to prove it. Right now."

"N-now?" It was not the cold or the wet that made the word come out strangely. I was having trouble believing that the moment I had been waiting for had at last arrived.

Richard's fingers went to the ribbons on my chemise, and then I realized what an awful wreck I must look. "Oh, Richard. You can't!"

His mouth fell open. And if I had been less distraught I might have laughed.

"What?"

"Look at me. My hair is all muddy. I'm a mess. I wanted to be pretty and—"

Richard burst into laughter, and in a moment had had whisked off my chemise and bundled me under the covers.

"Nessie," he said, removing his own clothes, "you are the most beautiful woman in the world."

From my nest of pillows, I watched him undress, and I did indeed feel beautiful. "You—you are a very handsome man," I ventured.

He laughed again. Oh, it was good to hear his laughter, clean and fresh. "I believe, wife, that you are a trifle biased."

"Perhaps," I agreed. "But just a trifle."

Then he was in the bed beside me, his body warm against mine.

Chapter Eleven

Afterwards, quite warm again, I stretched deliciously and smiled. Safe against the heat of Richard's body, with his arm around me, the things I had heard earlier were meaningless. How could I believe anything against him? My husband loved me. I knew it in the very depths of my being.

In my happiness, I recalled the child, Richard's child, and what I had promised her. "Oh, dear!"

"What is it, love?"

His lips were warm against my brow, his words of love burning in my heart as my body still felt the heat of our passion. I did not want to spoil our glorious time together, and so I hesitated; but I could not, in good conscience, put the task off any longer. "I told Sarah you and I would spend some time with her today. You are her father, and she should see more of you."

His whole body tensed, and though I lay just as near him, I felt a chasm opening between us.

"Nessie," he said, "do as you please about the child. I leave her entirely in your hands. Just understand, I don't wish to be involved."

I could not leave it at that. "But Richard, she's your child. How can you do this to her?"

His eyes had gone cold again. "Do what? I see that she has everything she needs."

I did not like to contradict him, but I saw that I must. "No, you do not. She needs her father's love."

He frowned. "I cannot give her that."

"Richard! After what your mother did to you, how can you be so cruel to Sarah? To your own child."

Richard sighed. "All right, Vanessa. I did not want to do it, but I see that I shall have to tell you the truth. Sarah is not mine."

I could not immediately take this in. "Not yours?"

"That's right. Caroline told me so herself."

"Then who is her father?"

"Caroline would not tell me." His eyes burned with pain. "She would not tell me his name, but she was quite sure the child was not mine."

"And that is why you stopped going to see Sarah? Why you ceased to act like her father?"

"Yes."

My heart ached for his pain. And for Sarah's. "Oh, Richard. You must not do this awful thing. Think! What if Caroline lied about this? Think what damage you'll be doing to your own child."

His frown deepened. "Why should she lie about such a thing?"

He did not know Caroline as well as I thought. "She lied about many things," I pointed out. "She lied whenever it suited her purpose."

"But if the child is not mine—"

"So what if she is not yours?" I persisted; I had to

132

make him understand. "What harm is done by loving an orphan, a foundling? In the child's eyes you *are* her father. How can she understand why her father does not love her?"

"You must make her understand," he said firmly. "For I cannot love her."

I could not believe that. I kissed his ear before I whispered in it. "We shall have many children, you and I, but in God's name and for His Son's sake, we must love the one that has already been entrusted to our care."

We spoke no more then, of Sarah or anything else, but once again explored the joyous union God had ordained for husband and wife.

Later, we rose and began to dress. I seemed to have suffered no ill effects from my fall and my exposure to the elements. Indeed, for the first time since I'd come to Greyden Castle, I felt warm and serene. And of course, I was feeling very happy to at last be Richard's wife in every way.

I stole an admiring look at his body as he bent to retrieve his shirt. Suddenly he drew in a sharp breath, as though something pained him. When he straightened, I saw that he walked with a limp.

I hurried to his side. "Richard, you have injured yourself. Oh, my dear, you did it helping me."

Richard smiled and touched my cheek. "No, Nessie. It has nothing to do with you. It's an old injury."

I thought of Roland's story. "How—how did you do it?"

His hesitation was almost imperceptible, but it was there. "I fell," he said. "When I was a boy. My leg acts up now and then."

"Where did you fall from?"

"The stable loft."

He did not go on. I badly wanted to hear his version of the story, but I dared not press him for it. He would not like my having discussed such matters with Roland—or anyone else.

I felt again a stab of disloyalty. If only my husband would confide in me. Then I would not need to gather information from his family and the servants.

I reached up to give him a kiss. "Richard, why did you not tell me about Penrose?"

At least he did not try to evade the question. He looked directly into my eyes. "I suppose someone has told you that Rosie is really his mother."

"Yes, the poor boy."

One of Richard's eyebrows shot up. "Poor boy! I did not suppose you had much sympathy for him."

"True, I did not. But with his mother as she is— Richard, can we get Rosamund some new gowns?"

Richard looked shocked. "Gowns?"

"Yes, dear. I was talking to Penrose earlier, and to Roland and your mother. They all agreed that it might be helpful to Rosamund to get her out of mourning."

Richard shook his head. "They all agreed, did they? Nessie, you are a miracle worker." He sighed. "It sounds like a fine idea, but I'm afraid it's only that. Rosie has worn black these eighteen years. How can we get her to change now?"

"I do not know," I said truthfully. "But Penrose said he would help."

Richard smiled. "Then perhaps you will succeed. He has a lot of influence with her. At any rate, it's worth the effort. Only do not agitate her."

"Of course not." I could not resist stretching up to kiss him again before I went to the armoire for a clean chemise. "And Richard—"

He looked faintly amused. "Already you are learning wifely habits."

I did not understand. "I am? What habits?"

"You have discovered the best time to ask for favors."

As the implications of this washed over me, I felt myself flush scarlet. "Oh, dear, I did not mean to—"

His laughter rang out again. How I loved the sound of it. "Nessie, my darling. What a gem you are. You may ask me anything you like at any time."

Emboldened by his words, I slipped again into his arms. "Then will you think about what I said about Sarah?"

Wonder of wonders, he did not push me away. The warmth of his arms still enfolded me.

"Yes," he whispered against my hair. "I will think about it. But Nessie, I can make no promises."

"I understand. But just think."

Roland must be mistaken, I decided as I donned my clean chemise and gown. Richard was too warm and loving a man to have tried to kill his brother. But why hadn't he told me the story himself?

"Nessie," Richard said as he did up my hooks, "would you really like to ride the stallion?"

"Oh, yes! Oh, Richard! I should love it!"

He hesitated. "I was thinking—but only if you really want to—no, it's too dangerous."

"Richard. What?"

"When you said you wished to ride Mercury, I did think that your doing so might quiet the talk."

I saw immediately what he was about. "Of course. If I ride him, people will see what a gentle animal he really is."

"That was my thought. But—"

I hurried into his arms. "Oh, yes, yes, yes!"

He smiled. "All right, you have convinced me. But you must promise me one thing."

"Yes, of course."

"First, we will go riding together. I'll show you the countryside. The landmarks. Places to avoid. And later, when you are accustomed to finding your way, you may ride out alone."

"Oh, yes. That will be marvelous." I kissed him once more and turned toward the door. "I must go to Sarah, my dearest. I promised her."

He nodded. I thought he almost smiled. At least he did not frown. "Since it has stopped raining," he said, "I'm going out to check the horses. I want to be sure the mare has suffered no ill effects."

I found Sarah in the nursery, staring at the fire. She did not speak to me or acknowledge my presence in any way.

Creighton frowned. "She's been like that these many hours, Your Grace. Won't move. Won't talk."

"Sarah?"

The child turned accusing eyes on me. "You didn't send for me. You lied."

"Here now—" Creighton began.

"It's all right," I interjected. "Sarah is right to be upset. I broke my promise to her."

Creighton drew in a sharp breath, and Sarah's eyes

widened. "Why?" Sarah asked. "Why did you do that?"

I drew up a chair so I could face her on her level. "I didn't mean to," I explained. "I went for a ride and I got lost. On the moor."

Her small face paled. "My mama hated the moor. She said it was the godawfulest country."

"I thought it rather beautiful," I said softly. "But I didn't watch where I was going, and so I got lost. Then, when I was trying to find my way, a storm came. The horse bolted and threw me."

The child climbed down from her chair and surveyed me solemnly. "Did you get hurt?"

"Just a little. I got the wind knocked out of me."

She nodded. "Then may I still sit in your lap?"

"Of course."

She climbed up and settled herself. "Did the horse run away, Nessie?"

"No, dear. Your father came along right then and brought me home."

Her lower lip came out to register her displeasure. "You didn't send for me."

"No, Sarah, I didn't. I was wet clear to the skin. I had to get washed and dried off, to change my clothes. And—" I could feel the flush rising to my cheeks—"I was very tired so I took a nap. But as soon as I could I came to see you. To explain what happened. I am sorry. Will you forgive me?"

"Yes." She put her little arms around my neck and kissed my cheek. "Will I get to see my father now, Nessie? Please?"

Her eyes were downcast, and I knew from her expression that she expected another disappointment. Suddenly I couldn't bear it. Richard must learn to love

137

her. I would do anything to make that happen. "Yes," I said. "Get your cloak. We're going to the stable."

Creighton shook her head; but she said nothing, and within minutes Sarah stood ready.

"Now," I said as we moved down the hall, "you must be good."

"Yes," Sarah replied. "Then my father will love me." She looked up at me with eyes full of tears. "I must have been very bad. That's why—"

"No, Sarah." I could not let the child go on like that. "You are not bad."

She shook her head. "I am. I know I am."

"How can you know such a thing?"

"My mama said so. She said I was a bad bad girl."

My heart skipped a beat. Oh, the things Caroline had to answer for. Perhaps Rosamund wasn't so far off in wishing her to burn in eternal fire. "When was this?" I asked.

"When I found her book."

"Her book?"

Sarah nodded. "She wrote in it. And she kept it hid."

My mind raced. Caroline writing in a book. Why hadn't I remembered that Caroline always kept a diary? If only I could find it. Perhaps it would tell me something about Sarah's father.

"I just wanted to see if it smelled pretty like her," Sarah told me. "But she said I was a bad bad girl."

"You were not a bad girl," I said firmly, remembering the day Caroline had found me in her scent bottles. "You were just curious."

She thought about this as we descended the great stairs. "Nessie, what is curious?"

I smiled. "It means wanting to learn new things. All

children are curious."

"And it's not bad?"

"Not at all," I said. "Sarah—" I chose my words carefully. "Do you know where your mama kept her book?"

Sarah shook her head. "No, Nessie. That day I saw it she was in the funny room. At the top of the stairs. Where it's so dark. I hid up there to surprise her." Her face puckered. "She scolded me and told me I was bad. I didn't mean to be bad."

"I know, dear." We had reached the bottom of the stairs. "But come, let us forget all that for now. Let's go see the horses."

"And my father."

"And your father," I repeated. How strong the bond of love must have been before Caroline's hateful words destroyed it. Why, I wondered again, should Caroline tell her husband such a hateful thing? Even if it were true, and something—some feeling in me—insisted that it was not, what had she to gain by telling him such a thing?

I could come to no firm conclusion. There were possibilities, of course. Perhaps she was jealous of the child and sought to bring Richard's attention back to her. That was certainly possible. Or she might just have wanted to hurt him, and knowing his love for Sarah, she knew also where to deal him the most painful blow.

The second possibility seemed far more likely to me. Caroline did nothing that did not benefit *her*. That much I could be sure of.

By this time we were following the path to the stables. "I like the sunshine," Sarah said with a little smile. "It's warm and bright."

The stable door was open, and we went in, Sarah's

small hand trustingly in mine. *Please God*, I begged. *Don't let him hurt her more.*

"There's the pretty horse," Sarah said. "And there's my father."

Richard turned. His face took on that closed expression, but he did not frown.

"Good day, Father," Sarah said. "Nessie brought me to see the horses."

Richard's look informed me quite clearly that he had divined my intent. But all he said was "So I see."

Sarah pulled me toward the stallion. "Look, Nessie, isn't he pretty?"

"Yes, Sarah."

"Can I pet him?"

"Of course." I bent to lift her and then paused. Perhaps . . . I straightened and put a hand to my back. "I seem to have a crick here. From the fall I suppose."

Richard frowned. "Maybe we should have Dr. Sanderson—"

"No, no. It's nothing. Here, Sarah, we'll try—"

"You'll do nothing of the sort. I'll do it." He strode forward and lifted the child into his arms.

Such a look of joy shone on her face that I had to swallow a huge lump that appeared in my throat. She wrapped one small arm around his neck. "Thank you, Father."

His stern expression did not fade, but I thought I saw something in his eyes—a warmth that had not been there. He stepped closer to the stallion, and I followed. "First," he said, "you must let him smell you. Put out your hand like this." He showed her how to extend her hand, palm up. "Sometimes," he said, "we give the horse a treat."

Sarah giggled, and I realized with a pang that this was the first time I had heard her laugh. "Like a tea cake?" she asked.

Richard nodded. "Yes, only horses prefer carrots. Now, when you give him the treat, you keep your palm flat and your fingers together. That way he will not make a mistake and bite you."

"He has big teeth," she said bravely, "but I still like him."

Toby appeared from out of the stable's recesses. He was carrying a carrot which he presented to Sarah.

"Like this, Father?"

"Like that."

She took her bottom lip between her teeth. Plainly she was frightened, but she did not mean to give in to her fear.

She put out her hand, and the stallion took the carrot. Sarah looked at her fingers. Then she giggled again. "His nose is soft. It tickles."

Richard's stern expression was softening. I knew he could love this child. I thought perhaps he already did. At least I could pray so.

Then, all unaware, Sarah tossed her golden curls. I saw his lips tighten into a thin line. Was he thinking of Caroline and her lie? Or was he using that as an excuse to cover up his real feelings? Perhaps he didn't want to see Sarah because she reminded him of the wife he had so passionately loved—and lost.

Sarah seemed to sense some change in the man who held her. She cast me an anxious look, but I could not help her.

"It's time to get down now," Richard said. "Tell the horse good-bye."

Sarah sighed. "Good-bye, horse." She turned to Richard. "Father, do you think someday I might have a pony?"

Richard hesitated only a moment. "When you are big enough," he said. "Perhaps."

She looked about to press; but I shook my head, and she did not go on.

He started to set her down, but she threw both arms around his neck and kissed him. "I am going to be a very good girl," she announced.

Richard looked startled. He set her on her feet. "Yes, I'm sure you will be." He looked at me. "You'll excuse me, Vanessa, but I have some work to attend to." Then he strode off, leaving us both to sigh loudly.

"Do you think he likes me any better now?" Sarah asked, peering up at me. "I was very good."

"Yes, Sarah, you were."

How sad for the child. I remembered my own childhood. Papa had been strict and sometimes angry, for I had been anything but a model child; but no matter how he yelled, I knew my papa loved me.

My heart ached for Sarah, but I took her hand in mine and smiled at her. "Come, dear. Let's go look at the other horses. And tomorrow we are going to see about some new dresses."

Chapter Twelve

The next few days were busy ones. Every morning Richard took me riding, at first on the black mare, but after a day or so, on the stallion. I came to know the moor—each fallen cairn, each peaked hill, the miles of gorse and scrub, and furze and sedge, the bogs whose quaking surfaces were to be avoided and the clear rippling streams where horse and rider could pause for refreshment. To some the moor might be a barren place, but to me it was heaven on earth.

I grew ever closer to my new husband. I lived for those golden hours we spent alone together—on the moor and in our marriage bed.

And every afternoon I spent some time with Sarah, getting to know my new daughter and letting her get to know me.

Early one afternoon toward the end of the week Richard came into the library bearing a package. He gave me a strange smile as he thrust it toward me. "Here is the doll baby you promised Sarah."

I hesitated and offered him a smile. "Will you not give

it to her yourself?" I asked softly. "It would please her no end to have it from your hand."

He shook his head. "Vanessa, my dear, I have thought and thought about what you said. But it is no use."

"But Richard—"

"No. Don't you see? There is no point in encouraging the child when I have no feeling for her. That is cruel."

I did not believe that he had no feeling for her, but I knew it would serve no purpose to say so. It is unfortunate, but sometimes a man must be led by devious ways before he is willing to face the truth.

"May I at least say that you brought the doll for her?" I asked.

He hesitated.

"That is actually what happened." I hurried on before he could give me an outright refusal.

"All right," he said finally. "But do not encourage her."

Richard might have known that the child needed no encouragement from me. Every look from him, every word of his, was precious to her. There was no way I could keep Sarah from being encouraged by any attention from her father, no matter how small. But I did not tell my husband that either, for it was my dearest wish to bring him and his daughter together again, to make us one happy family. And I would do anything I could to make that happen.

"I shall take it to her now," I said. "She will be very pleased."

He nodded. "But do not be too long, my dear. Remember, this is the afternoon the dressmaker is coming."

* * *

The way to the nursery seemed shorter and brighter than usual. Because of my good spirits, I supposed. And because things between Richard and me were now so good.

Sarah was playing before the fire. When she saw me, she cried, "Nessie!" She sprang to her feet and ran to greet me.

Then she spied the package I carried. "What is that?"

"This?" I laughed. "This is for you."

"A present?"

"Yes, my dear."

"A present from Uncle Roland," she cried.

I was startled. Was Roland in the habit of bringing her presents? "No. This is from your father."

Sarah's expression changed to one of awe. "From my father. This is from my father?"

Clutching the package tightly, she hurried to the hearth rug, but she did not rip into the package as an ordinary child would. Instead, she sat staring at it, repeating over and over, "This is from my father."

"Why don't you open it, dear?"

Slowly she removed the string and unwound the wrapping paper. "It's my doll baby," she cried. "My father remembered. He got me my doll baby."

I nodded. I was finding it difficult to speak because of the great lump in my throat. I sank down on the rug beside her, and together we examined the doll.

It was a very good doll, well made, with hair the color of Sarah's, and a sweet smile on its face. It was wearing a nice little dress, too, and had been wrapped in a piece of flannel.

Finally I had mastered myself well enough to speak again. "Do you like her?"

Sarah's eyes gleamed in the firelight. "Oh, yes." She

cradled the doll against her breast. "You will teach me how to be a good mama? Like you promised?"

"Yes, Sarah. What shall you name your baby?"

Sarah hesitated. "I don't know. What do you think?"

"She's your baby," I said. "And you must name her."

The child hesitated. "My mother did not name me."

I stared. Sometimes she said the strangest things. "Of course she did. With your father's help."

Sarah shook her head. "No, Nessie. She turned her back on me." She repeated the words like a litany. "I heard Grandmother say so. My mother didn't want me."

Looking up, I met Creighton's eyes. The nurse was nodding. I swallowed an oath that would have shocked even Papa. The things Caroline had done to her child were beyond my comprehension. Then and there I decided something must be done about it. And then and there, I made a beginning.

"Your mother was sick," I announced.

Sarah frowned. "No, she was strong. She went riding every day. And then she died."

I put my arm around her. "Your mama was sick in another way."

Sarah's eyes widened, and she looked up at me. "She was?"

"Yes. She had a sickness that kept her from loving anyone. Even her own family."

The child considered this. "You mean she didn't love my father either?" Evidently Caroline's lack of love was no news to her.

"No, dear. I'm afraid she didn't."

Sarah rocked the doll and looked at me. "But you love him. And I love him."

I hugged her to me. "Yes, Sarah, we do."

146

She kissed me on the cheek, and then she kissed the doll baby in the same place. Her eyes were quite serious as she asked, "My father loves you, doesn't he, Nessie?"

"I think so." I began to wonder where all this was leading.

"Then *he* doesn't have the sickness." She turned hopeful eyes to me. "And maybe he will love me? Someday?"

"We will pray so," I told her, fighting the urge to take her in my arms and weep. Tears would gain us nothing. It was action we needed. Action, and time. "Now, let us wrap up your baby. You must rock her to sleep. The dressmaker is coming to measure for our new gowns, and I'll be sending for you."

Sarah nodded and began to rock there on the rug, crooning a wordless little song to the doll baby in her arms.

Creighton followed me to the door. "'Tis the song *he* used to sing her," she whispered, tears in her eyes. "I haven't heard it these many years."

The dressmaker arrived in the middle of the afternoon. I sent a servant to inform the dowager and another to tell Rosamund and Penrose. The dowager sent back a terse refusal. Her gowns, she said, were more than adequate, and her presence would not be helpful to Rosamund. In truth, I was just as glad to be without her icy gaze on me.

But Penrose soon came in, bringing his mother with him. "Sit here," he said. "You're going to be so pretty."

"Jeffrey must like them," she told her son. "I cannot get anything he would not like. You know how particular he is."

147

Penrose patted her hand. I had never seen him wear such a tender expression. "Yes, Mother. I know Father likes to see you dressed well."

Rosamund nodded. "Yes, Penrose. Thank you. You're a good boy."

"Now," Penrose said. "Remember, you must not talk to Father while the dressmaker is here."

Rosamund's bottom lip protruded like a surly child's. "I don't see—"

"You know how Father is. He doesn't like too many people about." He patted her hand again, and she seemed appeased and smiled at him. There was no denying it—Penrose was very good with his mother. My estimation of him was beginning to change.

Looking at mother and son, I wondered what kind of story the dressmaker would take with her when she left us. Penrose and Rosamund were both wearing unrelieved black, and the circles under Rosamund's great eyes were big and dark. It was obvious the full moon had been hard on her.

But I had Mrs. Brewster sent in anyway. No doubt stories about this household were already rife in the parish. The dressmaker was a small plump woman, with the ever ready smile of those who make their living from the public. She was followed by three stout young fellows carrying bolts of cloth. The young men sent covert glances at Penrose and his mother and shuffled their feet nervously.

I indicated a sofa where they could put down their bundles. "You may go to the kitchen," I said. "Cook will fix you something."

Bobbing their heads in thanks, they hurried out.

All went well at first. Rosamund stood docilely while

148

her measurements were taken. Then she sat again to examine the materials.

On my instructions there were no blacks, no browns, no grays. There were only cheerful colors, in lighter shades.

Rosamund smiled often. She chose a pale green, a medium blue, a yellow that would not go well with her sallow complexion, but which I prudently said nothing about, and then, just as I thought everything was going to finish satisfactorily, she found an orange silk. The yellow would be bad enough, but Rosamund sat, rubbing the silk between her thumb and forefinger. "I like this," she said. "I want a ball gown made of this."

"Yes, it's lovely," agreed Penrose. "Still, don't you think the rose is nicer?"

Try as he might—and he did try—Penrose could not dissuade her. She wanted a ball gown of orange silk, and because we could not afford to agitate her, we were forced to let her order it.

Penrose led her away then, and I was left alone with Mrs. Brewster. "A sad case," she said, shaking her head.

I had already made up my mind that I would tolerate no more people like the vicar's sister. Therefore I put on my sternest look. "I beg your pardon?"

Mrs. Brewster had the good sense to look embarrassed. "Nothing, Your Grace. Will you be wanting some gowns for yourself?"

"Yes," I said. "And for Sarah." I rang for Gerson and told him to send for the child. "I should like some warm gowns," I said. "I find the castle very drafty."

"She said you wouldn't last long here."

"She?"

The little dressmaker's mouth pursed as though she

had tasted something sour. "Cressadine Varish. She came to order a gown the other day."

"Indeed." It took very little to suppose what kind of lies Miss Varish had served up—no doubt at every opportunity. "I hesitate to say it, since Miss Varish *is* the vicar's sister—" I lowered my voice to a conspirator's tone—"but I do think she has a rather active imagination."

The dressmaker's smile became more genuine, and she did not bother to mask her feelings. "That she does, Your Grace. 'Tis the most active thing about her, I fear." And like two school girls we giggled.

By the time Sarah skipped in, I was confident that the dressmaker was on our side.

"Nessie!" Sarah skidded to a halt and turned suddenly shy. "I've come to be measured," she said primly, crossing the room to my side.

"Well," said Mrs. Brewster, indicating the bolts of cloth. "What colors do you like?"

"Colors?" The child's eyes lit up. "Not black?"

"No," I said, wondering how I could have forgotten to tell her this most important thing. "Your black gowns are too small. We shall give them to the poor."

Sarah made a face. "The poor will not like them. They are ugly things. Oh, Nessie. Do look at the pretty colors!"

I crossed to the sofa that held the stacked bolts of material. "Tell me, which do you like best?"

"You mean I get to choose?"

"Yes, Sarah."

To my surprise she frowned.

"What is it, dear?"

"What colors will your gowns be?" she asked.

"I haven't chosen yet."

150

Her forehead puckered. "I want—Nessie, I want mine to be the same colors as yours. That way everyone will know."

I waited for the rest of the sentence, but nothing more was forthcoming. I sensed the dressmaker's eyes upon me, but I had to ask. "What will they know, Sarah?"

Sarah's smile was angelic. "That I am *your* little girl."

The familiar lump rose in my throat. "Thank you, Sarah. But that is not—"

"Your Grace—" the dressmaker looked apologetic for interrupting me, but she went on—"I can make the child's gowns from the same bolts as yours. Like as not it'll save on material, and it'll be no bother for me. None at all."

I hesitated. How would the others feel if Sarah began wearing gowns of the same material as mine? Would Penrose be provoked into saying more hateful things about Caroline? I already knew that the dowager would say something cutting, and what of Roland? I had not seen much of him in the last few days, and in my happiness with Richard I had not thought about him either; but I did value his good opinion of me. Would he think I was meddling where I meant only to help?

Sarah's little face was still turned up to me. Her eyes begged, and her bottom lip quivered. "Oh, please, Nessie."

The child needed this evidence of my affection, and so I nodded. "Very well. And save the scraps for us, please, Mrs. Brewster. Sarah has a new doll baby, and we shall use them to make her some clothes."

Mrs. Brewster smiled at Sarah. "Of course, Your Grace. 'Tis a lucky child the young lady is, to be having such a mama."

Sarah's smile lit the room. She turned and threw herself into my arms. "It shows already," she cried, and I could only hug her to me and swallow hastily.

Later, with Sarah in tow, I went in search of Richard, but it was Roland we found. "Uncle Roland," Sarah cried, running to him. "Wait till you see!"

"See what?" he asked, scooping her up and swinging her around.

"My new dresses," she cried. "So many colors. And all like Nessie's."

Roland's eyes went to mine, and there was a question in them.

"Sarah could not decide—" I began.

"Nessie!" The child hugged her uncle. "Nessie is teasing me. I want my gowns to be like hers. Because—" she paused and sent me a smile—"that way everyone will know."

Roland was no quicker than I had been at divining her meaning. Something happened in his eyes—a flash of something that I could not read. I thought perhaps he was upset over someone else getting Sarah's affection, but then I realized that I was being ridiculous. A man as kind and friendly as Roland had been to me would be glad to see the child have someone to love her.

"That's wonderful," he said. "You will be the prettiest little girl for miles around."

Sarah laughed. It did my heart good to hear her so merry.

"And," she said, giving him a strange look, "my father brought me a present."

Another peculiar expression crossed his face, and his

eyes came again to me. "It's true," I said. "Richard brought Sarah a doll."

"Yes," Sarah said. "She's very pretty."

Roland smiled. "Like you and your mama."

Sarah frowned. "My mama—"

"The doll is going to have some dresses, too," I interrupted. "We're going to make them."

I was suddenly embarrassed by what I had told Sarah. I had meant only to ease her pain; but as usual, I had not thought through to the results of my actions, and I had not thought to explain to her that her mother's sickness was not a fit subject for discussion with others.

Fortunately Roland did not have long to tarry. He set Sarah on her feet. "That will be nice," he said. "You be a good girl for Vanessa."

Sarah smiled. "I am a very good girl. Nessie says so."

Roland seemed startled at this, too. Then he managed another smile and hurried off.

Sarah came and tugged at my hand. "Let's go back to the nursery," she said. "I want you to see the bed I made for my baby."

I did not have an opportunity to see Richard alone until we stood in my bedchamber that night. I really did not like to bring up the subject; I knew it was not one he cared to discuss, but something within me insisted that Sarah was Richard's child, demanded that she be given the love that was her birthright.

So I said, "Sarah was very pleased with the doll."

He was removing his jacket, and he turned away to put it on a chair, saying nothing.

"You should have seen her. She was especially pleased

153

that it came from you."

He started to say something then, changed his mind, and clamped his mouth shut. I should have taken warning, but I was always foolhardy about what I thought was right. And I was so sure of this.

"Sarah has some strange ideas," I continued, "about her birth. It seems she heard the dowager say that Caroline did not want her, that her own mother had turned her back on her."

A fierce look crossed his face, but his tone was mild as he replied, "I'm afraid it's true. Caroline did not wish to become a mother. It interfered with her good looks and her social life."

I had no doubts about that. Caroline had never cared for anyone but herself. "But what a thing for the child to hear."

He frowned. "My mother doesn't mince words. She and Caroline were always on the outs. As you well know, Mother has no regard for me, and she cares little for the child. Except, perhaps, to use her against me."

I stepped out of my gown. The things he was saying about the dowager, though unpleasant, were probably true, but that did not change matters. Whether he had sired her or not, this child was Richard's responsibility. "Oh, Richard, the poor little thing needs love and affection."

Richard faced me then and stopped undoing his shirt. "Nessie, you must understand. I wish the child well. Truly I do. Give her all the love you can. God knows she needs it. But do not expect me to act the father to another man's bastard!"

The harsh word echoed in the room. His expression was so stern that I hesitated, not knowing whether it would be best to fight or retreat; but I have always been a fighter, and the words forced themselves out of me. "The child is a human being," I cried. "A tiny little girl. How can you be so heartless?"

I could see he was struggling to control his temper. His face grew even sterner, and his knuckles turned white. "I am not heartless," he returned, biting off each word. "I am behaving as any man would."

Perhaps he had some kind of twisted right on his side—I had never understood the workings of the male mind on these matters—but I still thought him heartless. Perhaps that was what goaded me to an action I would always regret.

"Sarah rocked her baby," I said. "She sang it a lullabye." I hummed a few bars of the song.

Richard stood as though he had been dealt a death blow. He gave me such a stricken look that my mouth went dry and I could not make another sound.

Then, as I watched, he gathered up his clothes and went off through the connecting door without so much as a word. He closed the door quietly behind him, and I was left, standing there with my chemise half undone, to the realization that in my zeal I had driven my husband from my side. For the first time since we had really become husband and wife, I would have to sleep alone.

Chapter Thirteen

I finished my undressing, put on my gown, and climbed into bed. It took me a long while to settle down, distraught as I was over Richard leaving me in such a startling fashion. More than once I glanced at the connecting door with longing. Papa had always said I had too much pride, and surely it was holding me back that night.

I told myself that I did not see how I could be held responsible for Richard's precipitous withdrawal. After all, I was only trying to make things right between us.

Or perhaps it was the memory of his pain-filled eyes that held me back. At any rate, it was obvious the man wanted to be alone, and I was too kind—or too cowardly—to intrude upon his privacy.

So I twisted and turned in the bed we had so lately shared—and as I did, I realized that I had not told him about the sickness story I made up to help Sarah or about her wanting gowns the color of mine. Now I did not see how I *could* tell him. After this, the first mention of Sarah was quite likely to send him off into another stony silence.

In the short week that had just passed, much had happened. Already I had grown used to the comfort of Richard's body beside me at night. Without him there, the bed seemed huge and empty, but finally I fell into a fitful sleep.

My slumber was disturbed by a series of strange dreams. In one the whole household had assembled in the great hall. It was even darker and gloomier than usual, but the flickering candles showed a horrible scene. Everyone had surrounded Sarah, and they were calling her distressing names. She was crying and calling for her father; but he stood with his back to her, unhearing and uncaring, and when, in the dream, I approached him, he turned his back on me, too.

That scene faded and I saw Sarah, seated on the hearth rug, rocking her baby and humming the lullabye. "Don't worry. *I* will love you," she whispered to the doll. "Mamas *should* love their babies."

Suddenly the dream doll began to wail. Its cries grew louder and louder. Slowly I struggled back to consciousness. I opened my eyes and saw that the candle I'd left burning was just a stub, soon to go out.

I sighed. The dream had been so real, so vivid, that for a moment I thought I'd heard—

I stiffened and caught my breath. That was not a dream. That cry was real, as real as my own labored breathing. And it was the cry of a babe.

The haunting babe! My mouth went dry and my body cold and hot at the same time. Three nights in a row, the legend went, and then Death was supposed to come for the hearer.

I forced myself to breathe slowly. There was no need

157

for panic. I was safe enough. I had not heard the babe for over a week, not since Richard had taken to sleeping in my bed.

At that time it did not occur to me to wonder about this strange coincidence. I only wished Richard were with me. The babe's cries were frightening to hear, and yet it seemed in such misery that I almost longed to go comfort it.

But even a person who often acts before she thinks does not leap from her bed to go seek out a ghost. So I lay there, wondering if Richard could hear the babe crying and wishing I had told him about hearing it before.

I had some thoughts, too, of bursting through the connecting door and throwing myself into his arms, but if he could not hear the babe, he would not believe me. And, since it had not cried on any of those nights that Richard had been with me, perhaps it did not mean to cry for him. Perhaps its cries were meant only for me.

If I ran to him, the cries might follow me, and I did not want him to hear them. Not ever.

Not that I believed the legend, of course—logic said it could not be true—but a week in the castle had made some dents in my common sense approach to things. I knew there was no haunting babe, yet still. . . .

I lay in my bed, waiting with bated breath for the next cry. I tried to persuade my rigid body to relax. It had been a long and tiring day, and I was weary. But, logic or not, I could not seem to dissipate the tension. My body was wound tight as a spring.

The minutes ticked away, and the room remained silent, the only sound my own breathing. Finally my body began to relax. I would just go to sleep, I told myself. In the morning this would be nothing but a bad dream.

Perhaps, I thought, clutching at straws, perhaps the babe's cry *had* been a dream, and waking in the middle of the dream, I had imagined it real.

Some part of me recognized this for what it was—a patent evasion of the truth—but another part took comfort in it. That was it, I told myself. It was all a bad dream. In the morning I would laugh at it. I turned on my side and willed myself to relax.

But there was to be little rest for me that night. Soon something else alerted me. I could not say exactly what it was. I sensed a change in the room—something I could not see, but definitely a change. The candle sputtered and would soon go out.

I leaned over to replace it and then I realized. The air had changed. There was a sweetness. . . . My heart rose up in my throat. Caroline's scent was filling my room, and I knew I was not imagining it.

Should I run and get Richard? But to what avail? He could not force the scent to leave, and it would bring back to him memories of Caroline, memories I did not want him to dwell on.

The sweet scent grew stronger. I was sure I had never heard of a ghost that wore scent, but Caroline had always had her way in life. Perhaps even in death. . . .

I was being ridiculous and I knew it. Caroline was not haunting me. This scent thing was a trick to frighten me off, but it would not be successful because I did not intend to be frightened. I might be a little queasy in the stomach, only it was not from fear but from inhaling the overpowering sweetness of the scent.

The babe's cries came again, and I could swear they were closer. Imagination, I told myself sternly. Sheer imagination.

But soon I could not deny the fact. The cries *were* coming closer and closer. I could hear no other sounds, but that meant little. My ears were attuned to only one thing, the cries of the haunting babe.

How, I wondered, did one release a ghost from its painful existence? There must be some way to do that.

Even Creighton had known very little about the ghost, only the bare bones of the story. I shivered at the aptness of the words.

The cries continued to grow nearer, thin plaintive cries, the cries of a child who desperately needed its mother.

Then the cries stopped. I shivered and waited. From outside my door came a voice. It was not Caroline's, and yet— "Van-ness-sa," it whispered. "Go home. Richard is mine."

He is not yours, I cried silently. *He is mine.* My fear began to turn to anger. Good righteous anger. Whoever was behind this hoax was not thinking straight. Why should Caroline have anything to do with the haunting babe? Caroline hated babies, and everyone knew it.

Perhaps, I thought, I could catch the person who was doing this. I was tired of having my sleep disturbed and my mind thrown into chaos. Since with me the thought is often immediate mother of the deed, I no sooner thought about this than I decided to do it.

Carefully I put back the covers and crept out of the bed. The stones were cold, as usual, but I had no time to look for slippers. I was determined to catch the trickster.

MORE PASSION AND ADVENTURE AWAIT... YOUR TRIP TO A BIG ADVENTUROUS WORLD BEGINS WHEN YOU ACCEPT YOUR FIRST 4 NOVELS ABSOLUTELY *FREE* (AN $18.00 VALUE)

Accept your Free gift and start to experience more of the passion and adventure you like in a historical romance novel. Each Zebra novel is filled with proud men, spirited women and tempestuous love that you'll remember long after you turn the last page.

Zebra Historical Romances are the finest novels of their kind. They are written by authors who really know how to weave tales of romance and adventure in the historical settings you love. You'll feel like you've actually gone back in time with the thrilling stories that each Zebra novel offers.

GET YOUR FREE GIFT WITH THE START OF YOUR HOME SUBSCRIPTION

Our readers tell us that these books sell out very fast in book stores and often they miss the newest titles. So Zebra has made arrangements for you to receive the four newest novels published each month.

You'll be guaranteed that you'll never miss a title, and home delivery is so convenient. And to show you just how easy it is to get Zebra Historical Romances, we'll send you your first 4 books absolutely FREE! Our gift to you just for trying our home subscription service.

BIG SAVINGS AND FREE HOME DELIVERY

Each month, you'll receive the four newest titles as soon as they are published. You'll probably receive them even before the bookstores do. What's more, you may preview these exciting novels free for 10 days. If you like them as much as we think you will, just pay the low preferred subscriber's price of just $3.75 each. *You'll save $3.00 each month off the publisher's price.* AND, your savings are even greater because there are never any shipping, handling or other hidden charges—FREE Home Delivery. Of course you can return any shipment within 10 days for full credit, no questions asked. There is no minimum number of books you must buy.

4 FREE BOOKS

FREE BOOKS

TO GET YOUR 4 FREE BOOKS WORTH $18.00 —MAIL IN THE FREE BOOK CERTIFICATE
T O D A Y

Fill in the Free Book Certificate below, and we'll send your FREE BOOKS to you as soon as we receive it.

If the certificate is missing below, write to: Zebra Home Subscription Service, Inc., P.O. Box 5214, 120 Brighton Road, Clifton, New Jersey 07015-5214.

FREE BOOK CERTIFICATE

4 FREE BOOKS

ZEBRA HOME SUBSCRIPTION SERVICE, INC.

YES! Please start my subscription to Zebra Historical Romances and send me my first 4 books absolutely FREE. I understand that each month I may preview four new Zebra Historical Romances free for 10 days. If I'm not satisfied with them, I may return the four books within 10 days and owe nothing. Otherwise, I will pay the low preferred subscriber's price of just $3.75 each; a total of $15.00, *a savings off the publisher's price of $3.00.* I may return any shipment and I may cancel this subscription at any time. There is no obligation to buy any shipment and there are no shipping, handling or other hidden charges. Regardless of what I decide, the four free books are mine to keep.

NAME

ADDRESS _____ APT _____

CITY _____ STATE _____ ZIP _____

TELEPHONE ( )

SIGNATURE _____
(if under 18, parent or guardian must sign)

Terms, offer and prices subject to change without notice. Subscription subject to acceptance by Zebra Books. Zebra Books reserves the right to reject any order or cancel any subscription.   ZBMS02

I crossed the floor and put my hand on the doorknob. There I hesitated. Should I go back for a candle? What if Caroline's ghost was really out there in the hall? Did I want to confront the spectre of my dead sister?

Or conversely, what if the haunting babe was out there, a floating luminescent bundle, wailing in the darkness?

The doorknob was cold, too, and my fingertips turned to ice. I was frightened—there was no doubt of that—but I was also angry. And when I am angry good sense can go begging.

So I turned the doorknob. As smoothly and carefully as I could, I turned that knob and eased open the door.

The hall outside my room was empty and very dark. No Caroline. No haunting babe. Not even, as far as I could see, a dead bird. On an impulse I stepped out into the hall. That was when I saw it.

Halfway down the hall a ghostly figure flitted. It was too far away for me to see it clearly. The hall was very dark, lit only by a few guttering candles in the candelabra halfway along it. But the apparition—or whatever it was—appeared to have the shape of a person and was of a greenish-white hue.

"Van-ness-sa," it whispered and motioned to me with a ghostly appendage.

Forgetting that I wore only my flannel nightdress, I stepped out after it. I was too angry to be properly afraid. I meant to put an end to this charade so we could live our lives in peace.

The figure did not float in the air, rather its whiteness reached to the floor. But it moved very swiftly. Though I tried my best, I could not catch up to it.

Then it paused. My straining eyes could make out no doorway where it stood, but the hall was very dark. The figure beckoned to me once more, and then it vanished, as suddenly as if it had been a candle flame snuffed out. Or as if it had stepped right through the wall.

I stood there, shivering from cold and fear, and tried to decide what I should do. My anger was rapidly deserting me, and I was growing colder and more uncomfortable by the minute.

I like to think it was the cold that decided me, not the fear, or perhaps for once good sense came to my aid; but at any rate, I refused the spectre's invitation. Instead of following it, I turned and retraced my steps to my bedchamber. I was not dressed for chasing ghosts.

I scurried inside without a backward look and pulled the heavy door shut behind me. Doors, of course, are no protection against ghosts, but I steadfastly refused to believe that Caroline was haunting me. There was some completely logical explanation for everything that had happened to me.

Jumping into bed, I began to chafe my frozen feet. If Caroline *were* a ghost, I asked myself, pursuing the logical idea, how would she behave? Would she give me teasing glimpses and whispered warnings?

Not likely. In life Caroline had been brutally frank. She had always felt her beauty granted her that privilege, and she exercised it to the fullest. That day she found me among her scent bottles, she had not suggested or urged; she had commanded. And with great and immediate force.

A ghostly Caroline, I reasoned, would be no different from a living one. Had she had the power to haunt me, she would appear before me in a blazing white fury and give her commands, fully expecting them to be obeyed.

My feet were warmer now and my mind clearer. I lay back under the covers and continued to think. Someone wanted me to be frightened—that much was plain—but I still could not understand why anyone should want to drive me off.

My husband loved me, his brother was my friend, Penrose and his mother had seemed to be growing reconciled to our marriage, and even the dowager had become almost bearable.

Why now? I asked myself. Why, when things had begun to look better, did this whatever-it-was have to come after me? And why did it do so only when I was alone? Did he or she know that? Or was it merely chance? There were too many questions and no answers.

I did sleep, finally; but my slumber was not restful, and by morning I felt even more exhausted. Richard was already gone when I went down to breakfast. Perhaps that was just as well. I was in a waspish mood and inclined to snap at the least annoyance.

Consequently, I gave myself a good talking to, and that, along with my breakfast and a strong cup of tea, settled me down. Soon I began to feel more like myself. After all, the disturbances of last night had done no real harm. I could easily survive an occasional restless night.

So, when Penrose came in, leading his mother, I resolved not to mention anything about ghosts and the like. "Good morning," I said to Rosamund.

She looked startled, but with a glance at Penrose she replied, "Good morning."

Penrose smiled sweetly at his mother, and then he

looked at me. "Good morning, Vanessa. Did you sleep well?"

In spite of my resolution, I almost lost my feeble hold on my temper. How dare he taunt me so? But his smile seemed genuine, so I swallowed hard and said, "Yes, thank you."

Penrose nodded. "I was up long reading the latest books from London. Have you read the new poet?"

The boy's somber clothes suddenly made more sense to me. "You mean Lord Byron?"

Penrose smiled, pleased that I knew the poet he meant. "Yes, isn't he magnificent? So free."

Privately I thought Byron too inclined to morbidity, and Papa had contended that the man simply never grew up; but I did not say these things. Certainly Penrose had reason enough to be morbid. How could a boy in such a situation be anything else? So I nodded. "I have read some of his works."

Penrose's face took on a glow. "'Childe Harold' is just wonderful."

For a moment he looked the boy he really was—young and full of life, longing for adventure. I wanted to reach out to him as I had to Sarah, but I knew better. Young men could not be treated like little girls. Not with impunity.

"What is your favorite?" I asked, wanting to prolong this good moment with him.

"'Cain,'" he said. "Cain has everyone against him. Including God." He sighed. "Yes, Byron is very good, but he has not written enough about death." He smiled at me, his eyes strangely bright. "Death, you know, is the ultimate adventure. If you go to meet it properly."

"Properly?" I echoed, trying to get my bearings in this

strange discussion.

"Yes. With spirit and fire."

I felt a wave of relief. "You mean in battle?"

"Perhaps." His glance went to his mother, who was smiling with animation into the emptiness on her other side. "Some of us are weak," he continued, "and some of us are strong."

I did not like the tone of this. A boy who takes a brother-killer like Cain for a hero might—

Oh, my God! My heart seemed to lodge in my throat. Richard! Richard had almost been another Cain. Thank goodness that had not happened.

"What do you suppose makes some of us weak?" I inquired, carefully refraining from looking anywhere near his mother.

Penrose shook his head. "I don't know. But surely death is preferable to some kinds of life. Perhaps a person who ends another's miserable existence is doing that person a favor."

This kind of hypocritical cant didn't suit me at all. It sounded far too much like an excuse for murder. "God gives life," I said, perhaps more strongly than I should have, "and He takes it away."

Penrose's dark eyes bored into mine. "Why does He give? And why does He take?"

The words of my catechism came into my mind: The proper purpose of man's existence is to glorify God. But I knew instantly that this was not the answer to give a disturbed boy. How could a boy who had never known an earthly father picture a heavenly one? Let alone one who subsisted on glorification.

I sighed. "I'm afraid there are some things beyond our understanding."

Again his glance went to his mother, and his expression grew bitter. "Indeed there are," he said. "Indeed there are."

He hesitated. He looked at his mother again, then he looked at me. "I am writing a poem," he said. He lowered his voice. "It's about the haunting babe."

I nodded. Here was my chance to get more information. "Do you know—is there any way to release the babe?"

His eyes gleamed with unholy glee, and I suppressed an urge to shudder. "You believe in it!" he exclaimed. "I knew it."

"I am interested in the story," I said, trying belatedly for dignity. "That is all it is, you know—a story."

"That's what your sister thought. She would not listen."

I did not want to hear this, but I couldn't stop now. "Listen? Listen to what?"

"The babe's cries are a warning—not to persist in a course of action." He leered. "It was common knowledge what course of action Caroline was following. She did not heed the warning"—he shrugged—"and Death came for her."

What was he talking about? "But Creighton said nothing of this. She only said—"

He laughed, that awful sinister laugh. "She said if you hear the babe three nights running, Death is coming for you."

I nodded.

"That's true enough. My mother told me the rest of it. She said the babe tried to warn her father. It tried to warn him before he killed my father. But Grandfather didn't listen. And he died."

"But—your grandfather didn't die immediately, did he?"

Penrose shook his head. "No, I remember him—a little—but he did die."

I was growing rather exasperated with this story. After all, we are all mortal and must die eventually.

Still, I felt I must pursue it. "And you say the babe warned Caroline?"

Penrose shrugged. "That's what she told my mother. They were never close, of course." His eyes shifted to my face. "I'm afraid your sister was a selfish woman. At any rate, she cared only for the company of men."

"A whited sepulchre," Rosamund announced.

Penrose and I exchanged glances.

"She was," Rosamund went on. "She was beautiful on the outside, but inside she was full of filth. She stank."

"Mother—"

Rosamund frowned. "It's true. All of it's true. That Jezebel, that—"

"Mama, please—" For the first time I saw Penrose embarrassed.

Rosamund stopped and stared at me. "Who are you?" she asked suddenly.

"I am Vanessa," I explained. "I am Richard's new wife."

She frowned. "New wife. New wife. Yes, I remember. You ordered me gowns." She frowned and turned to Penrose. "Where are they? Where are my new gowns?"

"They are coming," I hastened to reassure her. "Our order was rather large. It included some gowns for Sarah and me."

Rosamund's face softened. "The girl baby. Such a

beautiful baby. I wished she were mine."

I glimpsed his pain before Penrose could hide it. No wonder he had said hateful things to Sarah. He wanted all his mother's attention, and considering all he'd been through, that was quite understandable.

"Yes," Rosamund continued. "Such a lovely girl baby. I had no girls, you see. And that awful woman never went to see her child. She never held it."

Rosamund's great dark eyes grew wide with horror. "She told me more than once. She said she hated that baby. Poor little baby."

Rosamund was right about that, I thought. But she wasn't finished. Her eyes gleamed with zealous fire. "I warned her. I told her babies should be loved—" she patted her son's arm—"but she wouldn't listen." Rosamund sighed. "I was glad when they told me the horse killed her."

"Mama—"

"No, Penrose." She eyed him sternly. "I *was* glad. Because she was an evil woman. There was no good in her. No good at all." She smiled at me. "But don't you worry. She's paying. She's burning."

At that moment Rosamund's private circle of hell seemed quite an appropriate place for Caroline's eternal sojourn. I knew the great God was merciful, though. And I knew it was not up to me to decide.

"Come, Mama," Penrose cajoled. "Eat your breakfast."

Her attention thus distracted, Rosamund obediently began to eat. Penrose crumbled a roll between his fingers. "No one knows for sure," he said softly, "but Mama said the story goes that the babe will only be silenced if a woman willingly joins it."

A cold draft seemed to creep under my shawl. "You

168

don't mean—"

"Yes, I do. A woman must deliberately sacrifice her life. And then the babe will be set free."

"But—but that is suicide. It's a mortal sin!"

Penrose shrugged. "No one is going to do such a thing." He grinned at me. "Besides, as you say, it's only a story."

"Of course." And the matter was left there, for the time being.

Chapter Fourteen

Several days passed. Richard and I still rode together in the mornings. No mention was made of the night he had left me alone; he behaved as if nothing untoward had happened and so did I. Every evening he followed me up the stairs to my room.

For my part, I was careful not to bring up the subject of Sarah, but in spite of my care—or perhaps because of it—I could feel some constraint between us. It made me uncomfortable, as if I were out of touch with some vital part of myself.

Still, I enjoyed our rides. The stallion began to respond to me, to send me a whuffled greeting when I entered the stable, to shake his mane and show his eagerness for a run. Soon now I would be able to ride alone, to roam the moor in perfect freedom. I would be glad for that, though I would miss my rides with Richard. I knew the work of the estate kept him too busy for our daily rides to continue indefinitely.

Perhaps there would be others to share the moor with on occasion. I doubted that the dowager rode, but perhaps Rosamund went out with Penrose. If she didn't, perhaps we could persuade her to ride again. And surely Roland—

I pushed the memory of his kiss out of my mind. It lingered only because it had been a mistake. My husband's kisses were far sweeter.

So I set myself to enjoy Richard's company. Truth was, I did not know quite how to conduct myself. I am not by nature a person who thinks before she speaks; so, as not to say the wrong thing, I grew rather silent, not saying much at all.

Richard remarked on this one morning as we skirted a bog.

"I hesitate to tell you," I replied. "I do not want to make you angry with me."

He swung his horse closer to mine. Our knees touched for a moment, and he smiled at me. "Nessie, my dear, tell me. Please."

I took a deep breath. "I do not speak often because I am afraid."

He looked startled. "Of me?"

I shook my head. "Not exactly. Well, it's just—Sarah is so much on my mind that I often wish to speak of her. And—"

He sighed. "And you know I do not want to hear."

I contented myself with a little nod, though many words were racing through my mind.

"You are right," he said. "I do not wish to hear, but neither do I wish you to become silent like this. So say what you please, and I will listen to you."

Still I hesitated. "You will not leave me? As you did the other night?"

"No, Nessie. I won't leave you. The other night—it

171

was not what you said that bothered me. It was the lullabye. I had no idea Sarah would remember it."

My nervousness transmitted itself to the stallion. He pranced about and was hard to control. For a minute I was busy with him and said nothing. But I could not stop them; the words insisted on coming out. "It's the lullabye you sang to her when she was a baby."

"So you know that," he said. "Go on. What else have you been wanting to say to me?"

"The gowns we ordered from Mrs. Brewster will be delivered soon." I hurried on before I should lose my nerve. "Rosamund ordered a ball gown of orange silk. We could not dissuade her. And Sarah's—Sarah's gowns are made of the same colors and materials as mine. She begged me, and I told the dressmaker to do it." I glanced at him and swallowed. "Does that displease you?"

He shook his head. "No. I told you, I bear the child no animosity. I'm glad she's taken to you." He half-smiled. "You've no more to tell me? That is all?"

I wished that were true. "No. There is one thing more."

His smile wavered. "You might as well tell me everything."

"I made up a story for Sarah. To make her feel better about her mother."

His frown was fierce and instantaneous. "What kind of story?"

"I told her that Caroline suffered from a sickness."

His frown changed to bewilderment, but I hurried on. "I told her that this sickness kept Caroline from loving her daughter." I could not stop now. I must tell him all of it. "I told Sarah it kept her mother from loving anyone."

He considered that for a moment. "Including me," he

172

said with bitterness. "And how did Sarah respond to this story?"

I determined to talk to him frankly. He was, after all, my husband. I had that right. "She seemed to accept it. You must understand why I did it. She said her mother had told her she was a bad bad girl. I could not let her go on thinking she was bad, thinking that was why her parents did not love her."

I waited, but he was true to his word. He did not show anger and he did not leave me. But he was silent for such a long time that my nervousness began to increase. Finally he said, "You may be more right than you think. At any rate, I see no harm in your story. And perhaps it will do the child some good."

Relief flooded over me. "Oh, Richard, thank you!"

I leaned toward him and our lips met, but only briefly. The stallion was eager to be away. He pranced and fretted beneath me, tossing his mane and dancing about.

"Time for a run," Richard said. "Follow me."

The sun was high when we returned to Greyden Castle. We left the horses to Toby's expert care and went up the walk, laughing and happy, our arms around each other's waists. But as usual the castle cast a pall over my joyful feelings.

And I was right to feel so, for inside, huddled in a corner of the dark hall, Creighton waited. She held a bundle in her lap, and when she saw me she rose and hobbled forward. "Oh, that wicked child," she cried. "She's as wicked as her—"

"Creighton," I interrupted. "What is it? What's wrong?"

She thrust the bundle at me. "Just look!" she cried. "Just look at what she did to her doll baby."

I unwrapped the blanket. The doll baby was intact, but its beautiful golden hair was a sticky mass of what looked and smelled like apricot jam.

Richard's frown grew more fierce by the moment. "You're right," he told the old nurse. "She's ruined it."

There was no doubt that the doll was a sticky mess, but something told me there was more to it than that. I knew Sarah loved the doll. Why should she try to ruin it? The best way to find out was to ask the child herself. "Where is Sarah?"

Creighton wrung her hands. "I don't know, Your Grace. She's gone."

"Gone!" My heart rose up in my throat. "What do you mean—gone?"

Creighton pressed her hand to her heart. "When I found what she was doing, she ran out. I couldn't catch her. I don't know where she went."

Richard moved instantly to action. He motioned to Gerson. "Get the rest of the staff. Have them search the castle."

Gerson looked uncomfortable. He cleared his throat. "Ah, Your Grace?"

"Yes?"

"I found the front door ajar. A while back."

My mind went instantly to the most dangerous place— the break in the castle wall. "The cliff! Oh, God, no!" Without waiting for Richard, I whirled and rushed out the door. The walkway stones were slippery and overgrown with moss. Several times I almost fell. Brambles and briars clutched at my skirts, but I pushed through them, my heart pounding. "Sarah!" I called.

"Sarah, where are you?"

I turned the corner and skidded to a halt. There was no sign of the child. The railing was intact, no break in it. But Sarah was so small. She could have slipped under it. I stood there, panting, afraid to go any farther, afraid to look over the edge to where the sea crashed on the rocks below.

A hard hand descended on my shoulder and dragged me back. "Vanessa!" Richard cried. "For God's sake, be careful. You might slip and fall."

"I can't look. Is she—is she down there?"

"Stay here," Richard commanded, guiding me toward the castle wall. "I'll look."

I leaned there against the stones, breathing heavily. I heard his quick intake of breath. Did he see Sarah? On shaking legs I hurried to his side.

"Oh, no!" There on the slippery wet rocks lay a bundle of black rags. "Sar-ah!" The wail was torn from my throat, and I surged forward as if I could go to her. I felt Richard's hand on my back. For a minute it seemed to be urging me forward, and then he tangled it in my hair and pulled me back from certain death.

His arms wrapped me close against him. "Vanessa! Stop it! You must stop it."

"Sarah! Oh, Sarah. She's dead. And it's our fault."

He held me in a fierce embrace. "No, Nessie. Listen. That's not the child. That's not Sarah."

Still in his arms, I wept bitterly. "It is. It is. I know it is."

"Look again," he said. "There's no sign of her hair. It's so bright. You know it would show against the black rocks."

He was right! I looked again and saw. The rags were

only that—rags that had been washed ashore, perhaps from some passing ship. As we watched, the water pulled them apart, and one by one, they floated off.

"Oh, God, thank you," I cried. "But Richard, where is she? We must find her." I still leaned against him, my limbs trembling from the fright I'd had.

Richard swung me up into his arms. "We'll go back to the castle," he said. "Maybe they've found her already."

"Yes," I said, clinging to him, clinging to hope. "They will have found her by now. She must be safe."

Sarah had not been found. The whole family had assembled in the great hall. I was aware of them only in a general way. My attention was all on the butler. "We've searched everywhere," Gerson said, "but there's no sign of her anywhere in the castle."

I am not usually given to hysterics; but the events of the past weeks had left my nerves on edge, and the need to cry overcame me. I buried my face in my husband's waistcoat and sobbed like a heartbroken child.

Richard put me down on a divan. "Attend to my wife," he told Creighton. "I have an idea."

I tried to go after him, but my limbs simply would not carry me. And, though I knew it helped nothing, I could not keep myself from weeping.

"There, there, Your Grace. He'll find her." Creighton patted my hand awkwardly, obviously unsure what to do next.

I closed my eyes and struggled with the sobs. Papa would frown and call this female carrying on. He would tell me to stop it instantly, and if he were here, I *would* stop it.

Suddenly I felt a hand on my hair. I opened my eyes to find Rosamund stroking it as she might a child's. "It'll be all right," she soothed. "Richard will find her. Richard is good."

Richard is not good, I thought. *How can he be good when he does not love his daughter?* But I did not say anything, and to my surprise, I found myself comforted by Rosamund's presence.

"You'll see," she said. "He'll find her." She smiled at her son. "Penrose used to run away. Richard always found him."

Penrose looked a trifle annoyed at having his youthful pranks detailed. I managed to stop sobbing long enough to say, "Yes, I know, Rosamund. I know children often run away. But she is so little. And why, why did she do this to her doll?"

Rosamund eyed the doll now resting on a table. "Why?" she asked. Evidently she had no answers either, for she said no more.

Bringing my sobs further under control, I sipped the hot tea Gerson brought me. I was feeling foolish for having acted in such a vaporish fashion, especially in front of the frosty-faced dowager and Roland. I did not care so much about the dowager—she would dislike me no matter how I behaved—but Roland was my friend. I did not want him to think me a silly female.

I should have approached this with logic, as Papa would have. Logic was the way to figure things out.

I turned to Penrose. "When you ran away, where did you go?"

"Sometimes I went to the North Tower."

I started to my feet, but Gerson shook his head. "It's been searched, Your Grace. The child is not there."

"And sometimes I went to the oaks."

I shuddered. Surely those twisted shapes would frighten Sarah. "I don't think she'd go there."

"And sometimes I went—"

The front door opened. I leaped to my feet. "Richard! Oh, thank God! You've found her!"

In his arms he held a pale, big-eyed Sarah, her face smudged with dirt, pieces of straw still clinging to her dark dress.

I rushed to them, to touch her, to make sure she was really there. "Where did you find her?"

"In the stable," he said grimly. "Hiding in the corner of the stallion's stall."

"The stallion—" I remembered the others and broke off. "Bring her over here. Please."

I settled on the divan again, and he put the child in my lap. She smelled of the stable, but I did not mind. As ever it was a good smell, and now doubly comforting.

"She will not talk," he said, frowning down at us. "She hasn't said a word."

"Of course not," Rosamund replied calmly. "You have frightened her by your frowning." She took her son's arm. "Come, Penrose. Vanessa will do better without us."

While I stared in astonishment at such perception on her part, off they went, chatting cozily together.

Roland sent me an encouraging little smile and offered the dowager his arm. "Rosamund is right, Mama. We should go, too."

Richard cast me an exasperated look. "Vanessa, I—" Then, apparently thinking better of saying anything, he turned on his heel and limped out.

"Creighton," I said, "please go order some hot water

178

for a bath and wait for us in the nursery."

The nurse did not look happy, but she obeyed. "Yes, Your Grace. I'll go now."

Sarah and I were left alone. "Now," I said, smoothing back her hair, "you must tell Nessie why you ran away."

She sniffled and rubbed her eyes. "Creighton was angry. She screamed at me."

At least the child would talk to me. "What did you do to make her angry?" I asked softly.

She sniffled again. "Nothing, Nessie."

I took the doll baby from its place on the table. "Why did you spoil your pretty doll baby?"

The tears ran down her cheeks, leaving tracks through the grime. "I didn't mean to spoil her," she sobbed. "I thought it would work."

"Thought what would work?" I asked.

"Creighton told me once about people that color things with berries. Indians, I think."

"Yes. I believe Indians do that."

"I didn't have any berries, so I used apricot jam; but it wouldn't work. It got all sticky."

I thought I was beginning to understand. "You wanted to color your baby's hair?"

Sarah nodded. "Yes. I named her Nessie. She should have hair like yours."

"Oh, Sarah." For a moment I could not speak another word. The child had given me the greatest compliment of my life. I could not scold her for that.

I remembered then where Richard had found her. "Why did you go to the stable when you ran away?"

"I like the horses. I wanted to find you, but you were riding."

I nodded. "But why did you go into Mercury's stall?"

"He's yours," she said. "He belongs to you. Like me."

The poor child, so desperate for affection. I hugged her to me again.

She turned her little face up to me. "How will we fix my doll baby?" she asked, as though she'd asked me for help a hundred times in her short life, as though I were her mother.

I smiled and patted her hand. "I think we can wash the jam out, but I don't know if we can change the color of her hair. It is really very pretty. You know, when I was a little girl, I wished for golden curls like yours." Like Caroline's. But I did not say that.

Sarah frowned. "My hair is like my mama's. I don't want it to be like hers. I don't want to be her little girl. I want to be yours."

"You are mine," I said. "And you always will be."

She peered at me, her mouth puckering. "What about when that baby comes? Grandmother says when you have a baby of your own, you'll forget all about me."

The dowager again. Could she never control her tongue? "Your grandmother is wrong," I said firmly. "I would never forget my Sarah. You are my oldest daughter. You will be a big help to me."

She hugged me then, with the familiar stable smell still upon her. "Come," I said, picking up the doll baby. "It is time for baths. For both of you."

Later that night, in our room, I explained to Richard. "She thought orange jam would color the doll's hair," I said, wondering how I could tell him the rest without seeming to boast.

Richard frowned. "But why should she want the doll

to have orange—" He stopped and stared at me, and then he smiled. "I'll wager that doll is named Nessie."

He took me in his arms and wrapped one of my curls around his finger. "She wants the doll to have hair like yours." He kissed my forehead. "You have made your second conquest," he said with a chuckle. "First me, then Sarah. Soon you will have Mama eating out of your hand."

This unlikely prospect sent us laughing into each other's arms. It was good we had that laughter to remember. We were not to have much cause for merriment in the future.

Chapter Fifteen

The next morning the rain began—a dismal steady downpour that soon drenched everything. Because of it Richard cancelled our ride. Because of it the arrival of the new gowns was postponed. And because of my disappointment at both, everyone seemed even more peckish than usual, including me.

The dowager commented unfavorably and with icy detail on the way my hair was dressed. Meanwhile, Rosamund would converse with no one but the invisible Jeffrey, and a disconsolate Penrose moped about like a sick dog, breathing heartrending sighs and muttering lines of morbid poetry. All the while, I fretted.

Richard and Roland were the lucky ones, I thought with a tinge of resentment. Rain could not keep them indoors. I even considered going out to ride in the downpour myself; but I'd been fortunate not to take sick after my first drenching on the moor, and even I thought twice about tempting fate again so soon.

So I resigned myself, though not with any great patience, to a day spent indoors. The morning I occupied with various household tasks, which, to my great annoyance, did not go as I wished.

In the early afternoon I amused myself by spending some time with Sarah, but when Creighton put her down for her nap, I found myself again at loose ends. If I went back down to the library, I was bound to run into one of the family, and in my frettish temper I was very likely to say something unkind.

I had determined not to do that, no matter how much I was provoked. Anger would not help anything, and it might well make matters worse. I knew myself—and my temper—and I knew I would be better able to stick to my resolution if I stayed alone.

When I came out of the nursery, I was still undecided. Stepping out into the hall, I remembered leaving there that other day, the day I went to the North Tower. My rides with Richard and my preoccupation with Sarah had kept me from returning to the tower room; but I had certainly meant to do so, and today seemed an opportune time.

I picked up a candle and holder from those kept on the table in the hall. With the rain outside there would be no sunlight to come through the tower slits. The room would be dark and gloomy, even worse than the castle halls, but I did not care about that. In my present dark mood, I knew I was better off by myself.

Pausing in the archway, I looked up. The spiral staircase seemed narrower and darker than it had before. Papa had always said I was stubborn. When I'm determined I press on, regardless of any setback. And so up I went. Still, I set each foot down carefully. A fall here could well prove fatal.

Belatedly I realized that I had told no one of my

destination, but I did not want to turn back to look for a servant. I did not intend to stay in the room that long. I wanted only to have a little time to myself—the time I would have had with Richard had we been able to ride.

The door creaked in protest as I pushed it open. In the dim interior I could just make out the shapes of the desk and chair.

With the light of only one candle and no sunlight to brighten it, the room looked quite somber. Dark shadows lurked in every direction, and the armoire became a great threatening beast; but I was beyond being frightened by shadows. Logic, Papa would say. The good Lord gave you a mind. Use it.

So I took my candle and traversed the room. It was quite empty of anything threatening. Just as logic had told me it would be.

I sat down at the desk. In spite of its gloominess, in spite of the fact that it had been Caroline's room, I liked the North Tower. Perhaps I should make it mine. My own private place.

I smiled. The servants would not bother me there. Nor anyone else. Caroline had used this place to meet her lovers. I would use it to be alone. To think.

First I would refresh my memory of what was in the desk. I opened the drawer and found paper, pen, and ink. When I saw them, my thoughts went immediately to Papa. After my first brief note to say we had arrived in Cornwall safely, I had not written to him again. It was not that I didn't want to, or that I had forgotten about him. How could I forget Papa?

But I had never been good at concealing my feelings from him. I did not want him to feel sorry for me or to think that I had made a mistake in marrying Richard.

Whatever our problems might be, I loved my husband dearly, and I wanted Papa to think well of him.

Certainly things at Greyden Castle were far different from what I had expected them to be. The idyllic life I had envisioned had not included Richard's relatives or visits like that I had endured from the vicar and his waspish sister.

That was it! I would write Papa an account of Cressadine Varish's visit, an account slightly altered. I would describe for him Miss Varish's person and character, and report to him her remarks about the stallion. I knew Papa would agree that such a splendid animal should not be put down.

I would not, however, tell him what the vicar had said about complaints to the magistrate. I did not even want to think of that.

I could tell him about Sarah and her doll baby. He would laugh at the apricot jam and be glad to know the child had formed an affection for me. And I could tell him about Rosamund and Penrose, even about the gimlet-eyed dowager's distasteful habit of criticizing everything I wore or did.

But I intended to say nothing about Caroline's death—or anyone's suspicions regarding the cause of it. That was all they were, anyway, suspicions.

With a smile I readied my quill and opened the ink. I knew Papa would be pleased to hear from me.

Sometime later I looked up from my pages and stretched. Keeping a happy tone to my writing was not quite so easy as I had hoped, and I wanted to keep the tone happy. Above all I could not have Papa descending on us in alarm, and he was quite apt to do just that if he suspected something was wrong.

185

A chuckle tickled my throat. Putting Papa and the dowager in the same castle would make for some extraordinary verbal battles, I had no doubt about that, but much as I would love to see him, I did not want such a thing to happen. Caroline had caused him enough pain. I did not want to cause him more.

I reread my letter, considering each word. It sounded all right. I should be able to—

I thought I heard a creak on the stairs. Could Sarah be sneaking up to surprise me! I waited, but there was no other sound. So I turned, just in time to see the door swinging shut. I leaped to my feet, but I was too late. I was only halfway there when I heard the key turn in the lock.

"Wait!" I cried. "Don't go. I'm in here!"

There was no sound from the other side of the door. I knew I had heard the turning of the key, but still I went to try the doorknob. It was useless. The door was securely locked.

The candle, already quite short, chose that instant to smoke and flutter. The room seemed immeasurably darker, colder. I pulled my shawl closer about me. I must not panic.

Forcing myself to move slowly, I retraced my steps to the desk. Think, I told myself. And so, while my candle shed its slender circle of light around me, I sat and thought.

First, I thought that I was cold and getting colder. Well, I could do something about that. The coverlet was still on the cot. I would wrap myself in it.

Second, I thought of the darkness. When night fell, this room would be in utter blackness. What if I heard the crying babe then? What if the apparition came to taunt me?

My knees had begun to tremble badly. "Do not panic," I said aloud. "Think. What would Papa do?"

That was easy. Papa would look for a way out, and if there were none—as was surely the case here—he would simply compose himself and wait to be found.

They *would* find me. I was confident of that. The question was—when? No one knew of my whereabouts, and I would not be missed for some hours. Hours. I shivered. I had no desire to spend long lonely hours in this cold and dreary place, but it appeared I had no choice.

After a few moments I crossed to the bed and took up the coverlet. It was blue silk, cold, almost clammy to the touch. I shivered, but I wrapped it around me anyhow. It would help to keep me warm.

Then I turned my mind to the whys and wherefores of my predicament. One thing I knew for certain: It was no apparition that had locked me in the room. Ghosts had no need for such antics; they had fear on their side.

This so-called ghost had not appeared to me or tried to frighten me in that way. Instead it had crept up the tower stairs, softly, carefully. But not softly and carefully enough to avoid that telltale creak. Ghosts did not have the weight to make a stair tread creak. It was definitely a human who was doing these things.

This was another warning. Someone still wanted to frighten me, but I had no idea why. I had harmed no one. I knew nothing.

Now, why had that thought occurred to me? What could I know that would threaten anyone? Caroline. I knew Caroline. Did someone think she had told me something?

The servant! Perhaps it was the servant that Caroline had been meeting before her death. Perhaps he thought I might discover something of his identity. Perhaps he thought there was something in that very room, some clue he had left that would lead us to him.

I should search for it, I thought. But in that instant the candle guttered and went out, leaving me in blackness.

I sat quite still. The sensible thing, I told myself, was to go to the cot, cover myself as best I could, and to wait.

But my limbs did not want to move. The darkness around me seemed a palpable presence, pressing in on me. I began to suffer difficulty in breathing. My heart raced. Like a living thing the darkness tried to smother me. Panic began to descend on me, but just before I lost control, I called Papa's image into my mind.

I straightened my shoulders and spoke sternly to myself, just as Papa would have. "There will be no more panic, Vanessa. You are in no real danger."

I did not quite believe that. In spite of my determination to be sensible, I knew quite well that I *had* heard a baby cry; I *had* seen a ghostly figure. These things were not products of an inflamed imagination. They were quite real events. Certainly most people would have found them threatening.

I forced myself to my feet, pointing myself toward where I thought the cot lay. Each step into that impenetrable blackness left me weak and trembling. It was ridiculous, I told myself, to feel as though some abyss might suddenly open before me. The tower floor was made of solid stone, as were its walls. The door was locked. If someone opened it, I would hear the turning of the key.

I managed to move myself across the floor until my probing foot touched the cot. With a sigh of relief I wrapped the coverlet around me and lay down to wait.

Time passed slowly, so slowly. In the darkness I tried to estimate what time of day it was. What was Richard doing? Had he come home yet? Had he looked for me? Would he go to the nursery? Or would he attend to other business and not know I was missing until it was time for the evening meal?

In spite of the coverlet I grew colder and colder. Several times I contemplated rising and making the circuit of the wall, just to get my blood going a little, but it was so dark I could not bring myself to move.

During those long lonely hours I thought of Papa. I pictured his dear familiar face and remembered things he had said to me, things we had done together. I thought of Sarah and how far she and I had come in caring for each other. I even thought of Roland and the stolen kiss.

But mostly I thought of Richard and my love for him. How glad I would be to see him. I thought of him taking me in his arms and holding me close. Then this nightmare would be over. *But why didn't he come?*

Eventually I lost all sense of time. It seemed days rather than hours that I had been a prisoner in this darkness. Several times I started up, thinking there was someone at the door, but there was no one. And so, when finally the key turned in the lock, I thought I had imagined it, and I did not move.

Suddenly the room was flooded with light. I sat up, clutching the coverlet, trying to see. "Who—who is it?" I cried.

"Vanessa!" Richard took me in his arms. Behind him I saw Gerson, holding aloft a lighted candelabra. "What happened?" Richard asked. "What are you doing here?"

I shivered against my husband's chest, hardly daring to believe he was there at last, at last I was found. "It was

189

raining and we missed our ride. I thought I would explore. So I came here."

"But how did you get locked in?"

"I was writing a letter to Papa. It's over there on the desk. I heard a creak on the stairs. Then the door swung shut and someone locked it."

Richard frowned. "It doesn't make any sense. Who would do this to you?"

With Gerson standing right there I did not care to expound on Caroline's amorous meetings with the servants. "I do not know," I said, then sighed. "Richard, what time is it?"

He frowned. "It's going on bedtime. I didn't return till late afternoon. We didn't know you were missing until you didn't come to dinner."

"Dinner." For the first time I considered my stomach and realized its empty condition.

Richard leaped to his feet. "You must be starving. I know I am—now. Actually, no one has eaten. We've all been busy looking for you."

"Then we shall all eat together," I said, getting to my feet and returning the coverlet to the cot. "And Gerson, I want this room well stocked with candles."

"Yes, Your Grace."

Richard frowned, but he did not forbid me the use of the room. "And have the lock removed from the door," he added. "I do not want anyone locked in here again."

"Yes, Your Grace."

"Richard—" I began, but he silenced me with a quick kiss.

"Come," he said. "It's dinner time."

* * *

190

The meal was delicious, and for once the conversation was pleasant. Everyone seemed to be on their best behavior, and though no one referred to my ordeal, I thought it must be the reason for such unusual kindness.

Richard and I were not alone again until we went to bed. "Now," he said as soon as the door closed behind us, "I want you to tell me everything that happened. From the beginning."

As I undressed, I once more reported the details of the afternoon's experience.

When I finished, Richard's eyes held mine. "I don't like it, Vanessa. Is this the only strange thing that has happened to you since you've been here?"

I did not lie to him. I could not. "No, Richard."

He did not look surprised. "What else has happened?"

I hesitated, but I was tired of coping with all this alone. Perhaps Richard could help me get to the bottom of it. Besides, husbands and wives should not keep secrets from each other. "I have heard the crying babe."

His expression hardened into a fierce frown. "Vanessa."

I was sorry to upset him, but I knew what I had heard. "I have heard it," I repeated. "The second night I was here I heard it. And again later."

He did not look convinced. "Vanessa, the haunting babe is a legend, not a reality."

I stepped out of my gown and went for my nightdress. "That may well be. But legend or not, I heard a baby crying. I know I cannot prove it, but I also know what I heard."

I let my chemise fall to the floor and pulled my nightdress over my head. "And both nights there was the scent."

His eyes grew darker. "What scent?"

191

"Caroline's scent. I woke to find my room filled with it."

He seemed perplexed. "Caroline's scent? Why should anyone want to use that?"

I climbed into bed and Richard followed me. "I don't know. But I'm afraid that's not all." I told him about the dead bird and the ghostly figure that had beckoned to me to follow it.

Richard crushed me to him. "Thank God you were sensible," he said fiercely. "There are secret passages in the walls. Places you might disappear into and never be found."

I loosened his grip, struggling to get my breath. "You mean you don't know where they are?"

"Not all of them. I know where the priest hole is, but very little else."

I stared at him. "But this castle was built long before the persecution of Catholic priests. Why should it have a priest hole?"

Richard nodded. "I suspect some of the rooms were originally secret prisons. There were many such places long ago. Troublesome people disappeared and were never seen again."

Troublesome people. I shivered. Someone obviously found me troublesome. "Richard, who do you think is doing this to me?"

He shook his head. "Some of it sounds like Penrose's pranks. The dead bird would be a joke to him. But I don't know where he would get Caroline's scent. They were hardly friendly."

"The armoire!"

Richard stared at me in puzzlement.

"The armoire in the North Tower," I explained.

"There was a bottle of her scent in it. Richard, I suspect she met someone in that room, a servant with whom she was—"

His face hardened and he sighed. "She said she saw ghosts there. She said she didn't intend to go near it again. Ever."

Much as I loved him, I felt some exasperation. Why did he always want to believe the best of her? And after all she had done to him? "I think that was to keep others away. So she would be undisturbed." I told him about the witch story she had used to keep me from her trysting place in the woods.

The pain on his face was terrible to behold. I wished that I knew some way to ease it. But only time—and the good Lord—could do that.

"There are many male servants here," he mused aloud. "Any one of them could go to the North Tower without being observed. No one else went near it after Caroline started talking about ghosts."

I snuggled close in the circle of his arm. In spite of all that had happened to me that day, I was happy. There were no more secrets between us.

Then I remembered. The knowledge that I had shut out of my mind came back with a rush that left me shaken and sick at heart.

Richard had had Caroline's scented handkerchief under his pillow. Richard must know where to find her scent.

Chapter Sixteen

Another woman might have pulled back in terror or run home to her papa with a head full of suspicion, but I loved my husband passionately. It never entered my mind that *I* might have cause to fear him. Then I thought only that he still loved Caroline, and such knowledge was bitter as gall to me, who wanted to be the sole object of his affections.

Yes, that night I still refused to consider the possibility that Richard had anything to do with Caroline's death. It was true that he knew where to find Caroline's scent, but so might many others. It was one of them who was trying to frighten me away, not my husband.

I spent a fairly peaceful night with Richard beside me. Several times I awoke with a start, thinking I had heard the haunting babe's cry, but except for Richard's steady breathing, the room was always silent. Each time I uttered a sigh of relief and returned to sleep.

We woke to a day of sunshine. Richard and I had our ride, and he left to attend to estate business. That afternoon Mrs. Brewster returned, her stout young men bearing our new gowns. They deposited their bundles on the divan and retreated to the kitchen.

Summoned from the nursery, Sarah bounced in. "They've come," she cried, skipping to my side. "Oh, which ones are ours?"

I smiled at her enthusiasm. So did Mrs. Brewster. I could not help hoping that the dressmaker would report to the parish how well the duke's daughter got along with his new wife. We could use something good to counteract the malicious lies the vicar's sister must be circulating.

Penrose and Rosamund came in, too. In spite of all our efforts to calm her, Rosamund dug through her gowns, shoving them right and left, until she found the orange silk. Then, clutching it to her bosom, she began to dance around the room.

I exchanged glances with Penrose, but we dared not stop her forcibly. When she was thwarted, she had a terrible strength, and we had learned it was best to let her have her way.

Sarah, intent on the new gowns, paid her no mind. And Mrs. Brewster focussed all her attention on us. Or so it seemed.

"Which one shall you wear today?" I asked Sarah.

"Today?" she asked, as though she could hardly believe it.

"Yes, indeed. Today. We must get all those black things ready to give the poor."

Sarah glanced at my blue gown. "I want a blue one," she cried, running to give me a hug. "Oh, Nessie. They are so beautiful."

Half an hour later, she returned, looking an entirely different child. Her golden curls shimmered, and the new gown brought out the color of her eyes.

The sight of her set my heart to sinking. The dress made her resemblance to her mother even more marked. How was I to get Richard's love when Sarah was there, a constant reminder of the woman he had loved and lost?

Sad to say, for a few moments I considered giving up my efforts to bring father and daughter together. If I relegated Sarah to the nursery, Richard would find no fault with me. Indeed, I knew he would be happy with such an arrangement.

But I could not do it. I knew Sarah needed her father. She needed him, perhaps, even more than I needed him. So I must continue in my efforts to bring the two of them together and pray that my love for him would eventually make him forget Caroline.

The dressmaker had left us a great bundle of scraps, but Sarah was too full of life to think of sitting still to make doll clothes. She whirled around the room, then stopped to admire herself.

"Oh, Nessie," she cried again, just as Roland entered the room.

"My God!" Roland stopped in the doorway, his eyes widening in surprise.

Sarah ran and threw herself into his arms. "Isn't it beautiful?" she cried, wrapping her arms around his neck.

"*You* are beautiful," he said, lifting her. "You look just like—"

Something in the child's face stopped him in midsentence.

"I *do* look like Nessie," she cried. "You saw it."

Roland's smile was gentle. "Actually, you look more like your mama."

Sarah's lip came out in a pout. "I don't want to look like her. I want to look like Nessie."

Roland's smile included me. He sat down, perching Sarah on his knee. "You cannot do anything about your outsides—how you look," he told her. "That's one of the things we can't do much about."

I wondered if he was thinking about being born second, but from what he had said to the dowager, being second did not seem to bother him.

"But we can do something about our insides," he went on.

Sarah looked puzzled. "No one can see my insides."

Roland's smile grew warmer. "I'm talking about the sort of person you want to be. You can't make yourself look like Nessie, but you can act like her."

Sarah's pout was disappearing. "But how will anyone know?"

"They'll know," Roland assured her, "by the things you do. If you're kind and you think of other people. If you try to help. They'll know you learned these things from Nessie."

His speech made me a little embarrassed. It was difficult to listen to a recital of my virtues, especially since I so well knew my faults.

Sarah had been thinking this over and now she smiled. "All right," she said. "I'm going to be like Nessie that way." She kissed his cheek, then slipped off his knee to tug at his hand. "Come, I want you to see the rest of my dresses."

Off they went to exclaim over her gowns. I could not help noticing how good Roland was with her. Thank goodness someone had been there to give the child some sorely needed affection. If only Richard would see how much she needed his love. But he would not. He could not.

The dowager entered just as Sarah and Roland came to her last gown. "Mama," Roland said, "did you see Sarah's new gowns?"

"Very pretty," said the dowager in a voice that would have frightened an ordinary child.

Sarah only nodded. "Mine are like Nessie's," she said proudly. "Because I'm her little girl now."

The dowager scowled. "That is not possible. You will always be your mother's child. Sad as that may seem."

Roland sent me an embarrassed glance. "Mama, please—"

But even Roland could not silence the dowager. She stared him down. "That's the truth. Why shouldn't I speak it?"

"It's not true," Sarah cried, her little face puckering in distress. "Nessie is my mama now."

"Vanessa is your aunt." The dowager wrinkled her nose as though she smelled something distasteful, her favorite expression when she looked at me. "She's also your stepmama. But she will never be your mama."

"She will! She will!" Sarah burst into tears and ran wailing from the room.

I got to my feet to follow her, but first I had a few things to say to the dowager. She might pick at me, and I would remain silent; but when she hurt the child . . . "I have tried to be civil to you," I said, "because you are Richard's mother. But this is the outside of enough. How can you be so cruel to your own grandchild?"

The dowager's lip curled. "Hasn't Richard told you that either? The child isn't his. She's some fly-by-night's bastard."

198

Roland was obviously distressed at such plain speaking. "Mama, please. None of this is Vanessa's fault."

His mother sniffed. "She had no business coming here. Neither did the other one. But this one won't last either."

I could not take any more of her disdain. With an apologetic look to Roland I left the room.

Once I would have thrown something, screamed and vented my frustration, but now I went to the nursery. If I was to be Sarah's mother, I must put the child's needs before mine.

Sarah was seated before the fire, great tears rolling down her cheeks. I took her in my lap. "Sarah, dear. Why are you crying so?"

She buried her face in my neck. "I want—I want to be—your little girl."

I smoothed her hair, so like Caroline's. "Then there's no need to cry. Because you *are* my little girl."

She raised her head and sniffled. "But Grandmother said—"

I saw immediately what I had to do. I wondered why I hadn't thought of it sooner. "Sarah, remember when we talked about your mama?"

She nodded.

"Remember that I told you she was sick?"

Her eyes met mine, full of trust. "Yes, Nessie. I remember."

"Well, your grandmother is sick, too. She cannot love anyone either."

Sarah's forehead wrinkled into a frown.

"Do you understand?" I asked.

"I think so. But—"

"But what, Sarah?"

"If my mama had that sickness—and Grandmother has it—" Her voice quavered. "What if I get it?"

She looked so serious that I was hard put not to laugh. But I would not insult her feelings in that way. "No, Sarah," I said. "You cannot *get* this sickness. It isn't catching."

She started to smile, then frowned again. "Nessie, are you sure?"

I hugged her to me. "I am very sure," I said. "You and I, we will always love each other."

She sighed and returned my hug. "And my father. We will always love my father."

"Yes, dear. We will." But I could not help wondering —would he ever, really, love us?

Some time later I left Sarah playing happily with her doll. When I was with her, I could keep my anger in check, but the minute I stepped out into the hall, all my good feelings deserted me. The dowager was mean-spirited and vicious. In comparison, she made Caroline look almost saintly. The thought did not amuse me as it might have once.

I sighed. The castle and its inhabitants were pressing in on me again. If only Richard were here, we could ride again! I was sorely in need of a good gallop.

The second the thought crossed my mind I knew I'd have to do it. Surely Richard wouldn't object to my riding alone now. I knew the roads and the moor, and the stallion was used to me.

Minutes later I had hurried into my riding clothes and was at the stable. Toby grinned and touched his cap. "'Tis a nice day, all right, Yer Grace. Which animal will you be wanting?"

Mercury chose that moment to whinny and toss his head. Like me he was feeling the need to be free. "I'll take the stallion," I said. "He's eager to go."

I was halfway to the main road when I heard someone coming up behind me. "Vanessa, wait."

Roland's mare soon caught up with us. He frowned. "Must you ride that beast?"

I patted the stallion's neck. "He's a beautiful animal."

He made a gesture of dismissal. "Yes, but he killed—"

I did not want to hear about that. "*If* Mercury did it, he had good reason."

His eyes widened. "You mean you think it's all right to kill—"

"Of course I don't. But if Caroline went into the stall and beat the horse, then it was not his fault."

"You mean she provoked him." Roland nodded wisely. "Then you believe the stallion did it."

I sighed. This subject was not one I cared to pursue, but I felt obligated to defend the stallion. "Actually, I'm not sure I do."

He frowned. "But if the horse didn't kill her, then who did?"

"I don't know that. I only know I trust the horse."

He leaned toward me. His face that was so like Richard's, was serious. "Vanessa, I am worried about you."

"Me! Why should you worry about me?" The stallion chose that moment to skitter sideways, almost into Roland's mare.

For a minute our legs brushed, and I almost thought he meant to kiss me; but his mare pranced away and nothing happened. It was probably my imagination, anyway, thinking I'd seen something in his eyes, something that wasn't there at all.

"Why should you worry about me?" I repeated, mostly because I could think of nothing else to say.

Roland looked sheepish. "I should not have said anything to you."

"You have started now," I replied in exasperation. "You might as well finish."

Roland sighed. "It's just—Caroline died so strangely. I should not want anything to happen to you."

The stallion skittered again, but I got him under control. "Nothing is going to happen to me."

He frowned. "Richard's temper—"

I stared at him. "Whatever are you talking about? Richard has never even been angry with me."

Roland looked relieved, but a little unbelieving. "That's good. Perhaps he won't ever be. But his rages—"

Uneasiness crept into my heart, but I kept my face calm. The stallion, sensing my tension, began to fret even more at the reins. "What rages?" I asked.

"I told you about the stable loft. About him trying to push me out."

Why must he remind me of that? "But that was long ago."

"Of course. Forget I—oh, oh! Here he comes. I'll talk to you later." He cantered off.

Minutes later Richard rode up from the other direction. "Another ride today?"

I nodded. "I had words with your mother. I just had to get away."

He stared after Roland's retreating figure. "Who was with you?"

I hesitated for a fraction of a second. I did not know

why I should. I did not feel guilty. Certainly I had every right to speak to my husband's brother. "That was Roland. He caught up with me."

Richard scowled. "You were not riding together?"

"Only for a little way."

His scowl grew fiercer. Was I about to see one of those rages?

"I don't want you to ride with him," Richard said in a voice of command such as he had never before used to me.

Still, in spite of Roland's words, I was not afraid of my husband. "But he's your brother."

"I know that," he snapped. "And you are my wife. Obey my wishes in this, Vanessa. Roland is not fit company for you."

My mood had been far from good when I left the castle, and it was definitely not improving. "I fail to see—" I began, but that was all I had time to get out.

"Vanessa!" Richard thundered. The stallion pranced sideways, and I had to fight hard to control him. "I am telling you. Do not ride with my brother!"

I wanted to argue the point, but with the stallion carrying on so, my attention was divided. "Very well," I said, albeit with great reluctance.

Richard's expression smoothed out. "That's a good wife," he said and leaned over to kiss me. I swallowed my anger and returned the kiss.

My husband now looked as though nothing had upset him. I put a smile on my face. A good wife indeed! "I wish you could come with me," I said with a sweetness I did not feel.

He smiled and patted my hand. "I have some papers to attend to." He glanced at the sky. "You go ahead. Just don't stay out too long."

I nodded and gave the stallion his head before I should forget myself and tell my husband what I was really thinking. The great horse cantered away. I tried to enjoy the wind in my face and the feel of a good animal under me.

But my temper was up. Richard had no right to order me about like that. Well, perhaps he had the right. I *had* promised to obey him. But even Papa had not presumed so much.

Why was Richard so terribly unfair to his brother? Not fit, indeed! Roland was the only member of the family who had bothered to be kind to me, and now I was forbidden to ride with him. It wasn't at all fair.

Turning the stallion onto the moor, I pointed him toward a great jumble of fallen rocks in the distance. I knew this ground. I knew it was safe to let the stallion run.

When we reached the rocks, neither the stallion nor my anger was spent. I aimed him at another distant pile and off we flew.

We were almost there when I heard a sudden snapping sound. The same instant I went flying through the air, the saddle with me. Fortunately I did not land on any large stones, but again I had to labor to get air back into my tortured lungs.

The stallion waited patiently, and finally I was able to sit up. I checked all my limbs and decided that at worst I would suffer a few bruises. My saddle lay on the ground some distance away. I got to my feet and went to it automatically.

When I bent to pick it up, I gasped. The girth had been cut half through, up under the flap where it would not be noticed. Half the broken strap was frayed, but the other half was cut clean. Someone had wanted me to have an accident.

My hands began to tremble, but I paid them no mind. This was no time to get vaporish. I dragged the saddle to the pile of stones. I could not carry it far, but I marked the spot where I left it.

Then I considered my situation. It was a long way back to the castle. I must either walk it or ride the stallion bareback. I had no inclination for such a long walk, especially in boots designed for riding, but to mount the stallion bareback—and to ride astride—what if someone should see me? Someone like Cressadine Varish?

I glanced at the sky. It would soon be dusk, and the landmarks I knew would not be visible. I sighed and led the stallion to an overturned slab of stone. I would rather risk the bareback ride than be caught on the moor in the dark.

I spoke soothing words to the stallion as I used the stone to mount him. To my surprise he stood, meek as a lamb, until I turned him back toward the road. Then he kept his gait to a comfortable walk.

I leaned forward to pat his neck. "You're a good horse," I whispered. "A beautiful, good horse. And I won't let anyone hurt you."

Dusk was falling as we reached the stable. Seeing me astride, Toby let out a piercing whistle. The stallion, good animal that he was, never quivered.

Remembering himself, Toby rushed forward and grabbed the bridle. "Sure, Yer Grace, I'm sorry. But whereats your saddle?"

Richard emerged from a stall. "I was coming to meet you," he said. Then he, too, noticed my unusual position. "My God, Vanessa! What are you doing astride?" He reached up to help me down.

"I had an accident," I said, recounting what had befallen me. "The girth was cut."

I heard Toby's quick intake of breath. "'Twas her," he muttered.

Richard frowned. "What are you talking about?"

The boy trembled, but he went on. "I seen her. The ghost of the late duchess."

"Nonsense!"

Toby quailed, but he stood his ground. "I did, Yer Grace. I seen her. She were standing right there, right outside the stallion's stall."

"You're imagining things," Richard said.

Toby shook his head. "No, I ain't, Yer Grace. She left—" he reached into the tack box—"she left this."

My knees went suddenly weak. There in Toby's hand was a handkerchief. It was not as white as it had once been; but the monogrammed C was still plain, and I had no doubt that a hint of Caroline's scent clung to it still.

Chapter Seventeen

There was no discounting the reality of the handkerchief, but Richard adamantly refused to believe in a ghost. Someone else had dropped the handkerchief, he said, someone who wanted us to believe that ghosts existed.

I wanted to think as he did. It would soon be the full moon again, and I would be left alone while he attended to Rosamund. Under such circumstances the prospect of ghosts was not one I really cared to consider.

Logic told me that ghosts hardly went about cutting girths. Someone earthly wanted to do me harm. Perhaps even— I pushed the thought aside.

The accident was clearly meant for me, since it was the sidesaddle that had been damaged and I was the only one who used it. This was not a much pleasanter consideration, however, than the possibility of ghosts, and so I tried to put it from my mind.

For several days I could not ride. I fretted and fumed around the castle, nursing my bruises and my temper, until Richard brought home a new girth. His instructions to Toby were quite explicit: Every part of the saddle was to be inspected before it went on the horse, and Toby was to be held personally accountable for my safety.

The days passed and the full moon drew nearer. It hardly seemed possible that I had been at Greyden Castle less than a month. One night as Richard and I prepared for bed I said as much.

He smiled at me. "You have made my life bearable again, my dearest."

As compliments go, this was not the best I'd ever heard; but still, it gladdened my heart, and it prompted me to speak what was on my mind. "Richard, soon it will be the full moon."

He nodded and hung his coat over the back of a chair. "Will you go to Rosamund then?"

He frowned. "I must, Nessie. No one else can manage her."

"Not even Penrose?"

"No, not even he."

I climbed into bed and sighed. "I do not like to sleep alone."

Taking his place beside me, Richard chuckled and drew me closer.

I flushed. "You know what I mean. I want you with me. I cannot sleep when you are gone."

He kissed my forehead. "I don't like to leave you, Nessie, but if you stay in bed, you should be safe enough."

I snuggled closer. "But, Richard, I cannot sleep."

"We'll have a pot of tea brought up. Maybe that will help relax you."

I had to smile at my husband. He was sometimes a most amusing man. How could he possibly think that a cup of tea was a reasonable subsitute for a husband? But I loved him dearly, and I knew that for his sake I would suffer through the full moon, whatever it might bring me.

The next night the maid brought up a pot of tea. It was cozy to sit in bed with my husband, sipping and discussing our day. Richard told the staff to make the tea a nightly ritual, and I began to look forward to it.

More days passed. Sarah was blossoming into a lovely little chatterbox. Every day she grew dearer to me, but I was no more successful in bringing her and Richard together than I had been before. I thought often of the book Sarah said her mother wrote in. But, though I went several times to the tower room especially to search for a diary, I could find no sign of it.

The dowager grew ever more insulting, her comments on every aspect of my life sharp and stinging as winter rain. I had often to bite my tongue to keep back the bitter replies I wanted so badly to make.

Penrose had no trouble getting Rosamund to discard her black and wear her new gowns. The yellow made her look ghastly, but next to the orange silk it was her favorite. Penrose and Richard complimented her daily, no matter what she wore or how she looked.

Roland was not much about. Truth to tell, I missed his cheerful company. He was the only person in the household who behaved in a normal fashion, and I rather looked to him to help me keep a sense of what was right and decent.

Then the night of the full moon was upon us. At bedtime Richard accompanied me to my chamber and tenderly kissed me good night. I wanted to cling to him and beg him to stay with me, but of course I did not. I was made of sterner stuff than that.

"I shall be back at dawn, my dearest," he said. "Sleep well."

I made no reply to such a sentiment. I doubted I should sleep at all. But I knew Richard and I knew his sense of duty. If Rosamund needed him, he would be there. I could not dispute that.

I took off my clothes, got into my nightdress, and climbed into bed. It looked as though it would be a long lonely night. The maid arrived with the teapot, and I had her put it on the table right beside the bed. Perhaps a good cup of hot tea would calm my nerves.

I checked the drawer to make sure I had plenty of candles. Since my entrapment in the North Tower, I had been unable to overcome a distressing fear of the dark. It was one thing to lie in the dark beside Richard and quite another to be alone, staring into frightening blackness.

There would be light from the moon, I knew, but I meant to take no chances. I did not intend to be trapped in the darkness again. My memory of that experience was too vivid to be easily forgotten.

The time passed very slowly. I finished my tea and slid down among the pillows. The sensible thing would be to go to sleep; but no one had ever accused me of being sensible, so I tossed and turned and counted enough sheep to overrun all of Cornwall.

Nothing helped. I was still wide awake. I lay there, contemplating the moonlight that streamed through my window. If only Richard were there in the bedchamber with me. I let myself go back in memory to our last lovemaking. I remembered it so well; I could almost feel his arms around me, his lips pressing on mine.

These pleasant memories worked where the sheep had failed, and soon I drifted off into slumber.

I don't know how long I slept, but a noise woke me. I could not tell what made it, but I knew it was real and that I had just heard it.

The candle was still burning. I lay there, rigid, waiting for I knew not what. And then it came. "Van-ness-sa," the strange voice whispered. "This is not the place for you. Go home while you can."

I bit my lip. Should I reply to this so-called ghost? Should I tell it I had no intention of leaving my husband and the child who had come to love me like the mother she had never really had?

I opened my mouth, but I closed it again without saying anything. Surely one did not argue with a ghost. I would wait it out. Ignoring whoever it was would prove just as effective.

But I had never been a person given to waiting things out. As Papa always said, I was far more likely to rush in and start fighting even before I knew what was at stake. If only I could see my adversary. Then I would have a better chance.

I had not forgotten Richard's admonition to stay in bed, but I found I could not obey it. This inaction was driving me up in the boughs. I must do *something* to change the current state of affairs.

Surely the logical thing was to find out the ghost, to discern its identity once and for all. That was what Papa would do. Then we could take steps to end this charade.

I threw back the covers, but I did not hurry. This time I was determined to think clearly. I drew on my robe and stepped into my slippers. Then I picked up the candle.

Halfway to the door Richard's words came back to me again. I knew I should not put myself in danger, but I simply could not bear this kind of thing any longer. I had to do something, and I would be careful.

I crossed the room and laid my hand on the doorknob. Like everything else in the castle it was cold to the touch. I shivered, but I did not turn back. I must discover who was behind these ghostly visits, and then I could put an end to them.

Carefully I turned the knob and opened the door. The hall was dark. No white figure lurked outside my room. I was not surprised. I had not expected to find anyone—or anything—right there.

Taking a deep breath. I stepped out. The figure was halfway down the hall, just about where I had seen it before. It lifted a ghostly appendage and beckoned to me.

And I followed.

It led me in the direction it had before, down the hall toward the North Tower. And, as before, it kept the same distance in front of me.

It stopped, finally, in what looked to be about the same place it had stopped the first time I had followed it. I paused, too. Should I rush down the hall and try to grapple with this intruder? Unmask him or her? The prospect was enticing.

But Richard's words of warning were still echoing in my mind, and as I debated with myself, the ghost vanished again.

I uttered an oath that would have set Papa to frowning mightily and left Richard, who had never heard me curse, blinking in astonishment. Then, holding my candle high, I continued down the hall.

My progress was slow because I was examining the inner wall as I went. I could see nothing out of the ordinary, and I was just about to give up and return to my room when there it was.

A section of the wall was tilted out, and behind it gaped a hole, just big enough to squeeze through. I approached it carefully, ready to scream, to fight, to run, but the light from my candle showed me nothing but a dark passageway.

I drew closer. I stuck my arm and the candle into the darkness. Nothing happened. There was no one there.

I stood, half in and half out of the hall. Should I step inside and follow the passageway to its end? I dearly wished to get to the bottom of this thing.

The ghost was no longer nearby—clearly it did not wish to be confronted—but the passageway was there. I could follow it.

I took one step forward, then another. Richard's warnings rang in my head, but I did not heed them. One more step and I was completely inside the passage.

My knees trembled. My heart pounded. I stood there, trying to decide which direction to go. Suddenly I felt a cold wind on my cheek, and my candle flickered and almost went out.

My heart rose up in my throat. Fear, bitter as bile, filled my mouth. I could not get enough air into my lungs. With a sob I rushed back through the gap and out into the hall where I stood quivering and gasping for breath. I could not venture into that blackness; my fear was too great.

I tried to mark the section of wall by dripping candle wax on the stones, and then I backed slowly away.

My progress back to my room was slow; I could not bring myself to turn my back on the dark hole that threatened there in the wall. But finally I reached my room and the haven of my bed.

As I climbed back into it, I reflected that it had not

been Richard's sensible warnings that had deterred me, but my own very real fear. I simply could not stand the thought of being trapped again in the dark.

It was just as well, I thought, pulling the covers up to my chin. Tomorrow I would take Richard with me. Together we would find the wax-marked stones and the passageway they hid. Together we would explore them. With him beside me, I could brave the darkness. With him beside me, I could do anything.

Incredible as it seems, I soon slept and I remained asleep until Richard returned to our room at dawn. The sound of him opening the door must have aroused me. As he climbed in beside me, I opened my eyes.

"You see," he said. "You slept undisturbed."

I did not intend to let him go on believing such foolishness. But he had been up all night, and I hadn't slept much myself. So I just mumbled something and rolled into his waiting arms.

When I woke again, Richard was gone. Some early business had no doubt called him away. I went down to breakfast. When my husband returned, we would look for the passageway.

Penrose came alone to breakfast. I surmised that his mother was still sleeping. The boy looked tired, as though he hadn't slept much himself. "Good morning," I said, determined to be cheerful.

Though Penrose looked exhausted, I no longer suspected him of being the ghost. I was convinced that the apparition was the creation of the servant who had been Caroline's lover.

"How is your mother this morning?" I asked.

Penrose frowned. "She's not at all well. She heard it last night."

Icy fingers sidled along my spine. Still, I had to ask. "Heard what?"

"The crying babe, of course." His smile was sinister. "Have you heard it again?"

I shook my head. "Did Richard hear it?"

Penrose filled his plate. "He said not."

I breathed a sigh of relief.

Penrose was still scowling as he took his seat. "He says she imagined it."

"Be fair, Penrose. Perhaps she did."

His eyes bored into mine. "But you heard it. You know the babe is real."

I chose my words carefully. "I heard crying. That doesn't mean it was the babe."

His eyes were bright, too bright. "It does. You know it does."

His hand went to his coat pocket. "I am still working on my poem. Do you—want to hear it?"

I did not. I did not want to hear any more about the haunting babe or any other supernatural apparitions. But the boy seemed so eager, and so friendless. I tried to smile and said, "Yes, of course."

In another situation I might have found some humor in all this. Certainly Penrose was too young to be writing about Death and apparitions. In his somber black clothes he looked very like a little boy playing at grown-up.

But I did not say that, and I did not laugh. Instead, I composed my features into a properly serious aspect. "Go ahead," I said. "I am listening."

Now that he had an audience, Penrose did not seem eager. He hesitated. "It's rough," he said. "Only a first writing. I'll be doing more work on it."

I nodded. "Go on."

He struck an eloquent pose and began:

Death has gentle arms,
Yet the haunting babe gets no rest.
Death holds for it no charms.
It wants its mother's breast.

Penrose looked at me anxiously, and I nodded. I was
no connoisseur of verse, but even I knew that this effort
was no competition for Lord Byron.

I managed to hold my attention to the poem until the
last lines.

When living woman gives up breath, oh, willingly,
Then—and only then—shall the haunting babe go
    free.

I shivered. Though Penrose's efforts were bad poetry,
the story of the haunting babe affected me strongly. The
image of a baby crying for its mother was a universal one,
and the thought that it had been crying so for lo these
many years was heartbreaking. I was conscious, too, that
soon I might hold my own babe in my arms. And I feared
for it.

Penrose was staring at me, and I realized that I had not
made any response to his work.

"Have you been writing poetry long?" I asked, not
wanting to give an outright opinion.

He shook his head. "Just for the last several years." He
sighed deeply. "If only I could write like Byron. Such
fire! Such beauty! He knows Death. He has seen him face

216

to face."

He stopped and clasped a hand to his pocket. "No more paper," he muttered, more to himself than me. "I must get that down. "Face to face, I met Death."

He was off, leaving his breakfast on his plate, but cramming a muffin into his mouth as he went.

I breathed a sigh of relief. I did not want to hurt the boy's feelings, but he was not a poet. Even I could see that.

I frowned and bit into a hot roll. Penrose should not be moping around the castle, worrying about a deranged mother and scribbling lines about Death. Other youths his age were out living life—away at school or cutting up with the village girls.

I did not wish for Penrose to take up immoral pursuits, though now that I was married, I could better understand the kind of trouble many girls got themselves into; but I would have liked to see him behaving as other young men did.

I sighed and finished my ham and roll. Where was my husband? He seemed never to be there when I needed him.

I drank up the rest of my tea and left the table. Why should I wait for Richard? It was daytime now. I would explore the hall and find the secret door. How proud he would be of me when I found it.

I would not go into the passageway, of course, not until Richard came home and could go with me.

The hall was dark, as usual, and the candelabra were too far apart to give any really good light. Still, I was determined. I took a fresh candle and lit it.

Finding the door to the passageway was not as easy as I had imagined it would be. The stones all looked very much alike. Three times I traversed the length of hall from my chamber almost to the archway that led up to the North Tower, but I could not find any trace of a door in the wall.

Wax drippings I found in plenty. It seemed that every other stone had candle wax on it somewhere, but none of them moved to show me a dark hole with a passageway behind it. I poked and pried, breaking several fingernails in the process and raising my temperature almost to the boiling point, but I was no closer to finding the doorway.

By the time I gave up, I was no longer sure I had seen such a passageway at all. What if the events of the past month had affected my mind? What if I had dreamed the whole thing? I had no proof. Nothing to show for my midnight excursion. Muttering under my breath, I went off to the North Tower where I could give vent to a series of colorful curses that turned the air blue.

Papa had never approved of females who cursed. He said it showed lack of taste. However, I thought the whole process was very useful. My cursing made me feel better, and since no one heard it, it harmed no one.

After I had rid myself of some of my irritation, I decided to give the tower room another going over. I set my candle on the table and took out another. Since my being locked in, Gerson had been very careful to keep the room well stocked with candles. The very next day he had had the lock removed from the door. It would close, but no one could be trapped in the room.

I lit the second candle from the first and began to explore the walls. I did not see how there could be any hiding places in the wall. The stones were extremely thick—far too heavy to be moved by a woman.

The herringbone pattern of the fireplace was in perfect

condition. No one had tampered with it.

That left the furniture. I took every drawer out of the desk. I checked each to make sure it had no false bottom. On my knees I reached far back into each recess, but there was nothing there. If the desk had once held Caroline's diary, it no longer did so.

I got to my feet. The cot was next. Carefully I removed the coverlet. It still felt clammy, but I didn't let that bother me. The room needed something warm, a woolen cover, but that would have been too commonplace for Caroline. She always had to have silk.

There was nothing in the coverlet. I removed the other bed clothes. I examined the mattress—for lumps, for tears, for seams—for anything that would indicate that her diary was hidden within, but the mattress held nothing.

I looked at the cot itself, but it contained no hiding places.

That left only the armoire. Before I opened it, I went over the outside. I examined each carving, pressing this tendril, that flower bud. Nothing happened. No secret panel slid open to reveal Caroline's diary.

With an exasperated sigh, I opened the doors. Everything seemed as I had left it. I lifted out the chest. The scent bottle was still in it, still as full as the day I first found it. The brush and mirror were there, too. I examined the chest; but it was just that, a chest, and it had no false bottom either.

I put the chest on the stones beside me. Could the armoire itself have a false bottom? I knocked and measured, and finally gave up with another sigh. The armoire held no secret hiding places.

I got to my feet. Perhaps Caroline had once hidden her

diary in this room; but it seemed apparent that it was no longer there, and I was no closer to discovering the identity of Sarah's father.

I wondered if Richard knew that Caroline's robe was still hanging there? I had thought his chamber empty of mementoes of her—until I found that handkerchief under his pillow.

I should get rid of the robe, give it to one of the servants. Or, better yet, send it to the vicar for the poor as we had sent Sarah's and Rosamund's black gowns. I reached out to take it then, but the thought occurred to me that Richard might be returning at any time. If I did not want him to see it—and I did not—then I would be better advised to wait till I knew he would be gone for some time.

I closed the armoire door. Soon now, I would be getting a reply to my letter to Papa. I would come here to write back to him. Time enough then to dispose of Caroline's robe. I shivered. Perhaps I would let a maid lift it out. I felt a real reluctance to touch this thing that had once graced my sister's beautiful body.

"You are getting morbid," I told myself. I snuffed out the extra candle and turned toward the door. "Sarah should be up from her nap. Go play with her."

Chapter Eighteen

The day went by in a normal enough fashion. As was far too often the case, Richard remained away. After I played with Sarah, I spent a pleasant hour conversing with Roland in the library.

It would have been pleasanter had I not kept thinking of Richard's supposed rages and the angry way he had commanded me not to go riding with his brother; but he had not forbidden me the library or ordinary conversation with his twin, and so I made the most of this opportunity for normal talk.

I asked Roland if he had ever heard Penrose recite his poetry. He wrinkled his nose in a gesture very like the dowager's. "Once," he admitted. "But it was really very bad." His smile was disarming, so warm, so cordial. Sometimes I almost forgot that it was Roland, and not Richard, that I was talking to.

"I'm afraid I offered too much criticism." Roland's eyes sought mine. "This is not a good place for the boy to grow up. Richard should have sent him away to school."

I masked my rising apprehension. Hadn't Richard told

me that he had offered Penrose this very thing? "I can understand Penrose not wanting to leave his mother."

Roland looked surprised. "Oh, he would have left her if Richard had wanted to send him."

Uneasiness was stalking me again. Why must Roland tell me such disquieting things about my husband? Richard had told me that Penrose refused to leave his mother, and I had believed him.

But now—Richard had kept so much from me, starting with the existence of his distressing relatives. Was this one more thing he had conveniently forgotten to tell me?

Roland smiled at me. There was something about his smile that made me uncomfortable. Perhaps it was the memory of that mistaken kiss, that fiery kiss. When I was with him, I never could tell whether his warmth was simple friendliness or something else, something that a man should not be thinking about his brother's wife.

"Poor Vanessa," he said, leaning over to pat my hand. "You are having a hard time of it, aren't you, my dear?"

"A little." For a moment I considered telling him about the ghost and the passageway, but I had no proof of what had happened. Even more important, I knew Richard would not like my taking his brother as confidant.

"It is very different here," I continued. "I am accustomed to very ordinary circumstances. Here everything is so unusual. Rosamund is ill. Penrose is strange. Your mama does not like me. . . ."

Roland sighed. "I know. Believe me, Vanessa, I have tried to get her to change, but Mama is quite set in her ways."

I thought the dowager a mean-spirited old harridan, but I could not say that to her favorite son. I did say, "I do wish she would be kinder to Sarah. The child shouldn't be told that her mother didn't want her."

Roland nodded. "You're right, of course. But that really wasn't Mama's fault."

I stared. "Not her—"

He frowned. "Sarah was listening outside the door. We did not know she was there."

"I thought she was kept in the nursery."

Roland shook his head. "Creighton is getting on in years. She cannot control the child." His smile grew tender. "It seems Sarah has taken a liking to me. Perhaps it's because Richard has so little time for her."

I could not dispute that. My heart ached for Sarah and her loss.

Roland continued. "That day she had slipped away from the nurse and was looking for me. When she heard us discussing Caroline, I suppose she was naturally curious and stopped to listen."

The poor child, to have heard such terrible things. "I am glad you have been such a good uncle to her, Roland. She is fortunate to have you."

His smile grew even warmer. "I confess I have quite a tenderness for the child, and I am glad you came into her life. She is much happier now."

"Thank you."

Gerson came then to announce dinner, and off we went to the dining room. My good humor evaporated, however, when I discovered that Richard had not yet returned. He was spending more and more time away from me, and I did not like it.

By bedtime my temper had risen several more degrees. The night before I had been visited by a ghost and almost lured into a dark hidden passageway, and today I had not even been given the opportunity to inform my husband of these things.

He came striding into my chamber as I was struggling with the last hook on my gown. He dropped a kiss on my forehead. "Good evening, my dear."

Good evening, indeed! I evaded his help. "Where have you been?" I knew I sounded like a fishwife, but I could not help it.

Richard raised an eyebrow. "I had estate business to attend to. You know I cannot always be in your pocket."

I laughed, but it was not with humor. "In my pocket! I am lucky if I get a daily glimpse of your face."

"Vanessa!"

I wanted to rant on a little more, but something in his expression stopped me. So I swallowed my next remarks and said instead, "But at least you are with me now."

A peculiar expression crossed his features. "My dear, I'm afraid not."

"What!"

"It always takes Rosamund a night or two to calm down."

"But Richard—" I felt a childish inclination to run into his arms for comfort. Instead I glared at him.

"I'm truly sorry, Nessie."

His use of my pet name only made me angrier. Why must I always come after everyone else in the castle? Why couldn't I be first for a change?

Richard gathered me into his arms. I knew I was holding myself stiffly, but I couldn't help it.

"It's just for tonight, Nessie. I promise. Tomorrow night I'll be back in your bed."

I could not believe that I had to face another night

alone. "Richard, last night there was a ghost—"

He scowled. "Vanessa, how many times must I tell you? Ghosts do not exist."

I kept a hold on my temper. "Very well. But there was a person—all in white."

Richard frowned down at me. "And where did you see this person?"

"In the hall and—"

"Vanessa! You left your bed?"

Too late I realized that I had let myself in for a scolding, but I had to go on. "I couldn't help it. It called me. I thought I could catch it." Spoken so baldly, my words sounded childish, even to me. Unfortunately, they were true.

Richard's frown grew fierce. "And did you catch it?"

"Of course not. It vanished."

"Vanessa, I told you. There are no—"

"I did not say it *was* a ghost," I interrupted. "This *person* went into a doorway in the wall." I was becoming exasperated. Why wouldn't he believe me?

For the first time Richard looked as if he did believe me. "A doorway? Where? What happened?"

"I followed down the hall after it disappeared. A section of the wall was tilted out. You could squeeze through the hole. I went into the passageway, but a cold wind almost put out my candle." I hesitated in the telling. I did not like to admit my timidity, even to my husband. "I grew frightened and came back out."

He crushed me to him. "Thank God! Tonight you must stay in your bed. Tomorrow we will find the door and the passageway."

I shook my head. "It's no use. I looked for it today, but I could not find it."

"We'll search again tomorrow." He stared at me intently. "I want your word that you will not leave this bed."

He looked so worried that my heart was touched. "You have it," I said.

"Good." He gave me another kiss. "Be a good wife now and obey me. Your tea should be up shortly."

I watched him go. Then I finished undressing and climbed into bed. I thought it very unlikely that I would do much sleeping that night. The ghost would know I was alone, but I determined that this time I would listen to Richard. This time I would stay safe in my bed, no matter what.

Before long the maid came up with the tea. I poured a cup and sipped slowly. Yes, I would be awake all night, waiting for Richard's return. I finished my tea and set the cup down. I could not believe it, but I was already feeling sleepy.

I checked the candles. There were plenty in the drawer. Then I found myself staring at the candle's flame. It was so beautiful I could hardly take my eyes from it.

Suddenly I jerked and opened my eyes. To my surprise I realized I had been sleeping sitting up. I slid down among the pillows. The urge to sleep would not be denied. I had to let my eyes close.

My dreams were nightmarish, far worse than any I had ever had. In my dream I heard a noise and tried to get out of bed, but my head was so heavy and my legs would not support me. The parts of my body were like strangers to me. They ignored my commands.

In my dream I called for Richard, but he did not come. There was only blackness and the suffocating feeling that

I could not breathe. I tried to move, but I was paralyzed.

Then a stranger appeared. He was dressed all in black, and a black hood swathed his head. He did not speak a single word, but wrapped me in a great cloak that covered my head. I struggled for air, for freedom, but the stranger was strong, much stronger than I in my weakened condition.

There was a lapse of time in which I could remember nothing. Then the cold night air revived me a little. Because of the cloak over my head, I could not see; but a man's arm was around me, and a curious rocking motion made me slightly ill. Finally, I realized I was on horseback.

Again I slept, but my slumber was shattered by the sudden stopping of the horse. I tried to understand this peculiar dream, but my mind was cloudy. I could not think clearly at all.

Suddenly I felt myself falling, but before I could cry out, I hit something soft. I fought the entangling folds of the cloak, but by the time I had freed my head, I could see nothing but a dark figure on a light horse, galloping away.

What a strange dream. I lay down upon the ground, wrapped the cloak around me, and slept.

I do not know how much later it was when I awoke. When I did, I saw that I was not in my bedchamber. My head ached fiercely. Hazily, I recalled my dreams, and then the realization hit me. I saw that the dreams were not dreams at all, but reality filtered through my drugged mind. Someone had drugged me—it must have been in the tea—entered my chamber and carried me off.

I sniffed and looked around. The air held the tang of salt. The sea must be nearby. The sand under my bare feet was cold and wet. I shivered. My nightdress was also wet, and the cloak was not much drier.

I huddled in the cloak, trying to think logically, trying to piece it together. What did this person hope to accomplish by abducting me and leaving me here?

It was true that I was afraid of the dark; but the night was bright with moonlight, and besides, no one knew of my fear but Richard. And even with my fear, I could manage until morning when I could make my way back to the castle.

I leaped to my feet. Why wait till morning? Papa had taught me how to navigate by the stars. There was no need to sit here shivering. I would be home before daybreak.

I looked around. Though I could smell it, I could not see the ocean. Sand stretched in every direction. Tall strands of grass swayed on softly swelling dunes, and in the moonlight the sand glittered like molten gold.

It was actually very pretty. If I had not been cold and wet, and fiercely angry, I might have been more appreciative. As it was, I spared only a passing thought for its beauty. All my concentration was on the stars.

Finally I nodded. The castle lay in one direction, the sea in another.

I was cold and tired. My head ached abominably. I wanted just to climb into my bed and sleep, but first I had to get to it.

I wrapped the cloak carefully around me. Because the stranger had needed to keep me from seeing him, he had had to leave me the cloak. How fortunate for me, I thought grimly.

It is usually better to be angry than to be afraid. Deliberately, I fueled my anger. Richard was going to hear about this! It was high time he took proper care of his wife. If he had been with me, this would not have happened. The ghost had never bothered me when Richard was there.

My direction set, I started out. The sand was damp under my bare feet. The night air was chill.

Since I had no idea how far the stranger had brought me, I also had no idea how far I would have to walk, but I was determined.

Then I remembered. The quicksand! The thought frightened me so that I stopped in midstride and almost fell. Perhaps that was it. The stranger meant for me to blunder into quicksand, and whatever I knew—or he thought I knew—would perish with me.

My legs gave out suddenly, and I sat down, right in the wet sand. If this was the stranger's intent—and it certainly seemed likely—then he had probably dropped me near a place where there was quicksand.

The beautiful golden sand took on sinister qualities. How could I take another step when the sucking sands might swallow me up?

The night air was quite chill. Even with the protection of the cloak, I was shivering. If only I knew more about this treacherous sand. There must be some way to recognize it.

Logic, I told myself. You must use logic. So I set myself to recall everything I knew about the subject, and pitifully little it was. Richard had told me that the sands could not be distinguished from others—until they were stepped into.

I certainly did not want to discover their whereabouts in such a dangerous fashion. I sighed. If the only way I could tell the dangerous areas was to let myself be sucked into one of them, then I was doomed to wait here till someone found me. There must be another way.

Of course! The quicksand would swallow anything. All I needed was a good heavy rock. I would drop it before me to test the way.

I looked around me. The moonlight made the beach shimmer. I squinted against the brightness, looking for a rock. I could see none within reaching distance, but about ten feet away lay one that looked just the right size.

Slowly and carefully I got to my feet. If I could just get to that rock. . . . I tested each footstep before I moved forward. Even so, by the time I reached the rock, I was soaked with sweat. I could never have made it home like that; the tension was too great for any human being to long endure.

I fell to my knees in the sand and pried the rock loose. I was panting for breath, and I hardly knew if I could go on; but I knew I must.

No one would come looking for me. No one even knew I was gone. I could hope for no help till long after daybreak.

I got to my feet and fixed on the stars again. Then I rolled the stone a few feet and followed it, rolled it a few more and followed it. No doubt this sounds like a long and tedious process, as indeed it was, but I had never been able to sit and wait. I had to do something to help myself.

I stopped to rest often. The stone grew heavier and heavier, but still I pressed on. Twice, just as I rolled the stone, clouds covered the moon, and the stone's path was obscured from my sight. So, when I could see again, I could only hope that I was walking in the right place.

The sky was beginning to streak with dawn's light when I once more sat down to rest. I was bone weary and did not know how much longer I could go on. And to make matters worse, I was starting to think some very uncomfortable thoughts. When I reached the castle, what then? Would I be safe? Or would I be in more danger?

Sitting there, I actually, for a small space, contemplated following the ghost's advice and leaving Greyden Castle. I would have done it in a minute if I could have persuaded Richard to go with me.

But heartsore and weary as I was, I knew that I could never leave Richard. I had married him for better or for worse, and only Death could part us.

I shivered. If the ghost had succeeded, if I had panicked and run wildly off into the quicksand, Death *would* have parted us.

Morbid, I told myself. I was getting as morbid as Penrose. Soon I would be writing odes to Death and his coming. Weary as I was, the thought made me smile a little. No doubt my poetry would be even worse than Penrose's.

Once more I lifted the rock and struggled to my feet. Then I heard it: the distant neighing of a horse.

My first thought was to call out and run toward the sound, but second thoughts stopped me. Why would anyone be riding on the beach at daybreak? Maybe my abductor had come back to see the job properly finished. Trembling, I dropped to my knees and huddled there, hardly daring to breathe.

The first light of dawn touched the beach, and far in the distance, silhouetted against the rising sun, I saw the figure of a horseman. Even in silhouette I could see that the horse was light. My heart rose up in my throat. I looked wildly around for a place to hide, but there was none. For the first time I gave in to despair.

"Vanessa! Vanessa!"

Hope sprang into my heart. That was Richard's voice. Once more I got to my feet. "Here!" I shouted. "Richard, I am here!"

It took him only minutes to cover the distance between us. He swung down and gathered me in his arms. "My love! I thought I had lost you."

Now that I was safe, I could give way to the tears I'd been holding back, but I did not cry long. I had too many questions to ask. "How—how did you find me?"

Richard stroked my tangled hair. "I came back to the room early. Rosamund was sleeping soundly, and I wanted to be with you. When I found you gone, I was terrified."

The stallion thrust his head between us, and I rubbed his nose. "But why did you come here?"

Richard frowned. "My first thought was that you had followed the ghost again, but then I saw the candle was still there. Even you would not follow without a candle. So I surmised that someone had taken you."

"Someone did!"

"Did you see who?"

"No. He wore a dark hood. And . . . and I believe I was drugged." I put my hands to my throbbing head. "At first I thought it was all a strange dream. Then I woke up and found myself in the sand."

Richard pressed me close. "My God, Vanessa! You are soaked."

"Nightdresses are not much protection against the elements, but he had wrapped me in a cloak so I had that."

"We must get you home," Richard said.

He set me on the stallion's back and swung up behind me. His arms closed around me protectively. As I leaned back against him, I asked, "Richard?"

232

"Yes, dear?"

"Why did you search for me here—on the beach?"

His voice sounded strange. "I didn't."

"I don't understand."

"I was frantic. I didn't know where to look or what to do. Finally, I went to the stable, and Toby told me the story of a horse who found his master when he was lost in a snowstorm. The horse seemed my only hope. So I showed your handkerchief to the stallion. Then I saddled him and gave him his head."

I sighed. "He found me. Mercury found me."

"Yes, dear." Richard's lips were warm on my neck.

"That should prove to people what a good horse—"

"Vanessa, perhaps it would be wiser not to talk about this." Richard's voice sounded strained.

"But the servants will talk. You know how that is."

"Only Gerson and Toby know you were missing." He sighed. "There has been so much talk about us. And all of it bad."

I thought of Mrs. Brewster. "Perhaps not all of it," I said. But I could appreciate his thinking. "I shall not mention it," I assured him, "but I cannot believe no one saw you leaving the castle. Word will probably be out before we reach home."

Toby saw us coming and rushed out, his face wreathed in a great smile. "He did it!" he cried. "The stallion found her."

"Yes," I said. "And thank you, Toby, for your help."

The boy bobbed his head. "'Tweren't nothing, really. His Grace, he were near out of his mind. And I just thought to trust the horse. Horses is smarter'n we give 'em credit for."

I smiled at that. "You're quite right, Toby. Horses are wonderful."

Richard swung down and reached up for me. It was pleasant to feel solid ground beneath my feet, ground that I could be sure would not swallow me up.

Leaving the stallion to Toby, we walked toward the castle together, our arms around each other.

Gerson opened the door, his face stolid.

"Hot water," Richard ordered. "Right away."

The butler nodded and turned toward the kitchen.

Now that I was safe, my strength began to desert me. I faltered and swayed, grabbing the bannister.

"Here now." Richard swung me up in his arms. "You're exhausted."

I did not argue. Right then I didn't feel as though I could take another step.

Soon my husband had me in my room. He stripped off my wet sandy nightdress and rubbed me with a blanket. By the time the hot water arrived, warmth was returning to my body. Richard dismissed the maid and washed me carefully with his own hands.

He pulled a fresh nightdress over my head. "But it is daylight," I objected.

He dropped a kiss on my nose and tucked me into bed. "So it is," he said. "But I think you'd best stay abed this morning."

He began to undo his cravat. "And I believe I'll join you."

His smile warmed me clear to my bones

"Nothing more is going to happen," he said, his voice firm, "because I am never going to leave you alone at night again. Never. I promise you."

Chapter Nineteen

As the day began I nursed Richard's promise to me and I slept.

When I woke, Richard was gone. Perhaps I should have been more upset about what had happened to me, but I had always been a stalwart sort. Papa always said I bounced back quickly. I was deeply in love with my husband, who had just that morning given me ample proof of his love for me. Perhaps even then I was carrying the child I had promised him. Our child.

I smiled and stretched. Then I rose, dressed, and went downstairs to silence my stomach, which was insisting that it had been overlong since last night's dinner.

I found the breakfast room empty; but though it was past noon, Gerson soon provided me with an ample repast, and I settled down to fill my stomach.

Some time later, I put down my empty cup and pushed back my chair. Now I felt I was ready to face another day.

Hardly had I reached my chair in the library when Gerson appeared. "Miss Varish has come to call, Your Grace."

I masked my surprise. "With the vicar?"

"No, Your Grace. Miss Varish is alone."

Something about that did not sit well with me, but as the duchess of Greyden I could hardly refuse the vicar's sister admittance. "Show her in," I said.

She came, wearing a plain black bonnet suitable for visiting the dead. It was so different from the bonnet she had last worn that I felt it must portend something dire. Still, I forced myself to smile. "Miss Varish, how kind of you to call."

She selected a chair and settled into it. Her little black eyes searched my face, and my heart fell. This visit was clearly not a coincidence. Cressadine Varish had heard something, and she was here to discover whatever else she could.

"You poor dear," she began. "Such a terrible experience."

A frontal assault. I raised an eyebrow and laughed. "Whatever are you talking about?"

"There's no need for dissimulation," she whispered. Her eyes were like a weasel's, quick and full of malice. "The whole village *knows*."

I swallowed a sigh. I hadn't thought Richard would be successful in hiding what had happened from the village gossips. Obviously something had been going about.

But I had made a promise to my husband. So I would tell Miss Varish nothing. Besides, though it was perhaps unChristian, I knew I should enjoy thwarting her plans.

I smiled sweetly. "What does the village know?" I inquired. "Do tell me. I am always eager to know the latest news. The French have not been acting up again, have they?"

Miss Varish gave me a look that would have melted a

lesser woman, but I, having recently survived encounters with a ghost and an abductor, was not about to let a mere woman get the best of me.

The vicar's sister snorted, an indelicate sound, and sighed loudly. "There is no use your denying it, my dear. I have come here to get the facts." She leaned forward, like a snake just before it strikes. "With the facts I can clear everything up."

I did not like the sound of the word "deny." What cause had I—except Richard's request which she could know nothing about—to deny anything? For a moment I almost forgot myself and decided that it would be better to give her the true story.

Then she leaned forward again, licking her lips, and I knew that the facts would not help us. Anything I might tell Cressadine Varish would be twisted and molded to fit the story *she* wanted to tell. It would be best to stick to my guns and not let her know anything.

I picked up my needlepoint. "What facts are these?" I asked, measuring a length of thread.

Miss Varish's nose wrinkled. "The facts of last night."

I frowned, as though to concentrate. "Last night. Let me see. Last night the family had dinner. His Grace was late getting home, some business in the village. He came in at bedtime. We talked a little and went to bed."

Her eyes looked as though they would start from her head. Her lips parted avidly. "And then . . ."

I could not help myself. She was such a terribly provoking woman. I put my hand upon my breast and affected dismay. "Really, Miss Varish! Such an indelicate question!"

For the first time I saw her falter and a flush rise to her pale cheeks. Then she gathered her forces. "I was not inquiring into your matrimonial life," she said stiffly.

I pretended surprise. "Oh, you were not? I beg your pardon, then. It certainly sounded to me as though you were."

She frowned. "I assure you, I was most certainly not. I have no interest in such details."

I contented myself with a soft "Indeed."

In spite of her embarrassment, Miss Varish did not give up. "It was the *other* events of the night to which I alluded."

I put on my most innocent face, the one Papa said would convince anyone but him. "I slept. I dreamed." I paused and sighed. "I am dreadfully sorry, but I cannot recount my dreams for you. I neglected to remember them. And then this morning I awoke."

For an instant I saw the malice deep in her eyes. This woman hated me, and I really had no understanding of why that should be so.

Then, just as I thought I had bested her, the door opened. I knew before I turned that Miss Varish's visit was no longer in vain. Her eyes had widened, and they gleamed with a kind of avarice.

"Softly, darkly, comes my love." Rosamund approached the fire, crooning to herself. "Softly, darkly, and his name is Death."

Miss Varish's mouth closed with a sharp snap. I had no hope that the words of Rosamund's song had escaped her. Before nightfall the whole village would know what Richard's sister had been singing.

And, of course, Rosamund was wearing her orange ball gown. Either she had refused the ministrations of her maid or she had forgotten and pulled her hair down afterwards. At any rate, it hung around her face in a mad

238

tangle that made her look even wilder. She sank to the hearth rug and wrapped one lock about her finger.

"Softly, darkly," she sang, wrapping the hair. "Comes my love," she sang, unwrapping it.

The gown's brilliant color made her pale skin and dark-circled eyes even more noticeable. She looked, indeed, as if her lover Death had already marked her for his own.

I wondered what I could do, but a look at Miss Varish's face assured me that nothing short of a visit from Death himself would keep her from spreading this latest bit of gossip over the whole of the parish.

The door opened again. Penrose looked around. "Mama?"

She appeared not to hear him, but went on, staring into the flames and singing. Calmly Penrose nodded to Miss Varish. He cast me a short apologetic look, then crossed the room to his mother. "Mama, come. It's time for our walk."

Rosamund looked up at him. For a moment she frowned. It was almost as though she had to call a part of herself back from some far distant shore. Then recognition came into her eyes. "Yes, Penrose. I am ready."

She took the hand he stretched out to her and got to her feet. "I like to walk," she said. "The sun is warm. The flowers are pretty." And Penrose and his mother passed from the room.

I reached for the bellpull. "I'll just order some tea," I said, striving to recreate some sense of the normal.

But Miss Varish could not wait for tea. She got hastily to her feet. "No, no, Your Grace. Do not bother. I'll just be on my way."

Off she hurried, to begin her rounds. I sank back into my chair, not knowing whether to laugh or cry.

Rosamund could not help her affliction, and certainly her entrance had driven all thoughts of me from Miss Varish's mind.

But I knew it was only temporary. Once she had spread her story about Rosamund, Miss Varish would remember me again. I wished I had been more successful in discovering what she *did* know, but the vicar's sister had told me little more than I had told her.

I sighed and rang for Gerson and a pot of tea. I was still sipping my first cup when he came back to say, "Another visitor, Your Grace. The dressmaker. She says it's urgent."

"Send her in."

Mrs. Brewster stopped right inside the door, her eyes downcast. "Mayhap I shouldn't have come," she began, her voice trembling.

I put on a bright smile. "Mrs. Brewster, do come in and sit down. May I offer you some tea?"

She looked startled. "No, no, Your Grace. I just came—" She advanced slowly and took the chair I indicated. "I know you can't stop it," she said, "but I thought you'd want to know about it."

"Know what?" I inquired, wishing that I had stayed abed. Whatever this was, it could not be good.

"It's that Miss Varish." The dressmaker stiffened in indignation. "Thinks she's God Himself, she does, giving orders right and left."

It was plain that my earlier suspicions were accurate. Miss Varish and Mrs. Brewster had been foes long before I arrived in Cornwall.

"She can be a little overbearing," I agreed. "What has she done now?"

Mrs. Brewster flushed and looked around as though

she feared someone would hear her. "It's an embarrassing thing to recount, Your Grace."

I nodded. "I quite understand, but I assure you, it is all right. Just go ahead and tell me."

The dressmaker took a deep breath. "Well, Your Grace, she was around this morning, before decent folk were even out of their beds, telling everyone how your husband found you on the beach after midnight, wearing naught but a nightdress. And how he dragged you home in disgrace, you being worse than—"

She faltered and flushed scarlet. "These are *her* words, you mind. Worse than that sister of yours." She gazed down at the floor again, afraid, no doubt, to look at me.

So that was it. I made my voice firm, courteous. "Thank you, Mrs. Brewster, for coming here to tell me. That took courage."

She looked up quickly, almost startled by my gratitude. Perhaps she had thought to feel my anger, but I could not blame the messenger for the bad news she carried. "The story is not true," I said.

"Indeed, Your Grace. I knew it couldn't be." She drew herself up. "I know a lady when I see one, and you're a lady, right enough. Besides—" she smiled—"I saw the way you treat the little one. The way she loves you." She shook her head. "You're not the sort to go sneaking out in the middle of the night. I'd never believe such a thing of you."

I kept my face calm, but my mind whirled. This information put things in a very different perspective. If I told Mrs. Brewster the truth, she would see that it spread. Undoubtedly many would prefer Miss Varish's version, but some, perhaps, might have second thoughts. Perhaps the story of an abductor would make people

241

think twice before accusing Richard of Caroline's death.

Richard had not wanted anyone to know, but that was to keep people from talking about us. Since they were already talking, and passing on lies, surely my telling the true story could do no harm.

Mrs. Brewster got to her feet. "I'll be going now," she said, obviously still troubled. "I just had to do what I could."

It was her actions that helped me make my decision. She had not poked or pried, or asked for any information. She had come only to help me. "Mrs. Brewster?"

"Yes, Your Grace?"

"Sit down again. Please. I have something to tell you. But only if you promise to repeat it to everyone you can."

Half an hour later she was on her way, and feeling quite satisfied with myself, I went off to the nursery to play with Sarah.

We had admired our matching gowns, chosen the day before, and were arranging the doll's hair in a style like Sarah's when the door flew open with a bang. I got quickly to my feet and turned to face my husband. Richard's face was livid.

"Why," he cried, quite ignoring the child who crept behind my skirts. "Why have you disobeyed my wishes?"

Sarah gave a little whimper. I knew how she must feel. Richard was a frightening sight, especially to a little one.

"One moment, Richard." I took Sarah by the hand and led her to the other room where Creighton had been dozing. "You stay here," I told the child. "I will be back later."

Sarah clutched at my skirt. "Don't go, Nessie," she begged. "He'll hurt you. Please!"

Carefully I pried her fingers loose. "Now, Sarah, don't be silly. Your father is upset over something. That's all."

She shook her head, and tears welled in her eyes. "He yelled at my mama. And she's gone."

I heard Creighton's quick intake of breath, but I had no time for this. "Sarah," I said firmly, "that will be enough. I am going to see what your father wants. I'll be back later."

Leaving her weeping in the nurse's arms, I marched out, past Richard and into the hall. My husband followed me.

"Vanessa," he began.

I kept walking. "I should prefer to have this discussion in the privacy of our room," I said. "Here, even the walls have ears."

He kept his silence till the door of my room closed behind him. "Now," he thundered, "I wish to know why you went against my express wishes."

I turned to face him. If this was one of his rages, it was indeed frightening, but I refused to be cowed by him. After all, I had faced Papa. "First," I said. "I was not the one who spread the story. Cressadine Varish was here this afternoon."

He cursed, and one part of my mind noted with pleasure his inventiveness.

"So you told her everything!"

"Indeed, I did not!" I sighed and looked at him mournfully. "Really, Richard. How foolish do you think I am?"

He looked a little sheepish, as though he was beginning to regret his outburst. "Then what *did* you tell her?"

243

I sighed again. "I told her nothing. And I was still telling her nothing when Rosamund came wandering in, wearing her orange ball gown and singing one of her songs about Death."

Richard frowned.

"After that," I continued, "Miss Varish left. Rather hurriedly."

Richard looked puzzled. "But the particulars are all over the parish."

"Which story did you hear?" I asked. "Was it the true one or the one where you discovered me on the beach with my lover and dragged me home in disgrace?"

If I had thought his previous curse inventive, I found this one even more so. At another time I might have congratulated him on it.

When he had finished, he crossed the room to take me in his arms. "Tell me who is spreading this slander. I will see him silenced." He scowled. "Or run through with my sword."

I laughed. I could not help it. The image of Miss Varish, wearing one of her flowered bonnets and dangling from Richard's sword, struck me as amusing. "You cannot do that," I said, reminding myself that this was serious business. "You cannot run the vicar's sister through. It just isn't done."

His expression lightened a little. "You're right, of course. But are you sure it was she?"

"Indeed. After Miss Varish left, having learned nothing except what her eyes told her about Rosamund, I had still another caller."

Richard shook his head. "I cannot begin to guess who it was."

"It was the dressmaker. She came to warn me of the

244

story Miss Varish was circulating." I looked him straight in the eye. "Since a story was already about, I thought it best to tell Mrs. Brewster the true one. I specifically asked her to spread it far and wide."

Richard frowned and I held my breath. Had I mistaken my husband?

"I see your reasoning," he said finally.

Slowly I released my breath. Then I kissed his cheek. "I was confident you would. Else I would not have gone against my promise to you."

"Yes." He gathered me closer. "Nessie, my dear wife—"

The door flew open. Sarah rushed in, her arms flailing, and began kicking and screaming at her father. "Stop! Stop! Don't hurt Nessie."

Richard could not have looked more surprised had he actually seen a ghost. I stepped between the two of them and took the weeping child in my arms. "Sarah, my dear. I am quite all right." I wiped at her tears. "Look now. See? I am fine."

Slowly her sobs eased. She touched my cheek as though to reassure herself. "He didn't hurt you?"

"Of course not, my dear. Your father would not hurt me."

She sniffled. "Nessie, are you sure?"

Richard came to us then and lifted the child out of my arms. "Sarah, Sarah," he said sadly. "I would not hurt Vanessa. You must know that."

She looked long into his eyes, then she managed a watery smile. "Yes, Father. I know. But I was afraid."

He gave her a questioning smile. "Are you afraid now?"

"No, Dada." The childish word took them both by

surprise. For a moment there was an awful silence. Richard's frown returned, and Sarah looked as though she would weep again. "I am sorry, Father," she mumbled.

He nodded and set her down. "Run along now. You've seen that your precious Nessie is safe."

Sarah looked at me, and I nodded and motioned her out. "Go back to the nursery," I said. "Creighton will be looking for you."

"Yes, Nessie."

I watched her go, and then I turned to my husband. "Thank you, Richard."

He frowned again. "For what?"

"For reassuring the child. Hers has been a difficult existence. We are all that she has, you know."

"Then," said Richard, his frown returning full force, "God pity the child."

His words could not reach me; for I had seen the look in his eyes, and I was sure. Richard loved his daughter. I had only to make him admit it.

Chapter Twenty

Though I studied the matter day and night, I was unable to think of a way to bring Richard and his daughter together. He still refused to visit the nursery, and I did not like to bring the child to the table where she was exposed to the dowager's sharp tongue and Rosamund's distressing songs. But I did not give up. I simply bided my time.

The magistrate came to call. He discussed the events of that strange night with Richard, spoke a few words to me, and left. The talk in the village died down—or so Richard informed me—and I began to hope that people had found something else to speculate about. Our life went on.

True to his promise, Richard did not leave me alone again at night. Every morning we rode together, and every night we spent in my bed. Soon, I promised myself as I woke each morning, soon I could tell Richard there would be a child.

The rest of the family did not change. The dowager still cut at me at every opportunity, and Rosamund still drifted around the castle, her brightly colored gowns making her look even more pale and wan.

Penrose and I tried to get her outside, to walk, but more and more she seemed not to hear us. One day after a particularly futile attempt to get her to walk with us, Penrose motioned to me to follow him. We crossed to the other side of the room. Tears stood in the boy's eyes. "I'm losing her," he said, his voice thick. "She is slipping away from me."

"Oh, Penrose, I am so sorry." I longed to take the poor boy in my arms and comfort him as I would have Sarah, but I knew I dared not. He was a man now, and he must behave as one.

"Don't say it's for the best." He glared at me through his tears.

My surprise was genuine. "Of course I won't. I should never say such a thing."

He swallowed. "Grandmother does."

I put my hand upon his arm. It trembled with his emotion. "Penrose, I will tell you what I told Sarah. Your grandmother is ill."

He pulled away, plainly unbelieving.

"It's true. Not in the same way as your mother." I sighed. "In a way your grandmother's illness is worse."

"What are you talking about?"

I hoped he would believe me. This had helped Sarah. Perhaps it would help him. "Your grandmother is unable to love. Just as my sister was unable to love."

Penrose eyed me suspiciously. "I have never heard of such an illness."

I shrugged. "Perhaps not. But you have seen the evidence of it. You've been living with it all your life."

He frowned. "But Grandmother loves Uncle Roland."

I should have known that was coming. Perhaps I did,

for my answer sprang to my lips. "Does she? Really? Is it love to cut your child off from his brothers and sisters? To smother him?"

Slowly Penrose lost his frown. "I think you are right about Grandmother," he said finally. "But my mother is fading, and I still cannot help her." The boy's face held such pain.

"I know. That hurts a great deal. I hurt, too," I said, "because I cannot bring Sarah and her father together. Because I love them both."

Penrose nodded. He looked into my eyes. "Vanessa, I— I—"

"What is it?"

"When you first came here, I— I hated you."

This did not surprise me, but I asked, "Why? You did not even know me."

The boy's eyes were clouded with regret. "Your sister—she was so nasty to my mother. I thought you would be like her, saying mean and vicious things."

I smiled at him. "I'm glad you've found out that I am not."

He nodded. "Vanessa?"

"Yes?"

"I'm sorry."

"That's all right. I've forgotten whatever you said."

His gaze faltered. "No, I didn't mean that."

"Then what?"

"When you first came, I put— I put a dead bird outside your door. I'm sorry for that. Will you forgive me?" The boy looked so stricken.

"Of course," I said. Then an idea came to me. "Did you dress in white or speak to me through the door?"

He paled so that I thought he might sink to the floor.

"God, Vanessa, no! Did someone do that?"

Belatedly I cursed my penchant for speaking before I thought. I tried to smooth things over. "Yes, but don't worry about it. It must have been a joke."

He frowned. "Do you think—might it have been Mama?"

I stared at him. "I don't know. Do you think it might?"

He sighed and tugged at a lock of hair. "Mama does strange things, especially when the moon is full."

I thought of the person who had abducted me. Rosamund was too frail to have lifted me onto a horse, but the ghost and the abductor need not be the same—or even connected. Perhaps more than one person wanted me out of Greyden Castle.

I would think about that later. Now the boy looked so distraught I had to help him. "It couldn't have been Rosamund," I said. "Richard was with her."

"That doesn't mean she couldn't have done it," Penrose said. "She often slips away from us."

"Well," I replied, and I never meant words more, "I don't believe it was she."

Penrose studied his coat sleeve. Then he raised his eyes to mine. "Thank you," he said. "For trying to help her. I shall never forget it."

Before I could say more he was gone. It was only then that I thought to wonder and to wish that I had asked him if he believed the crying babe to be a real ghost.

Just as I turned to follow him, Sarah came in, her eyes shining. She waved her hand, a cloud of color fluttered through the air. "Look, Nessie! Ribbons! Lots and lots of ribbons!"

I crossed the room and stooped to admire them.

"They're beautiful. So many different colors."

"To match each of our gowns." Sarah was so excited that she danced about.

"Where did you get all these lovely ribbons?"

"Uncle Roland brought them. Isn't it wonderful?"

I swallowed my disappointment. I knew Richard would not bring the child such a gift. I knew he still wanted nothing to do with her, and yet in that first instant, I had not been able to keep from hoping.

"Yes, indeed," I said. I looked up.

Roland was standing in the doorway, his face wreathed in a smile. He came into the room, still smiling. "It's good to see the child so happy." He sighed and his smile faded. "If only Richard—"

I nodded and straightened. "I know. It pains me, too. But we must hope. And pray."

Roland's eyes clouded. "Pray? I don't think prayer will help Richard."

I felt a stab of foreboding. Roland looked so strange. Could *his* mind be going, too? "Whatever do you mean?"

For a second he stared at me, then his face cleared. "Oh, nothing, Vanessa. Nothing."

I could not let it pass. Sarah was engrossed in plaiting her ribbons. She paid no regard to us.

"Were you thinking of his rages?" I asked. I didn't know why I should ask such a question. Richard's rages seemed to be a thing of the past. At least, I had never fully experienced one.

"No," Roland said. "Actually—" He paused and looked embarrassed. "There are still some people, Richard's enemies, who are spreading talk. This tale of abduction—"

So Roland had heard it, too. Mrs. Brewster had done

her work well.

"It was not a tale," I said. "It was the truth."

He looked upset, as though I had insulted him in some way. "Of course it was. But, Vanessa, why should someone do such a thing?"

I glanced at the child and lowered my voice. "I do not know. Except—I think perhaps it was Caroline's lover."

His eyes widened. "Her lover?"

I nodded. "I think she was meeting a servant in the North Tower."

He looked astonished. "A servant?"

Now that I knew him better, I could say to him what I had not dared to say before. "Yes," I whispered. "Caroline was not over nice in such matters."

A wave of revulsion swept over his features. I hurried on. "I think this servant believes I know something—something that might implicate him."

"And do you?"

"Of course not. Caroline never confided in me. She did not even like me."

Roland nodded. "I suspect she liked few women. She seemed to prefer the company of men."

A suspicion struck me. Why had I never thought of it before? "Did Caroline—" I could not go on. It was too embarrassing.

Roland caught the import of my question. "Yes," he said sadly. "She approached me." He shuddered. "Of course I said no. My own brother's wife—besides"—his smile warmed me—"she was not like you, Nessie. She was cold and selfish. Such a woman can only give a man pain. As she did Richard."

I nodded. It was a relief to know that at least Richard did not have this cause for enmity toward his twin.

"Vanessa?"

"Yes, Roland?" There was a curious look on his face, one I did not like.

"There is something—I have been wanting to tell you—I feel—"

Then Sarah ran into his arms. "Oh, Uncle Roland," she cried. "These are the prettiest ribbons in the whole world!"

He smiled at her. "I'm glad you like them." He stroked her long blond curls. "Why don't you go now and show them to your nurse?"

Sarah laughed. How rarely had I heard the child laugh. "Yes, Uncle. She will be happy. She likes pretty things." Sarah looked at me. "Are you coming, Nessie?"

I started to follow her, but Roland put a detaining hand on my arm. "Nessie will be there in a little while. You run along."

The child skipped off, clutching her ribbons, and I eased my arm out from under Roland's hand. I felt a sort of uneasiness. There was so much warmth in his smile, and he was standing so close to me.

"What is it?" I asked, wanting to get this scene over. Nervousness made my voice crack, and I took a backward step.

"Vanessa, this is very awkward. You are my brother's wife."

I did not like the sound of this, but I did not know how to stop him. And, as any woman would, I wanted to know what he meant to say.

He sighed. "From the first day I met you—when you flew into my arms and kissed me—"

"I thought you were my husband," I interjected hastily. "I did not know he had a twin."

Roland nodded. "And I did not know that you were his new wife. But from the moment our lips met—"

Heat flooded my body. "Roland, stop! You must not say these things to me."

He looked hurt, dejected; his dark eyes gleamed with tears. "Vanessa, my dear. You mistake my meaning. I would never— I did not intend to suggest—"

He looked so crestfallen that I hastened to apologize. "I'm sorry I misunderstood you, Roland, but then, what do you mean?"

"I only want you to know that I care for you deeply."

I raised a warning hand, and he hurried to add, "As a brother should. But if you ever need a protector—"

"Why should I need a protector?" I demanded. This whole conversation was quite unnerving.

"I do not know." He sighed. "I am doing this so badly. I only wanted you to know that you have a friend. You can always come to me. Always. No matter what."

He did not advance any nearer to me, and I pondered his words for a few moments. "I think I understand," I said then. "Thank you."

In a way it was comforting to know that I had such a good friend in the household—that someone truly cared for me. Someone besides Richard, of course.

Roland pressed my hand, but only for an instant. "I shall say no more about this. I just wanted you to know."

Then he left, and God help me, I could not keep myself from remembering his kiss. But he had not presumed upon that kiss. He was offering me nothing more than his friendship, and as God well knew, I needed that.

Richard was away most of the day. After Roland left

me, I went to the nursery. Sarah and I sorted out her ribbons, putting matching ones in her hair and her doll baby's. The child's joy was heartwarming, but it also saddened me. Why couldn't Richard be more like his twin? Why couldn't *he* love a child that wasn't his?

I had no answers to my questions, of course, and that night, after we had gone to bed and I lay snug in the circle of Richard's arm, the questions came back to plague me.

Sarah was not my child; yet I loved her deeply, and that love was in spite of, not because of, Caroline being her mother. In her entire life Caroline had never done a nice thing, a sisterly thing, for me. Indeed, she had treated me very shabbily, but I did not hold that against a helpless little girl.

I sighed, hoping Richard would hear and ask me why; but he did not, and soon the sound of his even breathing told me that he slept.

I eased myself out of his arm and tried to find a comfortable position in the big bed, but no matter how I arranged myself, sleep would not come.

I counted sheep. I counted horses. Horses were more interesting, but brought me no closer to slumber. Still I lay, staring into the darkness, wide awake as if it had been noon.

And so I knew I did not dream it. Out of the darkness came the wail of a baby. Terror clutched at me, and I rolled close against Richard's side. He did not stir. The baby's cry had not wakened him.

What did it mean? Why was the babe crying when Richard was with me?

It could not be Penrose playing a trick. I was convinced his apology that afternoon had been genuine.

It might be Rosamund, though to what purpose I had

no idea. She seemed to be drifting farther and farther away from us. She hardly ever spoke to me, and sometimes she did not even know Penrose. Still, it might be her. The workings of her mind were now so strange and convoluted that a sane person could not hope to follow them.

The babe cried again. I tried not to shudder. Should I wake Richard so that he could hear? So that he could know it was real? But even if I woke him, I had no guarantee he would hear the babe. It might not cry again.

I bit my bottom lip. Perhaps only certain people could hear it. I had better let Richard sleep. I was safe as long as I was with him, and according to the legend, the babe had to cry three nights in a row before Death would come.

The silence stretched on and on. I lay in the darkness, wishing I knew what to do to stop this. I could not, as Penrose's poem and the legend said, give up my own life to console the babe.

Under the covers my hands crept to my belly. Soon, soon, I prayed, a new life would be growing there. A life I hoped would connect Richard and his daughter.

I meant to include Sarah in everything that had to do with our child. I hoped—and prayed—that when Richard saw her helping me and loving the little one, he would forget his animosity. I expect I hoped, too, that seeing the baby would awaken in him memories of Sarah's babyhood and the love he had felt for her then. Given Richard's adamant stand on the matter, my hopes seemed futile; but they were all I had, and I nursed them carefully.

Once more the babe cried. My heart turned over. Could it be the servant who had been Caroline's lover, trying to frighten me? But surely by now he realized that

I knew nothing, that I was no threat to him.

If only I had some way to search him out. Did Gerson know who he was? Butlers usually knew everything that went on in a household, and a loyal one would have informed his master. When Caroline met someone regularly, Gerson most probably had known.

But he had not told Richard. That meant that he did not know or—I almost sat straight up in the bed—could it be Gerson himself who had been Caroline's lover? That would explain a great deal, including the stories that leaked out to Miss Varish.

My mind whirled madly, but finally, when the babe cried no more and I could come to no conclusions, fatigue overcame me and I slept, curled against Richard's side.

257

Chapter Twenty-One

I did not hear the babe again that night—or in the nights that followed. I did all I could to help Penrose with his mother, but it seemed she was getting more and more strange. It was difficult to reach her at all. Most of the time she would talk only to the invisible Jeffrey. The rest of us were not real to her.

As the full moon approached again, Richard grew silent and moody. I tried to give him an opportunity to talk about Rosamund. I mentioned her often. I spoke of the full moon. I did everything but ask him outright what he meant to do, but he did not respond to me. He remained silent and withdrawn, and I grew more and more worried.

The night that the moon came full, Rosamund wore the orange silk to dinner. The maids had reported difficulty in getting it away to be cleaned, and that certainly appeared to be the case. The hem was dirty and ripped in several places, and the bodice was spotted with food from earlier meals. I was surprised the dowager had not taken me to task for it. The dress was truly in sad shape.

But Rosamund did not notice that. She preened herself like a great lady and Richard and Penrose both paid court to her, complimenting her wildly. For a moment she seemed to regard them, then she was gone again, off in that strange world with her Jeffrey, laughing and singing her songs to him.

When the meal was served, she grew quiet. We were all quiet. Roland was absent, and for once the dowager kept her peace.

Afterwards, the others retired early to their rooms. Richard and I went silently up the stairs to our chambers. In spite of the quiet evening, my heart was heavy. Richard looked quite upset. Heaving a hugh sigh, he took off his coat.

I could bear it no longer. I had to make him talk to me. "You are worried about Rosamund," I said.

He frowned. "She will be all right. Penrose will stay with her. He shares her apartments."

His words were comforting, but I knew Richard and could see his concern. I could not let the matter rest. I had to press on. "But you are still worried."

He ran a hand through his hair. "Vanessa, I said I would not leave you alone. I gave you my word. What more do you want?"

I went and put my arms around him. If only I could wrap him safe in my love. "I know you promised. But my dear, I cannot stand to see you so concerned."

He kissed the top of my head. "I appreciate your concern, Vanessa. I know I am being ridiculous, worrying so. It's just that she gets so wild. I never know what she might do."

"I know, dear."

He heaved another sigh and began to help me with my

hooks. "Don't worry, Nessie. I will not leave you alone tonight."

"I know." I was not afraid he would break his word to me; but I was afraid that something would happen to Rosamund, and I knew that if it did, while I was keeping him from her side, in some obscure way I would hold myself responsible. It was not a pleasant prospect. Almost, I wished I could make him go to her.

Wait! There was something I could do. "Richard, put your coat back on."

He frowned. "Nessie! I said I will not leave you, and I meant it."

"There is no need," I said, refastening my hooks, "for I shall go with you."

"Of course!" His face lit up, and he grabbed me and kissed me. "Oh, Nessie. You are such a good wife. Hurry, let's go."

I reached up on tiptoe to kiss him. "One more hook, Richard."

The castle halls were cold and gloomy. A few candles were left to burn all night, but the halls seemed even darker than usual.

We hurried toward the apartments that Penrose shared with his mother, Richard almost at a run and I struggling to keep up with him.

"Ri-chard!" I panted, a stitch in my side making it difficult for me to breathe. "Please, slow down."

He shortened his stride, but only a little. I understood his alarm. I was anxious to get there myself, to be assured that his sister was safe.

The door to Rosamund's rooms stood open. Richard

hurried in. He looked in each room, but no one was there. "Gone!" he cried, turning to me. "That fool boy! Why didn't he keep her here?"

I looked around. Something white lay upon the writing desk. I crossed to it. "Richard, look! It's for you."

He broke the seal and began to read aloud.

Dear Uncle Richard,

Mama has asked me to write this to you. She has heard the haunting babe cry three nights in a row.

Richard cursed, then hurried on.

We are going. She wanted to go alone. But I must go with her. I am not afraid to die—

My heart threatened to choke me. They must not. "Die! Richard, where have they gone?"

He scanned the letter, then turned to me, his eyes wild. "He doesn't say. My God, Vanessa. Is he going to kill her?"

I tried to think. "No, no. He could not do that. Most likely she will do it herself. But why did she go out—the cliffs! The break in the wall!"

Richard dropped the letter and hurried out the door. I followed as fast as I could.

Down the halls we ran. Richard was getting farther and farther ahead of me, but I did not call out to him. He must get there. He must get there before this awful thing was done.

Just as I reached the top of the stairs, I heard the front door crash open. "Oh, please," I prayed as I rushed downward. "Let him be in time."

I hurried out the door—now standing wide—and around the corner to the pathway. It was still overgrown and tangled, but I scrambled through it as fast as I could, fighting the stitch in my side and struggling for breath.

Ahead of me I could hear the noise of Richard's passage. Then there was an awful shout. "Stop!" he cried. "Rosie, don't!"

A piercing wail almost drove me to my knees, but gasping for breath I hurried on.

Finally I came round the corner. Rosamund was nowhere in sight, but Richard and Penrose were struggling in front of the break in the wall. Back and forth they grappled, their faces contorted with their efforts. Glimpsing Penrose's terrified face, I thought for one awful moment that Richard was trying to push the boy over the edge.

Then I realized Richard was holding him back. The boy was trying to get to the cliff. "Mama!" he wailed. "Let me go!"

I wanted to help, but there was nothing I could do. Back and forth they struggled on the edge of that terrible cliff, while the rocks waited below.

My heart was in my throat, but I dared not get any nearer. Finally, Richard forced Penrose to the ground and held him there. I hurried to his side.

"Rosie," he panted. "She went over."

"My God!" Only then did I see the broken railing. I crept to the wall. Far below, a bright splash of orange spread out across the wet black rocks. Except for the gentle lapping of the waves against the silk, nothing moved. No one could have survived a fall like that.

I went back to Richard, who was still straddling

Penrose. "It's no use," I told my husband. "Rosamund is gone."

Penrose began to struggle again. "Let me up! Please! I promised to go with her."

"Penrose, no." I grasped his flailing hands and held them tight. "You must live."

His face twisted with his sobs. "How can I live without Mama? She's the only one who loved me."

"That is not true," I said severely. "I care about you. So does Richard. Else he would not have saved you."

The boy clung to my hands. "She was so miserable," he cried. "She wanted to go, and I could not let her go alone."

"I know. But Penrose, if she were well, she would want you to live. To be happy. To have the life that was denied her."

He stared at me. I couldn't tell if I was reaching him at all, but Richard could not keep him pinned there indefinitely. "If Richard lets you up, will you promise not to . . ."

He considered this for a moment, and I thought he might refuse. Then he sighed. "Yes, Vanessa. I promise."

I looked to Richard. In his eyes was misery to equal the boy's. "I wasn't in time," he said. "I grabbed, but I missed her."

I longed to help them, to ease their pain, but there was no help for this. All I could say was "Let us go back inside."

Richard frowned. "I cannot leave her—"

"Of course not. But you will need help."

"Yes, of course." Richard got to his feet and helped the boy up.

"Come," I said, herding them away from the cliff's edge. "Back inside."

We went into the library. Richard stirred up the fire and sent Gerson for men and ropes to bring up Rosamund's body. I persuaded Penrose to sit down on the divan. When the men left, he wanted to go, too, but Richard insisted that he stay with me.

"You've already made your farewells," I pointed out after they had gone. "And now your mama's spirit is free."

Penrose shivered. I took off my shawl and put it around his quaking shoulders. Then I sat down next to him.

He stared at me, his eyes wide with horror. "She said—oh, Vanessa, it was terrible. Mama said she killed Grandfather. And your sister. She said everything that went wrong at Greyden was her fault."

I thought of Rosamund telling me her father was burning in hell. And Caroline, there too. Why had Rosamund so suddenly decided to take her own life? Had she become sane long enough to realize what she had done?

"Did she say that she made the crying babe's noises?" I asked.

Penrose looked startled. "No, no. That is, I don't think so. She—she believed that her death would free the babe—like the legend said—because she went willingly. She said that in helping it, she would expiate her sins."

He buried his face in his hands. "Why didn't he let me go with her? My life has no purpose now. I know nothing but suffering and death."

This time I put my arms around him. Penrose sobbed on my shoulder like the little boy he had never had a chance to be.

"I know this does not seem possible now," I told him, "but the misery will pass. And you have one great consolation."

He raised his head. "I have?"

"Yes, indeed. You have known your mother's love. Many of us are not that fortunate."

"We are not?" His eyes met mine. "Vanessa, what do you mean?"

I made a quick decision. It was not a subject I cared to discuss, even to think about, but if it would help the boy. . . .

"Yes," I said. "I know whereof I speak. My mama did not love me."

He looked unbelieving.

"It's true," I said. "Caroline was her eldest, a copy of her own exquisite blond beauty." I sighed. "I was a gangly awkward carrot top. Mama had no time for me. I could never please her."

Penrose took my hand. "Oh, Vanessa, I am sorry. I did not know."

I shrugged. "It's all right. I had my papa's love, and it was good."

We sat in silence for a few moments while I considered the things Penrose had told me. Finally, I said, "Penrose, how could your mother have killed her father?"

He sighed and wiped at his eyes. "I do not know. I used to think that she only imagined she did it. That because she wished him dead she thought herself responsible. But when your sister was found like that—"

He swallowed. "And Mama said—she said she was

glad. And then tonight—tonight she said she killed that wicked woman." His eyes were apologetic. "That's what she always called Caroline."

The name-calling meant nothing to me. Certainly if anyone deserved such an adjective it was Caroline. Was it possible that Rosamund had killed her? "But how? How did she do it?"

"I don't know." Penrose sniffled. "She said she was sorry—for all the pain and grief she caused you. She said to tell you."

My heart almost turned over. Could Rosamund have been responsible for everything that had happened to me? Could she have brought the scent into my room, and acted the ghost, and cut the girth?

The answer to all was yes. The servants were used to seeing her in unusual places. No one would have remarked on it.

But the abductor had been so strong. How could a frail woman have lifted me, who is far from frail, onto a horse? "Do you think Rosamund was posing as a ghost to frighten me?"

Penrose considered. Finally, he sighed again. "Vanessa, I just do not know. Her mind was so different, so strange. Often she said things I could not understand. I knew all the words, but the sentences made no sense." He pulled out his handkerchief and wiped at his eyes. "I suppose she could have done just about anything. She might have feared you would hurt her. She was very fearful sometimes."

"But could she have lifted me?"

Penrose did not ask me the reason for my question. "I heard about the abduction," he said. "I don't know what Mama could do. The moon seemed to give her great

266

physical strength." He shuddered. "She talked to the babe before she—she—"

He began to cry again, great wrenching sobs. I put my arm around him. "There now, go ahead."

He did not cry long. "I must stop," he said. "The men will be returning." He wiped at his face. "I wanted to tell you before they get back. I wanted you to know. She told the babe she was coming willingly. The curse is broken."

I patted his shoulder. "Your mother was a good woman."

His eyes went wide. "How can you say that? She said she killed Grandfather."

"Penrose, that's what she said. She was ill. God knows that. He knows what she did, and He knows what was in her heart."

His bottom lip quivered. "I should have gone with her. She will be lonely."

"No, Penrose. She will be at peace. And if indeed there was a curse—which I am not entirely ready to concede—then she has lifted it, and the babe's spirit is free."

"Yes." He brightened a little, then he frowned again. "But after what she did—"

"She's safe now," I insisted. "Only God may judge her, and He is merciful."

"Even to—"

"Yes," I said quickly. "Even to her. And Penrose—"

"Yes, Vanessa?"

"I want you to remember that. And to remember that your grandmother is ill. Do not regard whatever she may say to you."

He looked about to cry again, and then he grabbed my hand and clung to it. "Thank you, Vanessa. You have helped me."

And none too soon, I thought, as I heard the front door open. Penrose leaped to his feet, casting aside my shawl. "They're back. I must go to her."

"Penrose, perhaps—" But he was already gone, and I hurried out after him.

The men had paused in the great hall, putting their blanket-wrapped burden on a hastily cleared table. Penrose lifted the edge of the blanket. Rosamund's face was peaceful and serene. For some reason the fall had not marked it at all.

I put my arm around the boy. "She is safe now," I repeated. "Remember that."

He bent and kissed her cold cheek. "Good-bye, Mama." He turned to me. "She'll wear her yellow gown."

Richard frowned. "Penrose—"

I put a hand on my husband's arm. "Of course, Penrose. I know she'd like that."

The boy's eyes told me I had understood him. In this last thing he wanted to please his mother, and I would see that he could.

Then he turned to Richard. "Did she—was it—" His voice broke and he could not go on.

"It was very quick," Richard said, his voice husky. "She felt nothing."

Penrose nodded. "That's good. She—"

"She should not have stood so near the edge. The stones are slippery." Richard's voice had changed. It carried a strange tone, almost of warning.

I saw immediately what my husband was about. Oh, why hadn't I thought to warn the boy?

There was a pause, and I thought Penrose would give it all away. Then he said, "Yes, yes. I tried to tell her. But—"

"We'll take her up to her rooms," Richard said. "We'll send for the vicar in the morning."

Penrose nodded and we watched them go. When we were sure we were alone, he turned to me. "Tell Uncle Richard what I told you," he whispered. "And tell him I won't let anyone know how Mama died." He frowned. "Do you think it wrong to deceive the vicar? You know suicides cannot be buried in the churchyard."

We all knew that. So we must keep the suicide note a secret. "Your mother did not know what she was doing," I replied, putting as much conviction as I could into my voice. "Therefore, she cannot be held responsible."

I led him back to the library where the fire still blazed brightly. "Why don't you wait here?" I asked. "When she's ready, we'll send for you."

Later, when all that we could do for Rosamund had been done, we summoned Penrose to sit with his mother and returned to our rooms.

First Richard burned Penrose's note in the fireplace. Then he ripped at his cravat. "Thank God the boy had sense enough to see what I was about—to say it was an accident—but why did he agree to such a thing in the first place?"

I put down my shawl and turned to face my husband. "He loved his mother."

"Loved her?" Richard's face contorted with anguish. "How was that love?" He tore off his coat and threw it in a chair.

My poor husband was suffering so. "Richard, she wanted to go, and she wanted to make her going worth something." I told him about the curse.

"There are no ghosts," he stormed. "She died for nothing."

I put my arms around him. "No, Richard. There was a babe—at least for Rosamund. And it is not what she did that counts as much as her reason for doing it."

He twisted free of my arms and turned away, but I followed him. "Richard, please, you must let her go. She's at peace now."

For a few moments he glared at me. I thought perhaps he would storm out. Then his expression softened. "You really think—"

"I really think God understands it all." I pulled on my nightdress. "And I know He is merciful."

Richard finished undressing and climbed into the big bed beside me. "I am weary, Nessie." He gathered me in his arms. "So weary. Perhaps Rosie was weary, too."

"Yes," I said, holding him close. "I'm sure she was. But she is at rest now."

I hesitated. I had just gotten him calmed down. I hated to tell him the rest of what Penrose had related, but Richard was the head of the family. He must be told. "Richard?"

"Yes, Nessie?"

"There is more. I would not bother you with it, but—"

He sighed. "But you must."

"Yes. Rosamund told Penrose that *she* killed your father."

"What!" He sat up in the bed and stared at me.

I saw that I had best get all of it out at once. There was no use delaying things. "And she told him she had killed Caroline, too."

He stared at me in horror. "Vanessa, my God! How can you say such things about my sister?"

270

"*I* did not say them," I reminded him. "She did. And certainly she should know what she had done."

Richard dropped his head into his hands. "Oh, God, my own sister."

"Then you believe it."

His eyes were clouded with uncertainty. "How can I tell? Did Penrose have any proof?"

"No. Only what she said to him." I reflected on this. "Tell me, Richard. How did your father die?"

He frowned and ran a hand through his hair. "He was ill. He had been for some time. And he got worse and worse. The doctor said it was his heart."

"And . . ."

He shrugged. "And one night it stopped."

The question had to be asked. "Could Rosamund have caused it?"

He sighed once more. "Perhaps. I do not know. In those days she was more active. She went riding. She went into the village. I suppose she might have found some way. Some poison." He groaned. "Oh, God. I just don't know."

I put my arm around him and pulled him close. "And Caroline," I said. "Could Rosamund have done that?"

His face was growing paler by the minute. "I suppose so. You know how she is—was—when the moon—my God! The moon was full the night Caroline died. I remember. I had just gone to bed—at dawn—when the servants came to say they had found her."

I sighed with relief. "Then Rosamund couldn't have done it. She was with you."

He shook his head. "Not the whole night. She slipped away once. It was almost like a game to her. It took me over an hour to find her." He dropped his head into his

271

hands. "Poor Rosie. I can't believe she's gone."

"She's at rest now, Richard. We must think of her son. We must make him want to live."

He stared at me. "I don't know, Vanessa. Those odes to Death he's always writing, and the terrible tricks he plays on people—the boy has always been strange. How could he be otherwise, raised in this house?"

"You are quite right," I agreed. "But in spite of those things he has a lot of goodness in him. It is up to us to bring it out. He is Rosamund's son. We must take care of him. For her sake."

Richard nodded. "Yes, Nessie. I see that."

"Thank goodness you were able to keep him from going over the cliff."

Richard paled. "I was reaching for Rosie. I got Penrose instead."

"You did what you could. You saved one of them."

He nodded. "Yes, yes. But why did he take her there? Why didn't he keep her in her room?"

"Rosamund was a grown woman," I said. "He is only a boy. He loved her and he wanted to please her."

"But—"

"Richard." I made my tone firm. "Please, do not ask the boy any questions. You cannot bring your sister back. And Penrose is already miserable. Do not add to his grief."

For a long moment Richard regarded me. Then he sighed again and pulled me close. "As usual, my dear, you are right. Do not worry yourself about it. I promise, I will not add to Penrose's burden."

Chapter Twenty-Two

The vicar came next morning. He perched on a chair in the library, looking for all the world as though a loud noise would make him cut and run. I reminded myself that this was not a humorous situation and steadied myself as best I could. Hysteria was hardly called for. Now, above all, I must keep stable and sane.

Penrose, summoned to speak to the vicar, looked ill at ease. I gave him a reassuring smile. We had rehearsed what he had to say, covering every question we thought the vicar might ask him; but there was always the possibility that something would trip him up, and that left us all jumpy and on edge.

My conscience did not bother me over much. True, we were practicing deception. Well, actually, we were lying. We knew Rosamund's plunge over the cliffs had been deliberate. But for her son to see her denied proper burial in hallowed ground—it simply was not fair. I was confident God would understand, even if the vicar would not.

As for deceiving the vicar, well, he was a man who put

his living above justice. Or so Roland had told me. So why shouldn't we put mercy above justice? That seemed ultimately fair to me.

It appeared that the vicar had some suspicions. He eyed Penrose severely. "I understand your mother was ill."

Penrose nodded, his expression sober. "At times she was not well."

The vicar frowned. "If she was ill, what was she doing out there—by the break in the wall—in the middle of the night?"

I felt called upon to interject. After all, Penrose was only a boy. His life had been difficult enough. He should not have to face this alone. "It was not the middle of the night, Vicar. Richard and I had not yet retired."

"That's right," said Richard from his place behind my chair. "It was only just bedtime."

The vicar did not look convinced, but he could hardly contradict both of us, no matter what his suspicions.

"Why were you out there?" He put the question directly to Penrose. And in quite a stern manner.

Penrose held up beautifully. "Mama wished to see the moon on the ocean," he said. "She was fond of the moon, and she loved the sea. We often took walks after dark."

The vicar stroked his jaw. "And how did she fall from the cliff?"

Penrose hesitated, and my heart fluttered up into my throat. I tried to think of some way to help him, but Richard's hand descending on my shoulder kept me silent. Much as I wanted to help, I knew Penrose must do this alone. If we interfered too often, the vicar would only grow more suspicious.

"I am not exactly sure," Penrose said finally. "She

him through this ordeal.

Roland and the dowager stood near us. Thank goodness they had come in a different carriage. Roland seemed preoccupied and distant, his face set. No doubt he was having hard work mastering his grief. A man, of course, did not show his sorrow in public.

The dowager looked no different than usual. I did not believe she had shed a single tear for her daughter, but I was surprised to find that she had not worn black, but a gown and bonnet of her usual gray. Not even in death could she show poor Rosamund any love.

The people of the village had come, whether out of respect for Rosamund or because Richard was their duke we had no way of knowing. At least they were there, and Penrose could take comfort in the ordinariness of the ceremony.

The vicar's words carried the usual comforting message about another, better, life to come. Once Penrose moved, as though the words were too much for him; but Richard put a hand on his arm, and he remained there between us.

The villagers all looked respectfully sad, but just as the vicar reached "Dust to dust, ashes to ashes," I looked up to find Cressadine Varish staring at us across the grave. Under her sober black bonnet those avid eyes were searching, seeking out weakness.

I had no doubt that she was already rehearsing the story she would tell about us. How, I asked myself, and why, did the good Lord permit such a creature on his earth? Then I remembered the deception we had practiced and the fact that my own slate was none too clean, and I forbore to judge.

When the first shovel of dirt hit the casket, Penrose

gave a low moan. Richard and I moved at the same time, and as our arms went around Penrose, they touched each other. Over the boy's head, Richard sent me a tiny smile. I let my eyes give my reply. With Cressadine Varish watching, a small smile could rapidly become the height of disrespectful levity.

After the ceremony was finished, we stood with Penrose while the villagers came, one by one, to pay their respects. And then, finally, we were alone.

"A minute," Penrose said. "Just a minute. And then I'll be ready."

Richard looked about to object, but I took him by the arm and led him back to the carriage. "He wants to say his good-byes," I told my husband.

Richard nodded. "Did you see my mother? Not even wearing mourning. That will mean more talk. Always, always, there is talk."

I put my arm around him. "Perhaps this will be the end of it. If Rosamund really—if she was the one—"

Richard sighed. "I don't know what to believe any more. "To think that Rosie—"

"Things will get better," I said. If only I could tell him now about the child. But it was too soon. Our child was still just a hope in my heart.

"Richard, can you do something about your mother?"

He raised a brow. "Like what?"

"Will you tell her not to say horrible things to Penrose? The poor boy has been through enough already."

Richard frowned. "I can tell her, but that will do little good. You know she pays no mind to me." He sighed. "I'm afraid, my dear, that you have come to the wrong

278

man. The only one who has any influence with her is Roland."

He looked about to add something to this, but then he shut his lips firmly.

Perhaps I *should* ask Roland to use his influence. Penrose was in such a delicate emotional state. He could easily be tipped in one direction or the other. Toward normalcy or toward—I did not want to think on that.

Later, back at the house, I turned to Penrose. "I have not had time to play with Sarah lately," I told him. "Will you go to her and explain?"

The boy fidgeted and looked ill at ease.

"What is it?" I asked.

"Vanessa, I—I have not been kind to Sarah. I have said—bad things about her mother."

I patted his arm. "Tell her that I sent you," I told him. "Tell her that I said you need a friend."

Penrose looked bewildered.

"She will understand," I assured him. "Oh, and Penrose, she loves stories. But please, don't tell her any about death and dying."

Penrose nodded. "I will not, Vanessa." He managed a little smile. "I will only tell her good, happy stories."

After the boy left the library, Richard raised a questioning eyebrow. "You sent him to Sarah? Why?"

I smiled at him. "She will be good for him," I said.

Richard frowned. "How can you be sure she will even accept him? In the past he has been most unkind to her. Tricks and taunts."

"Sarah has a forgiving nature," I said, sure I was right

279

about this thing. "She will see that he is sincere, and she will sense that he is in need of love. As she is."

Richard seemed disposed to argue this point, but he was prevented by Gerson announcing the first of many callers. Though we had decided not to observe many of the traditional funerary customs, we did mean to receive callers.

The day wore on. Everyone seemed quite respectful and kind, offering their condolences and saying all the proper things.

We did not summon Penrose back from the nursery. He was gone for some time, and I nourished a secret hope that he was lost in some childish game with Sarah, that for a moment he was free of his pain and sorrow.

Toward dinner time the stream of callers slackened, and Richard and I were alone. He sighed. "Perhaps that is the end of them."

I shook my head. "I'm afraid not, Richard. If you recall, Cressadine Varish has not yet made an appearance."

He sighed again and rubbed wearily at his eyes. "That woman is an abomination. She's made more trouble in this parish than any ten other people."

I had no disagreement with that, but I've always been of a curious nature. "How do you suppose she got that way?"

Richard stared at me as though I had suddenly taken ill. "What do you mean?"

"I mean that she did not come into the world as—as she is now. Therefore something must have happened to make her so."

Richard frowned and ran a hand through his hair. "There was some talk—long ago. Something about a man. He left her."

I nodded. "That explains it. The poor woman is missing love."

Richard smiled. "Nessie, every night when we go to bed, I expect to see your wings unfolding."

I felt the hot color flooding my cheeks. "Nonsense, Richard. I am far from angelic. I just think there are reasons, however twisted they may be, for the things people do."

He considered this. "And are you saying that if we knew the reasons we could forgive them?"

I thought of Caroline. Much as I knew I should, that it was the Christian thing to do, I did not think I could ever truly forgive her for what she had done to her husband and her child. "Perhaps not forgive." I sighed. "But perhaps understand a little better."

Richard pondered this. "Perhaps, but—"

Gerson appeared in the doorway. His usually bland features carried an overlay of distaste. "Miss Cressadine Varish," he announced.

Richard uttered a muffled curse. I composed my features to cover my distress. "Thank you, Gerson. Please show Miss Varish in."

She was wearing the dour black bonnet and an expression to match. I knew Richard was doing his best to be civil; but this was the woman who had spread tales about my supposed infidelity, and it was hard for him to contain his wrath.

She took a seat and arranged her skirts. "My condolences," she said.

"It was kind of you to call," I replied.

But Miss Varish was not interested in lesser game. She fixed her beady black eyes on Richard. "Oh, Your Grace. Your poor sister. What a dreadful life she led. Deserted like that. And then losing her mind."

I saw Richard swallow. I knew my husband, and I knew he was growing angry. Very rapidly.

"Rosamund's life was pleasant as most," he replied in a tight voice. "She was loved and cared for. None of us can ask more than that."

Bravo, Richard. I shot him a smile of congratulation. Miss Varish was not impressed. She renewed the attack. "Still, it must have been a trial. Having a child out of wedlock like that."

I thought I saw it then. Strange as it seemed, Cressadine Varish envied Rosamund her son. Penrose was visible evidence that Rosamund had been loved. Miss Varish had no such evidence.

Richard struggled with his temper. I knew the signs, and I grew fearful that I might really see one of those awful rages; but Richard mastered himself enough to turn to me. "You'll have to excuse me, my dear. I've something I must attend to."

"Of course."

He nodded to Miss Varish and was gone.

"Poor man," she said. "Carrying such burdens."

I almost agreed with her. Almost. But then, just in time, I realized what she could make of even such agreement. By the time she was through elaborating, my words could have been transformed to something quite different, and damaging.

Before I could think of what to reply, the door opened. Sarah came in, leading Penrose by the hand. Sarah was wearing a pink dress. I saw Miss Varish's eyes widen at

282

the sight of it. So, I thought, if my refusal to put Sarah back in mourning gave the vicar's sister something to talk about, well and good. Better that she should talk about me than about Penrose and his mother.

Sarah came straight to me, a smile on her face. "Nessie," she said. "Penrose knows the most marvelous stories. You must hear them."

The boy looked a little sheepish, but he did not move away or try to release his hand.

I smiled at them both. "I'm glad," I said. "But right now I have a visitor. Why don't you go back to the nursery? Later, I will come up and hear them." I turned to Penrose. "Thank you for looking after Sarah. Better take her back now."

"Of course, Vanessa." His tone was respectful, and his eyes gave me his thanks.

I swallowed a sigh of relief as the two left the room. Had she questioned him, I might well have lost my temper. Penrose did not need to suffer an inquisition by this hateful woman.

"Quite a big boy to be telling stories," she observed sourly.

I almost lost my temper then. The woman had been doing everything in her power to harm us. I was hard put to remain civil to her. And why should I? "He is helping me," I said coldly. "The nurse is old."

There was little use in explaining anything. A woman of Cressadine Varish's nature could not understand what I had hoped to accomplish by sending Penrose to the nursery. She could not understand the finer things of life. The healing power of a child's love would be to her mere fantasy.

"Yes, indeed." Though the words were in agreement,

her expression plainly said she didn't believe a word I said. Her eyes took in the room, looking, no doubt, for something unusual to report.

I left her to her looking. Knowing that my temper would soon reach the boiling point, I cast about in my mind for some excuse to rid myself of her presence.

While I was still searching for some reason, any polite reason, to send her on her way, the door opened again. Roland helped the dowager into the room.

I noted that Miss Varish's eyes lingered on the dowager's gray gown. "Good afternoon, Your Grace." Miss Varish's tone was subtly different. Evidently she thought more highly of the dowager than she did of me.

The dowager did not deign to reply but nodded regally and took a chair near the fire. Roland settled beside her. Why, I thought, why had they decided to come down, just when I did not need their presence, just when it would complicate matters no end?

"A tragic accident," Miss Varish commented, her eyes on Roland, her smile obsequious.

"Yes," he agreed. "Quite tragic."

My heart commenced to beat faster, but I reminded myself that Roland could not give away our secret. He did not know it. Only three of us knew that Rosamund had gone to her death willingly. Still, I would have preferred to have Miss Varish away from the castle. Let her harass someone else. It had been a long hard day, and she had made it longer and harder.

There was silence in the room for some seconds. The dowager stared into the fire, and Roland contemplated the painting above it. I determined to remain silent. Let the dowager and Roland provide some of the conversation.

The two said nothing. Finally Miss Varish broke the silence. She leaned forward with that particularly avid look of hers and said, "Such a frightful shame. I understand poor Rosamund was very ill."

Roland's features hardened, and he cast her a stern look. "We are all ill at times. It is a misfortune none of us may escape."

Miss Varish nodded, her eyes never leaving his face. "Yes, of course. But I do not believe that we are all in the habit of singing songs about the coming of death."

Roland shrugged and adjusted his cuffs. "I suppose my sister liked the melody."

Miss Varish looked pained and hesitated. "That is what her son told my brother. But she knew the words. I distinctly heard her sing the words."

Roland shrugged. "That signifies nothing."

For a minute I thought he had succeeded in subduing her, but she simply could not give up. "Indeed, it—" she began.

The dowager got to her feet and directed a frosty look at the vicar's sister. "I think you have been here long enough," she said coldly. "You may leave now."

For a moment it seemed the words did not reach Miss Varish's mind. I, too, was stunned. In fact, I was left momentarily speechless. The dowager had been quite rude, but I could not deny the fact that I was very glad of it.

Then the visitor flounced to her feet. "Well, I never have been so insulted!"

The dowager almost smiled. "Really? I should have thought you'd have heard much worse. But if you wish I can—"

"No, no!" Miss Varish edged toward the door as

though she were escaping a house full of madmen. "Really—" she began.

Roland got to his feet. "I'll just go to the door with you," he said, guiding her out. "It was most kind of you to come. You'll forgive Mama, I'm sure. She's a little . . ." His words faded as they made their way down the hall.

The dowager turned her frosty stare on me. "I can't imagine why you let her call. A most reprehensible woman," she observed, stalking out. "Worse even than your sister."

Chapter Twenty-Three

Our life slowly returned to normal, or at least as normal as life at Greyden Castle could be. I did not know what to believe about the things Rosamund had told her son. But the days passed and there was no sign or sound of the haunting babe. No ghosts whispered outside my door. No scent wafted into my room. It certainly looked as though Rosamund had been behind all the things that had happened to me, and yet, somehow, I did not feel relieved, did not feel that the bad times were truly over.

Perhaps, I told myself, it was because I had no way to confirm Rosamund's claims. Even more so, perhaps it was because Richard seemed so far away from me. I knew that he had undergone a great deal. Losing the wife he loved and then his sister, and in such peculiar and awful circumstances.

Sometimes he looked at me in such a strange way. At those times I remembered the dowager's violent and acid temperament, I remembered Rosamund's terrible illness, and most of all, I thought of Richard's rages—so vividly reported to me by his twin.

Could there be a possibility that my husband was suffering from some kind of madness? I pushed the thought aside, but always it came back. I had seen Richard very angry, but never with the kind of rage Roland had spoken of.

Now Richard was not angry at all. He did not shout or curse. Mostly, he sighed. He seemed enveloped in a terrible cloud of black melancholia, and that cloud darkened my life, too.

I tried my best to be a good wife to him, and he, in turn, was there with me every night. At least he did not withdraw to his own chamber. That would have been even more difficult to bear.

His body was there, but much of the time his mind seemed far away. Was he remembering innocent childhood days with Rosamund? Or was he tormenting himself with thoughts of some way he might have saved her, thoughts of what he *should* have done?

I knew from experience that nothing could be more futile. How many weary months I had spent wondering what I should have done to make my mama love me, before I finally realized that nothing would make that miracle happen. I wanted to help Richard, but I knew that this was one lesson he would have to learn for himself.

His refusal to have anything to do with Sarah still troubled me greatly, but sunk as he was in his grief, I judged it wiser not to push the matter. I could not make him see things my way when he was grieving so. I had not given up, I assured myself. There would be time. Plenty of time.

So life went on. I waited, and I prayed. I prayed diligently that Richard and I might be blessed with a child;

but I did not let concern with that keep me from mothering the children already entrusted to my care, for Penrose had, indeed, become once more a child. He spent most of his waking hours in the nursery with Sarah. Once he'd stopped tormenting her, the two had become fast friends.

My intuition had been right. Sarah had taken him to her heart, and her innocence was helping him to heal.

To my immense relief he had left off writing those dreadful odes to Death. Now he was composing funny verses for Sarah instead. Perhaps they were no better poetry, but they were funny. Every day he seemed more like a boy his rightful age, and best of all, he had learned to laugh.

I was heartened and pleased at the change in him, and Sarah was a daily pleasure; but still I felt something oppressive hovering over me, disaster waiting to strike. I went about almost cringing, continually expecting the worst. Yet nothing happened.

I examined all my feelings. I used every avenue of logic to consider what I was thinking and feeling. There seemed no reason for it. Yet still I felt as though I labored under a dark cloud of misfortune. Something dreadful was about to happen. Some part of me knew it and was waiting. Waiting.

I railed at myself for not being able to overcome such a patently foolish attitude. Anyone could see that things at Greyden Castle were better than they had been for a long time.

True, the dowager was still rude and unkind—she probably would never change—and Richard was morose and withdrawn; but the children were doing so well. Were they not the hope of the future?

I pushed my forebodings aside and set my mind once more on ways and means of bringing Sarah and her father together. Where there was a will, there must be a way, and I was determined to find it.

So it was that I began to visit the North Tower again. It was still a dark and dismal place, with little warmth or light. I did not venture there without candles aplenty. But I liked the privacy of it. Sometimes I would go there and sit in the stillness, just thinking.

I believed a child was growing within me. I was almost positive this was true, but I did not tell my husband. I did not want to raise Richard's hopes only to dash them again. In several days, no more than a week, I would know for certain. Then I could tell Richard, could see him smile as he used to.

Sitting there in the silence of the dark room, I wondered how Caroline had felt when she knew she would have a babe. From what I had heard, the prospect of a child had not been at all pleasing to her.

I spent some time trying to understand this. It was not that I could not comprehend it, because I thought I did understand Caroline's intense interest in herself and her beauty; but wanting a child as badly as I did, I could not really imagine how anyone could not.

One afternoon, some weeks after Rosamund's death, I sat at the writing desk in the North Tower. It was time to write another letter to Papa. He would be glad for the good news of the children. And the other, this cloud of apprehension that hung over me—I would not tell him about that.

I only told him good things. I hinted at the new babe and, following these thoughts, soon found myself dreaming of the future. And of our son. He would look like Richard, of course. Dark hair and dark eyes. I smiled. But then I frowned. He would also look like Roland.

It was hard for me to consider my feelings for Richard's twin. It was impossible that I should love him. I loved my husband. Nevertheless I felt a certain warmth toward Roland. How could I feel otherwise when he had been so good and kind to me? When he had always looked out for me and volunteered to be my protector?

I sighed. Life was so complicated. Richard had issued no more ultimatums concerning his twin; but then, these days Richard said little at all, and my attempts to draw him out inevitably met with failure.

For the hundredth time I considered what I could do to bring Richard and his daughter together, to make us a real family. I was convinced that Richard loved the child. More than once I had seen indications of it in his look, but his stubborn, misguided pride kept him from admitting it.

I was still certain Sarah was his child. If only I could find that diary. I was sure Caroline had kept one. She had always liked to record her conquests. But where had she put it?

With an exasperated groan I got to my feet and began to pace the tower. If the diary still existed, it had to be somewhere in this room. Before my arrival Richard had had my chamber completely refurbished and redecorated. There was nothing of Caroline's there, and I was grateful for that.

This room, however, had been left undisturbed. Caroline's chest of things was still in the armoire, her robe still hanging there.

Logic, I reminded myself. Use logic. But I had looked everywhere in this room and found—

Not everywhere! I stopped in midstride and hurried to the armoire. My hands trembled as I opened the carved doors. What if the robe was gone? What if someone had taken it? But it was still hanging there.

I reached out, but something stopped me. I did not want to touch it. Unreasonable fear tried to paralyze me, but I could not call a servant to remove the robe for me. I must take it out and examine it myself. Alone.

Papa, I thought. What would Papa do? I forced myself to lift it down. The velvet was cold against my fingers, almost slimy. It made me think of death and decay. I shivered. The robe still gave off a faint indication of Caroline's scent, and though I did not really believe in ghosts, I felt her presence in the tower.

For a moment I tasted panic, remembering my terror at her scent invading my room. I reminded myself that that was all behind me. There had been nothing supernatural about it. It was just a trick of Rosamund's—and she was gone. Gritting my teeth, I carried the robe to the cot.

If only the room were not so dark. I did not want to take the robe to my chamber, I did not want Richard to see it, and I did not want anything of Caroline's in the room that was now mine.

Carefully I ran my fingers over the material. It did not seem a likely hiding place for anything so bulky as a diary, but still I persisted. This robe was my last hope. We had not been able to find the secret doorway in the stones of the hall, and even if we had, I could not imagine Caroline using such a hiding place. She would not want anything to do with a place that smelled musty or might get her clothes dirty.

I examined every inch of that robe from its lacy collar down to the entire round of the hem. There was nothing.

Still I felt certain that her diary existed.

I hung the robe back in the armoire. I would dispose of it later. Then I lifted out the little chest and carried it to the writing desk.

I took out the scent bottle, laid the silver-backed mirror and brush on the table, and again checked the inside of the chest. There was no lining. No false bottom. It was just a small chest used to store things. With an angry exclamation I slammed it down on the desk. The mirror jumped.

I picked it up. The silver chasing on the back was intricate and detailed. Cupid leaned over Psyche as she slept. Idly I traced the pattern of a leafy vine, its intricate design teasing my fingertips. I bent to look more closely.

The design was so well done that for a moment I lost myself in the story. Then I sighed again. I must find a way to reach Richard, to make him accept Sarah as his daughter. Otherwise we would never know real happiness. And our new child. . . .

I picked up the hairbrush. It was quite heavy, with a large handle that fit awkwardly into my palm. How curious. Caroline had always favored small dainty things. Why had she chosen such an outsized brush?

I examined the back. The same scene decorated it. Cupid and Psyche now seemed stupid as my temper rose. I uttered an oath, and then, hearing myself, I sighed. I had promised myself I would stop cursing. After all, there were the children to consider.

This was all so aggravating, to feel so certain and not be able to prove anything. I looked down at the brush. In the candlelit dimness the silver chasing twinkled, but I did not see the beauty of the carving or the fine workmanship. I saw Caroline laughing at me. Once more she had bested me. Once more she had taken what I wanted, what should have been mine.

"No! I won't let you!" Grabbing up the brush, I threw it across the room. It bounced off the wall with a harsh explosive sound and fell to the floor.

"Well, Vanessa," I said, feeling more than a little foolish, "that was a childish thing to do."

I crossed the room to retrieve it. At least no one would know if it was damaged, and there had been no witnesses to my bad temper.

I bent to pick it up, and it came apart in my hand. My God! The handle was hollow, and sticking part way out of it was a roll of thin paper.

My fingers trembling, I carried it back to the desk. Carefully I unrolled the paper. There it was—cryptic little notes with initials beside them. I pored over Caroline's fine spidery writing, determined to learn everything I could.

There was precious little to learn. If the numbers were dates and the initials those of men—my head was swimming. Caroline had known intimately far more men than even I had imagined. She had been with some of them many times, and others only once.

I forced myself to go slowly. I did not want to miss something of importance. I had been at my task for some time when a noise brought my head erect. Hurriedly I stuffed the papers into the pocket of my gown. Then I sat very still, my hands in my lap, every cell in my body listening, waiting. My eyes were fixed on the door, and I strained to see more than the dimness would allow.

Though I sat in utter silence for long long minutes, every sense alert for the slightest sound, nothing more happened. I heard no more noises, and not a soul appeared.

Finally I decided that my imagination had been playing tricks on me. With a sigh I took the papers out of my pocket and spread them out again.

The record of Caroline's betrayal was a lengthy one. I had almost stopped, sickened as I was by the scope of her treachery, and then I saw it. I bent eagerly over the entry. "Told Richard Sarah not his. Served him right for bringing me here. Will never tell him she really is his. Let him suffer."

In stunned silence I read it over twice. At last, at long last, I had what I needed to bring Richard and his daughter back together. I could hardly believe it. At last we had a chance to be a complete family.

It was not good of me, but I also told myself that once Richard knew the extent of Caroline's infidelities, he would be so filled with disgust that he would stop thinking of her with longing.

My first impulse was to run out, to go to Richard and show him what I had found, but for once common sense moved faster than my feet.

Suddenly fearful, I clutched the papers to my breast. They were so important. I must keep them safe.

The voice of logic spoke again. The diary had been safe in its original hiding place for over a year. Why not return it there?

Carefully I rolled up the sheets and pushed them back in the handle of the brush. A little twist and the brush was whole. No one could ever suspect what treasure it held.

I replaced the mirror and brush, and the scent bottle, closed the chest and returned it to the armoire. Richard! I must go to him immediately with this wonderful news.

My heart was singing, and I wanted to shout it from the housetops; but I could not tell anyone else before I told

Richard. That would not be right.

This could be the news that would change his whole life, that would make everything right for us and the children.

I grabbed my candle and hurried out. It was all I could do to go slowly on the narrow spiral stair. But, I reminded myself, there was the new child to think of. I slowed my steps.

Reaching the hall, I hurried to my room. As I scrambled into my riding habit, I tried to remember if I had heard where Richard was going, but it didn't really matter. Wherever he was, I would find him and tell him the wonderful news.

Then I remembered something else. Sarah would be waking from her nap, and I had promised to read to her. Grabbing up my hat, I hurried to the nursery. The dark halls seemed somehow brighter and more cheerful. I laughed aloud. Things were going to be so different.

I entered the nursery quietly, knowing Sarah would still be sleeping. Penrose and Creighton were sitting side by side before the fire.

Penrose looked up from a lap full of papers and smiled. "Hello, Vanessa. I am making Sarah a story—about a horse with wings."

Creighton nodded complacently over her knitting needles. "'Tis marvelous the way she takes to him. Warms the heart, it does."

My own heart skipped a beat, and I almost blurted out my news; but Richard must hear it first. "I'm going out," I said hastily. "Tell Sarah I'll see her later."

Penrose frowned. "She'll be disappointed. So will I."

I patted his head as I would have Sarah's, thinking that just a few short weeks before I had been suspecting him of the most awful things. "I'll come in later. Before dinner. You can tell me your story then."

His eyes lit up at that. We must be careful, I thought as I hurried out. In our new-found happiness we must not forget to include Penrose.

I rushed down the stairs and out the front door, almost colliding with Roland in my haste.

"Vanessa!" He caught at my waist to steady me. "Where are you off to in such haste?"

"To find Richard. I've—I've something to tell him."

Roland smiled. "It must be something wonderful." He patted my arm. "Have a care, Vanessa. You are precious to us."

I blushed and backed off a step. I could not help it. Sometimes Roland's closeness made me uncomfortable. Certainly he had not presumed on his feelings for me; but I knew that he had them, and it was disconcerting to know that I was loved by my husband's twin.

"Yes, yes," I murmured. "I shall." I knew he was thinking my behavior quite odd, but I could not stop to explain.

I turned away, but Roland put a detaining hand on my arm. "I hope Richard is all right. These silent spells—" he sighed deeply—"they are like he used to have, before an awful rage. He was silent for weeks before he pushed me—and before Caroline's death." Roland paused and removed his hand. "But here, I am keeping you from your ride."

I nodded and hurried out to the stable, where Toby greeted me cheerfully and saddled the stallion. "His Grace has gone to the village," he said. "Told me he'd be home afore dinner."

"Maybe I shall meet him," I said absently as he tossed

me up.

I pointed the animal toward the village. As always it was wonderful to be on horseback. Eager for a run, the stallion needed a strong hand to hold him back. Instead I gave him his head, and we galloped off down the small road toward the bigger one.

For some moments I lost myself in the joy of the run; but finally I slowed the stallion to a walk, and then my troubles began. It was as if I had suddenly opened a door in my mind and a host of terrible thoughts rushed out. Thoughts I had refused to consider before now shoved and elbowed around in there like a crowd of demons.

I uttered an oath. I knew Roland meant well. His concern for me was obvious. But why must he remind me of Richard's rages now—when I had such happy news?

Even worse, what if Roland were right? What if seeing the list of Caroline's indiscretions brought on another of Richard's rages?

How had Caroline died? And why? I had never been able to believe that the stallion was responsible for my sister's death, but I had not carried the thought to its logical conclusion. Now I did. If the stallion was not responsible, then some person was behind this, some person who hated Caroline. This same person had tried to hurt me.

Without thinking I pulled up on the reins, almost startling the great horse into rearing. For the first time I let myself recognize the truth. Someone had really tried to kill me. It was a distressing thought.

Suddenly, somehow, I knew with certainty that it had not been Rosamund. I should have realized it earlier if I had not been trying to avoid facing the fact. I had not wanted to let myself think it.

Now the thought had escaped. It was there in the open, and I had to confront it.

One of my hands went protectively to my belly. Now there was this new life to think of, the new life that would bring us together, make us into a family.

But—who had wanted Caroline dead?

One by one I reviewed the members of the family. The dowager had hated my sister, but she could not have lifted me onto the horse. Penrose had believed his mother guilty of Caroline's death. Roland had refused Caroline's advances. And Richard—

Oh, God! Richard had by far the biggest motive. She had lied and cheated and dragged his name through the mud. She had destroyed his love for Sarah.

Richard could have killed her. In one of his rages he could have struck her and then covered it up by putting her in Mercury's stall, letting the horse take the blame. Then he had refused to have the horse put down—because, of course, he knew the stallion was innocent.

The things that had happened to me—being locked in the tower, the hauntings and the abduction, the accident on the moor—they had happened when Richard was not with me.

Why hadn't I seen it before? Richard could be the one behind everything. He had Caroline's scent. He knew about the secret passageway. He had access to the stable and the tower room.

Dear God! What was I going to do? Richard, my beloved Richard, might really have murdered my sister. And what did he intend to do to me?

Chapter Twenty-Four

The horse walked on for some minutes while I rode in stunned and horrified silence. I could not believe these awful thoughts were possible. How could I suspect my husband? Yet all the facts pointed to him. Every single thing I considered led back to Richard.

Finally I grew aware that I was still headed toward the village. I swung the stallion's head around. I could not face Richard while I was in such a condition. I must rid my mind of the terrible things I was thinking.

The ride back was dreadful. By the time I reached the stable I was near tears. I threw the stallion's reins to Toby and hurried up the walk toward the castle. I must get to my room before—

But I no sooner got into the great hall than Sarah was there, tugging at my riding habit and crying, "Nessie, Nessie! Guess what?"

I composed myself as best I could and tried to answer her. "Yes, dear? What is it?"

"Uncle Roland has promised me a present. A big, big present." She clapped her hands. "Do you think it's a pony?"

My head was whirling, but I tried to remain calm, to think of the child. "I don't think so, dear."

Sarah looked disappointed, but I could not comfort her then. It was all I could do to keep from screaming my misery aloud. "Please, dear, go back to the nursery now. You will get your present."

Sarah nodded. "Yes, I know I will. But first I have to find Penrose. I want him to be there when I get it." And off she went.

I turned toward the stairs. Roland came toward me out of the gloom. When he saw me, his face twisted into a frown. "Vanessa! My dear, you look absolutely horrible." Gently he pulled my arm through his. "Come, let's go into the library. You must sit down."

I let him lead me in and set me before the fire. I felt so strange, so unlike myself. Roland rang for tea and poured me a cup himself. He pressed it into my hands and watched while I sipped.

"Now, Vanessa, tell me. Whatever is wrong? A while ago you left here in such good spirits. And now you look as though you've seen a ghost."

I would ask Roland, I thought, my numbed brain trying to function. He knew his brother. Roland would tell me this dreadful thing could not be true.

"It's—Richard. I'm afraid—afraid that—" It was so hard to say the words. "It seems that—he could have killed Caroline."

Roland did not seem surprised. "I suppose he could have," he agreed. "But then everyone seems to feel she deserved it."

Horror washed over me. "But—"

Roland sighed. "Come, come, Vanessa. I do not believe it was premeditated. Probably it happened accidentally.

301

I'm sure Richard would never hurt you." Roland stared at me, his dark eyes thoughtful. "Richard is not a murderer. But why were you rushing off to look for him?"

I wanted to continue the discussion of Caroline's death, but I was afraid. Roland, too, thought Richard might have done it. Because of my fear I looked for something else to talk about. "I found a piece of Caroline's diary. It says—" I stopped suddenly, aware that I had said too much. This news should be told to Richard first.

Roland looked startled. Then he frowned, his dark brows coming together. "You will want to destroy it, of course."

"Oh, no!"

He raised an eyebrow. "Why not?"

"It—it contains proof that Sarah is really Richard's child." I could not help it. I had to tell someone, and he had been so helpful, so kind to me.

Roland shook his head. "I don't see how that could be. Caroline told anyone and everyone that he wasn't the child's father."

Poor Richard, I thought. How he had suffered because of my sister. Still he loved her. And perhaps had killed her. The thought almost took my breath away. "It's true," I said. "It's there in black and white. In her own handwriting."

Roland looked perturbed. "Could—could I see it? Perhaps then I can tell—"

"Tell what?"

He patted my arm. "How Richard may react to its contents."

I nodded. That made sense. I did not want to send

Richard into one of his rages. Had he been in a rage when he? . . . "Yes. Will you help me then? Help me decide how to tell him?"

Roland smiled. "Of course, my dear. But let's go before he comes in."

Minutes later we were standing in the tower room. Roland held both candles while I opened the armoire. "She hid the papers in the handle of her hairbrush," I explained, pulling out the chest.

I crossed to the desk, and Roland followed, putting the candles down there. I took out the silver hairbrush. "You just turn the handle," I told him. "Like this."

From beside me Roland let out a great sigh. "May I see them?"

"Of course." I turned and held the pages out to him. "You'll need to get close—"

To my surprise, he almost tore the papers from my outstretched hand. "Thank you," he said, his voice strangely husky. "Now I have everything I need."

Suddenly fearful, I looked up at him. Dear Lord! This man who stared back at me with frozen eyes and an evil smile could not be the Roland I knew. "Roland, what is it? I do not understand," I said.

He laughed. It was a sound of such complete evil that I swear the babe within me leaped with fear. My legs almost refused to hold me erect, and I struggled to keep my senses.

"Poor Vanessa," he said. "Poor, stupid Vanessa. Shall I explain it all for you?"

His eyes gleamed with a terrible madness. "Caroline was mine," he cried. "She loved *me*." He laughed again, that horrid laugh. "Mine! I did not care how many men she used. I knew she was mine.

"But then she said she was leaving." For a moment he looked like a bewildered little boy. "Running away with some country lout. I could not let her do that. She was mine. She could not leave me." He smiled again, and my blood ran cold. "I stopped her. She didn't get to go. Now she'll always be mine."

He took a step toward me, his smile turning tender. "You could have been mine, too."

"No!" The word burst from me in involuntary protest. To think that I had believed this man my friend, this man who had murdered my sister.

"Yes," he went on. "I offered myself to you. I would have loved you. Sarah, too. I would have made us into the family you wanted." He frowned. "But you say she's Richard's child. So she'll have to die, too."

Over his shoulder I glimpsed the door. It was shut, but I knew it could not be locked. If I could get to it, get down those stairs. . . . I made myself keep my eyes away from it. I must not let him suspect what I was planning. I must keep him talking.

"Why?" I asked. "Why did you do those things to me?"

He laughed again, but I controlled myself. I must not give in to my fear. If I panicked, I could not think. And to save myself—and the child—I had to be able to think, to plan. And to pray.

"At first I wanted to frighten you off," he said, still smiling that terrible smile. "I had everyone believing Richard guilty—until he brought you home. But if I could frighten you off, then he would look even guiltier."

I gripped the back of the chair with trembling fingers.

"But you were so kind to me."

He continued to smile. "Of course. I learned early to keep my true feelings to myself. Mama taught me that, though she is not good at it herself. Oh, Vanessa, if you had come to me, as Caroline did, you could have become my duchess."

I tried to think, to make sense of this nightmare. "But you are not the duke. Richard—"

"Yes, Richard is the duke." He nodded, his eyes gleaming. "And he's still alive. But you could have helped me. If he were convicted, it would all be mine."

"All—"

He smashed a fist down on the desk, making the candles jump. "I hate being second! I should have been born first. All my life I've suffered because of that stupid ten-minute difference."

He smiled again. How could I have ever thought that smile friendly? It was pure evil. "But no matter," he said. "That will soon be over."

"It will?"

"Of course. When Richard's second wife is found dead, strangled with a piece of her own petticoat, all the evidence will point to Richard. He will be sentenced to death." He chuckled. "And Greyden will be mine. All mine."

My heart threatened to choke me. Some part of me had known he meant to kill me, but to hear the words spoken aloud made it even more frightful. I prayed for strength. And wisdom. I had to make him change his mind.

"Roland, please don't do this. Just because Richard tried to push you out of—"

His laugh made cold chills slither down my spine. "Vanessa, you are such a fool. So gullible. Worse even

305

than my father. Richard didn't push *me*. I pushed *him*. That time it didn't work, but this time it will. You will be found, and Cressadine Varish will be glad to spread the word of Richard's guilt."

Keep him talking, I reminded myself. "Miss Varish? What has she to do with this?"

He licked his lips. "The poor woman is laboring under a misapprehension. She believes that I am in love with her."

That explained a great deal. But how could any sane woman have believed his lies?

I caught my breath. *I* had believed him. I had thought him my loyal friend. Even though I had my husband's love, I had believed his twin, and Cressadine Varish was a woman alone—and unloved.

Roland ran a hand up his coat sleeve in a caressing motion. "Women. Just give them a smile and they will do anything you ask."

He took a step toward me. The chair was between us, but it offered little protection. I must do something to stop him. "Roland, think, surely you wouldn't kill an innocent child?"

He shrugged. "I had some affection for Sarah, but that was because I thought her mine." He frowned. "We shall see."

"And Penrose. What of him?"

"I had hopes for him. But lately he's been changing. You've ruined him with your goodness. Probably I shall have to dispose of him, too." He rubbed his hands together. "Richard's shoulders are broad. He can take the blame for all."

I wanted to scream out my anguish for those I loved, so soon to die at this madman's hands, but screaming would not help them. I had to keep my wits about me, keep him talking. I was the only one who could prevent this tragedy. "So then, Richard really did not suffer from rages?"

"Of course not. He's disgustingly even-tempered. But that won't help him."

"Did you—" I had to ask him. I must know. "Did you kill your father, too?"

He looked amused. "No. And neither did Rosamund. I heard some of the things she babbled to Penrose, but she didn't kill our father. Wishing won't kill a person, you know, or I'd have been rid of Richard long ago."

"You—you did all those things?"

He nodded. "Yes. As I said. At first I meant only to frighten you, but later I thought perhaps you would die." He frowned. "Why didn't you? It would have saved me so much trouble."

His gaze went downward to where my hand had gone automatically to shelter my unborn babe. He chuckled. "So, it's that way, is it? Well, it won't do any good to plead Richard's brat to me. I'll be well rid of the lot of you."

He was so evil. How had he hidden it for so long? "But—but aren't you afraid you'll get caught?"

He shook his head. "Why should I be? I killed Caroline, and no one caught me. I did it with my bare hands." He frowned again. "Around her neck. I just squeezed. Then I made it look like the stallion trampled her." He took another step toward me. "You see, Vanessa, no one will suspect me. It's too bad you didn't come to me. That day you kissed me—that was good. I know we could have been happy."

The man was mad. How could he think that I . . . ?

"But you killed my sister."

He shrugged. "You didn't like her, and she hated you." His eyes gleamed. "You should have heard some of the things she said about you. And anyway, you weren't supposed to know I killed her. I made everything point to Richard."

He had. And he had done a good job of it, too. Even I, who should have known better, had suspected my husband.

Roland adjusted his coat sleeves. "I am very good at being friendly and kind. A second son needs ingratiating qualities, you know. He must survive in this cold hard world."

I decided to try another tack. "Why didn't you ask me outright? I would have come to you." I tried to make the lie convincing. "Even now, tell me what to do. We can still get rid of Richard."

For the space of a second I thought he might believe me. Then he shook his head, his expression rueful. "It's too late for that, Vanessa. I know you love Richard. I'm sorry, but you must die."

He sighed. "You are so beautiful. I could have loved you." He reached out toward me, but I backed away, pulling the chair with me. "Do not struggle, my dear," he said. "It will be much easier for you that way."

"You will be damned!" I cried. "Murder is a terrible sin."

Roland shrugged. "So they say. And if there is that hell that Rosamund was always talking about, I shall no doubt burn in it. But you see, one murder or six, it makes no difference. The sentence is still an eternity in flames. And anyway, I do not believe in hell."

Now I was certain he was crazy. No sane person would

thus defy his Maker.

"So—" Roland took another step toward me.

I backed away, still keeping the chair between us.

"Vanessa, you must stop this silliness. There's no escaping me." He sighed. "I hope you aren't going to be like Caroline. First she laughed. She didn't believe me, you see, but then she pleaded. She lied and lied."

In the dimness his eyes were terrifying. "She lied to me and then I killed her. But after she laughed, she cried—and pleaded. I hope you won't do that. It's so tiresome."

He took another step. Soon I would be backed against the wall, and he was much bigger and stronger than I. I had no doubt he could choke the life out of me.

Oh, God, I thought. My babe, my poor babe. Help me save it.

Roland stepped closer. What would Papa do? In desperation I lifted the lyre-backed chair and swung it sideways. I wanted to hit Roland in the head, but the blow fell short. The chair bounced harmlessly against his shoulder.

Still, it threw him off balance, and he went down on one knee. I did not wait to see more, but flew to the door and yanked it open.

The spiral stairs were dark. I could see very little, but I raced down them as fast as I could go. A broken neck from a fall would be better than death at Roland's hands. At least on the stairs I had a chance.

I scraped my knuckles on the wall as I tried to guide myself, but that pain was nothing compared to the pain in my heart. Our unborn child. Richard. Sarah. Penrose. All their lives depended on my winning free of the madman behind me.

Then something fell out of the blackness above me. It struck my temple a sharp glancing blow. I cried out and tried to go on, but a darkness that was not of the stairs threatened to swallow me.

I sank down on the cold stone steps. Fighting, fighting the encroaching darkness, I struggled not to slip into unconsciousness.

I tried to get back to my feet, to keep going, but before I could clear my head enough to get up, Roland was upon me. He grabbed me by my gown and jerked me upright. His face was close to mine, so close that even in the darkness I could see the whites of his eyes. Those eyes, peering into mine, were hideous in their evil.

"This is even better," he said, licking his lips as though he tasted something good. "Poor Richard's wife fell to her death on the tower stairs. In suspicious circumstances. No doubt *he* pushed her."

I tried to press back against the wall, but he still had a grip on my gown. "You are mad," I cried, hardly knowing what I was doing or saying. "You will be found out. You will be punished."

He shook his head. "Oh, no, not me. And after your death, my dear Cressadine will spread the proper tales." He frowned. "And this time the magistrate will be forced to act upon them. I'll see to that."

I tried to wriggle free of his hold, but he was too strong. "Now," he said. "Just a little push and it will all be over."

He let go of my gown to grab my wrist, and I did the only thing I could think of. I shoved him with all my might.

He lost his balance and fell. But just two steps. The curved wall kept him from going far. I watched as he lay still in the half darkness.

My heart was pounding in my throat, my knees were weak and wobbly, but to get to safety I had to step over him. Move, I told myself. I peered at him. He must be unconscious. Gathering my skirts, I crept down one stair, then two. He did not stir.

I stood on the step above him. I just had to step over his body. Then I could run to safety.

I lifted my foot. His hand shot out and closed around my ankle. My scream bounced off the wall as I went down.

Then the darkness rose up to greet me, soft comforting darkness. I could sink into it and forget my troubles, but somewhere was the nagging thought that I must not sleep, that if I slept now I would never waken.

I felt Roland's hands close around my throat. "Richard!" I cried, though no sound came out. Then I could no longer get my breath. My blood pounded in my ears like thudding footsteps. I fought. I kicked and I scratched, struggling desperately to save my life—and the life of my unborn babe.

Try as I might the darkness grew heavier and heavier. I knew it would not be long before I faced my Maker. In those brief moments while my life flashed before my eyes, I regretted most of my suspicions of Richard, who had always been a good husband to me.

Then, just as I thought my next breath would be my last, the constricting hands were gone.

"Mama, Mama!"

For a moment I thought myself already dead and the voice that of our child, dead, too, and welcoming me to heaven.

Then Richard said, "Vanessa! Vanessa, darling! Can you hear me?"

I pulled in great gulps of air and struggled to open my weighted eyelids. The staircase was flooded with light. I was lying on the cold stone steps, and staring down at me, their faces twisted in frowns of concern, were Richard, Sarah, and Penrose.

Praise God, I was not dead. And my loved ones were there.

Chapter Twenty-Five

"I—hear—you." My throat was raw and painful, but I made myself speak. I had to protect them. "Ro-land!" I squeaked. "Where is he?"

Richard frowned. "Don't worry, my love. We have him under guard."

Sarah threw herself upon me. "Oh, Mama," she cried again. The word was music to my ears.

I found that my arms would move, and I put them around her. "It's all right, Sarah," I soothed. "I will be all right."

For a moment I considered my body, searching it inwardly for signs of harm. Though I was stiff and sore, all else seemed well. The babe was too little to be harmed by my fall.

But consideration of my body brought to me the knowledge that I was lying on cold hard stone. I began to shiver.

"Vanessa!" Richard's voice rose in alarm.

"She's cold," said Penrose. "We should get her warmed up."

Richard peered down at me, his beloved face full of concern. "Are you injured anywhere?" he asked.

"No. I think not." I extended my hand. "Please help me get up."

Sarah drew back to give them room, and everyone, including the servants who held aloft the candelabra, stood watching as Richard and Penrose helped me to my feet.

I raised a hand to my head, which throbbed dreadfully. "He threw something. It hit my head." My knees sagged, and I leaned against the wall.

"We'll go down to the library. I'll send for the doctor." Richard bent to pick me up.

"I can walk," I protested. "Your leg—"

But Richard ignored that and swung me up into his arms. "You go first," he said to the children. "Penrose, take Sarah by the hand. Sarah, you listen to Penrose."

"Yes, Dada."

My heart rose up in my throat, but Richard did not reprimand her. Perhaps, I thought, he had not heard. Or perhaps, because of the stress of the moment, he would not mention it to her.

Penrose led Sarah down the spiral staircase, and Richard followed. I was concerned about his leg, but I was also glad to be carried. My limbs felt weak as jelly, and I doubted I could have taken more than three steps.

Penrose and Sarah reached the library first. "Here," Penrose cried as Sarah carried me in. "We fixed the divan in front of the fire."

"Very good," said Richard. He put me gently down, and Sarah brought pillows to prop me up, along with a cover to warm me. She tucked it around me like a little mother.

Richard pushed back my disheveled hair and examined the bump on my head. "Good," he said. "The skin is not broken. You'll have a big headache, but probably no more." He took a chair nearby.

I was beginning to feel a little steadier. My throat still hurt, but I knew it would heal. And, better yet, I knew we were finally safe. Then I remembered the diary. "Richard! I found Caroline's diary."

To my surprise he merely shrugged. "Caroline is gone." He looked at Sarah, and she ran and climbed into his lap. "We are a family," he said, gazing at me with such tenderness in his eyes. "You are the mama. I am the dada. Sarah is daughter. And Penrose is son."

My heart sang with joy at the wonderful news. Without thinking I said, "You have forgotten someone."

Richard looked puzzled. But Sarah giggled. "I know," she said, looking up at her father. "It's the new baby."

"New—" Richard began.

"Yes," I said. "I believe that next spring we will have a new baby."

Sarah put her arms around his neck. "I get to help," she said proudly. "Don't I, Mama?"

"Yes, dear." I smiled at her and then at the boy. "And Penrose will tell you both stories."

"Oh, yes!" His eagerness told me the boy had been waiting for me to say something that included him. I smiled at my family. We were safe at last.

"But tell me," I said. "How did you find me?"

"It was Sarah—" Penrose began.

"It was Penrose—" Sarah began.

Richard chuckled. Tears of happiness sprang to my eyes. It was so good to hear him laugh, so good to see us all together.

Penrose pulled up a chair. "It was like this," he said. "Sarah was looking for me."

"To tell him about the present," Sarah added.

Penrose nodded. "She saw you and Uncle Roland pass and followed you. She is very good at following silently."

"Very good," Sarah repeated, obviously pleased with the compliment.

"She followed you up the stairs to the tower room, and she heard you and Uncle Roland talking. She thought he was going to tell you about her present."

Sarah's bottom lip quivered. "He was bad. He was going to hurt Nessie. He was going to hurt my mama."

Richard hugged her close, and Penrose continued. "Sarah crept back down the stairs and ran to Gerson, but she was so frightened, she was crying about her mama."

"You *are* my mama," Sarah insisted.

"Yes, dear. I am."

Penrose went on. "Gerson thought she was crying about Caroline. Then I came along." He paused.

Richard smiled at him. "Thank goodness, Penrose understood her."

"I knew she called you Mama to herself," the boy said. "And she spoke of you that way to me. So I tried to make Gerson understand."

He looked down, obviously embarrassed. "But he thought it was some kind of trick. I—I have done such things in the past, but I would not do them now."

"I know." I hastened to assure him. "But if Gerson did not believe . . ."

Richard smoothed his daughter's hair. "The children started out alone to help you."

I shivered, thinking of that madman, of what he might have done to them. "Just the two of them?"

Sarah nodded. "We didn't want him to hurt you."

"But I did not see . . ."

Richard frowned. "I came in just as they were heading up the stairs, and they poured forth their tale." He smiled at them fondly. "I am quite proud of them both. At any rate, as soon as I understood, I called some servants and we hurried to you."

"And just in time," I said, with a sigh of relief. "But Richard, I must tell you. I found a piece of Caroline's diary, and it says that Sarah is—"

He cast me a warning look. "Sarah is *my* little girl," he said warmly. "Some part of me has known it all along."

Sarah nestled against him contentedly, but then she frowned. "Dada?"

"Yes, dear?"

"What's wrong with Uncle Roland? Why was he mean to Nessie?"

Richard looked to me. I sighed, and then I knew what to say. "Remember," I said, "when I told you how your mama and grandmother had a sickness?"

Sarah nodded. "I remember. They can't love people." She smiled. "But we didn't get it. We can love." She looked up at her father. "I love you, Dada."

Richard hugged her to him. "And I love you, Sarah."

A lump in my throat made it impossible for me to speak. Penrose took the hand I stretched out to him. "I think I know," he said. "Uncle Roland had a kind of sickness, too."

Sarah looked puzzled. "But he loved me. He brought me presents."

Penrose nodded. "Yes, but his sickness made him hurt people. Isn't that it, Nessie?"

"Yes, Penrose. That is it."

I looked at my husband. There were still a few things I needed to tell him. I squeezed Penrose's hand. "You and Sarah saved my life," I said. "You're a wonderful brave boy."

He blushed. "You are my friend," he said simply. His flush deepened. "You will not mind if I don't call you—Mama?"

"Of course not. I understand perfectly. Will you do something for me now?"

He got to his feet, every inch a gentleman. "Of course, Vanessa."

"Please take Sarah to the nursery." Sarah looked about to protest. "You may tell your nurse all about the excitement."

Sarah gave her father a hug and kiss. Then she hopped down and slipped her hand into the boy's. "You will let me tell it, won't you?"

"Of course," replied Penrose, smiling at me. And off they went together.

Richard came to sit beside me on the divan. He put an arm around me. "Oh, Nessie, my love, if I had lost you. . . ."

"I love you, too, my dearest." Then, because I was still shaken from my ordeal, I blurted out, "Someday you will forget how you love Caroline and love me the same."

He frowned. "How I love Caroline? What do you mean?"

"I know she was more beautiful. More—practiced. I know you pined for her." I swallowed. "I found her handkerchief under your pillow one of the nights you left me alone."

"The night you smelled Caroline's scent in your room?"

"Yes, Richard. But it's all right. I know you loved—"

"Vanessa, for God's sake! Will you stop saying that?"

I stared at him. "But—"

"You are wrong," he said wearily. "I did not pine after Caroline, and I was not the one who put the handkerchief under my pillow. When I found it, I threw it away. I knew several days after I'd married your sister that I had made a mistake."

I could not believe my ears. "Several days—"

"Yes. And I kept thinking about a carrot-topped young girl I'd seen and wishing I'd waited for her."

It was incredible. All these weeks I had been hating my dead sister because she had Richard's love. And she had never had it!

"Oh, Richard! And I loved you. That is why I never married. No man could compare to you."

He kissed me then, tenderly, carefully.

"Now that the children are gone, I must tell you. Caroline's diary says—"

He put a finger across my lips. "It's better that I don't know who her father is. I shall love her, I promise you."

I pushed his finger aside. "But it's you!" I cried. "You're her father."

He stared at me. Then joy broke over his features. "Oh, Vanessa, my darling. What wonderful news." He put his hand gently on my stomach. "And this, this is glorious."

I had a sudden image of Roland's evil smile. How that man had deceived us all. I shuddered. "Oh, Richard. Your brother was going to kill me. And Sarah and Penrose, too. And he was going to fix the blame on you. All these years he has hated you."

Richard sighed. "I know. That time—when I fell out of

the stable—Roland pushed me. He told my father I pushed him, and Father believed him. He had a way with people, Roland did—so open and friendly—but it was all a mask. I saw behind it that day at the stable, but no one would believe me."

"What—what will happen to him?"

Richard frowned and pulled me close. "I will talk to the magistrate. Perhaps he can send Roland out of the country. To the Americas, perhaps."

"And your mother?"

He frowned. "We cannot have her in our household. I see that now. She is not good for the children." He sighed. "I think we should leave here. There are too many dark memories for the boy."

"Yes," I said. "Oh, yes. Where shall we go?"

Richard smiled. "I was watching you with the children, and I thought—perhaps we can find a place near your father. I have—"

"Oh, Richard! How wonderful. Sarah will love it there. Penrose, too. It will be so good for him."

"I thought you would like that."

So our nightmare ended. Roland was shipped off to the Americas while the dowager elected to stay on at Greyden Castle with a small staff of servants. I suppose she wanted to hold on to her memories—since she had nothing else.

Richard moved the rest of the household, anyone who wanted to go, including Toby and Creighton, to Wiltshire, where we all live happily together, the past a dim memory. Sarah and Penrose are flourishing, and Papa does his best to spoil all his grandchildren, including the new little Rosamund.